Other Books by Joyce Carol Oates

NOVELS

The Assassins
Do with Me What You Will
Wonderland
Them
Expensive People
A Garden of Earthly Delights
With Shuddering Fall

SHORT STORIES

The Goddess and Other Women
Marriages and Infidelities
The Wheel of Love
Upon the Sweeping Flood
By the North Gate
The Hungry Ghosts
The Seduction
The Poisoned Kiss, Fernandes/Oates

CRITICISM

New Heaven, New Earth:
   The Visionary Experience in Literature
The Edge of Impossibility:
   Tragic Forms in Literature

PLAYS

Miracle Play

POEMS

Anonymous Sins
Love and Its Derangements
Angel Fire
The Fabulous Beasts

ANTHOLOGY

Scenes from American Life:
   Contemporary Short Fiction (EDITOR)

Joyce Carol Oates

Crossing the Border

FIFTEEN TALES

OAT
copy 1

The Vanguard Press, Inc., New York

The stories in this collection have appeared previously in the following maga-
zines, often in different versions: *The New York Times Magazine*; *Chatelaine*;
The Malahat Review; *Family Circle*; *Prairie Schooner*; *The Fiddlehead*; *The
Canadian Fiction Magazine*; *Playboy*; *Michigan Quarterly Review*; *Queen's
Quarterly*; *Epoch*; *Fiction*. To all these, acknowledgements and thanks are due.

To my parents

Caroline and Frederick

Contents

*C*rossing the Border

Evan, the young husband, hurries from the men's rest room at the Sunoco station near Tiger Stadium in Detroit, pale and stricken and angry, and Renée, his wife, sits helpless in the car to wait out another session. She is miserable with the heat.

A few blocks away is the bridge. They are about to cross the border after a long drive from the South. Their new country will be a northerly country. But the border is no more than three minutes away; it will be hot there also. In Florida she studied the map and daydreamed of fresh air, chilled from the Arctic, a ceaseless cleansing wind . . . knowing at the same time it was unreasonable to have such thoughts. She knew better. Her daydreams hinted at wonders, but she knew better.

At this point the Canadian border dips down, flowing in a southwesterly direction between Lake Huron and Lake Erie, graceful as if it were water and not dense and stubborn, like earth.

Crossing the border at this point means traveling south, southeast.

But it won't be as hot as New York City, probably; certainly not as hot as Florida.

Once he accused her of wanting to die—scrubbing the kitchen walls and floor in the heat. *What? But why?* He walked away, he was always walking away. Ninety-five degrees and the air conditioning that didn't work right. *But I don't want to die,* Renée had protested.

She rarely lied.

A curiosity. You traveled south from Detroit to enter Canada. Something to mention in a letter home. She might have mentioned it to Evan; couldn't remember. She couldn't remember if he had bothered to reply.

Pain took the form of silence with him.

Sorry. Sorry. Sorry. Sorry!

Euphoria: words. Excited proclamations. Apologies. Hand squeezing, forearm stroking, light airy married-lovers' kisses: on the cheek, on the back of the neck (embarrassingly damp).

Just as they had been preparing for this trip for weeks, without speaking much about it, so on the final morning they said little. Life was a matter of detail, of things to be done, arranged, shut off, completed. Like grace, such silence.

Wordless, he was very real to her. Walking heavily on his heels, giving the impression of being a much larger man. The floors of the rented house shuddered when he was barefoot . . . as if he were deliberately bringing the fleshy part of his foot down hard, to hurt himself. Strange vulnerability, weakness of the heel: not mythology but physiology.

Wasn't everything?

They got into the habit of going barefoot much of the time in Florida. Might have been dangerous: spiders, roaches. Scorpions? Of course there were snakes but only outside, rarely near the house, rarely in populated areas. Renée had seen a few large

snakes but they had always been dead. On the road. Run-over by
traffic many times, safely dead, harmless because dead, though
Renée could not help but stare at their mangled bodies in an
exquisite, bewildering terror. Must run over them, must drive
over. What if still alive? But no. Impossible.

Sometimes she kicked off her shoes in the car. Drove barefoot,
her foot confidently on the gas pedal. Of course it seemed peculiar
to her—her childhood had been spent in an expensive but poorly
heated apartment on Manhattan's West Side, and during the
summer her parents usually went to Maine, where it was so often
cold, drizzling, the beach pebbly, that she had had to wear shoes.

Why aren't your things packed yet?

Impatient, thudding around without shoes, beginning to feel
a little euphoric. They were escaping, after all. Released, free,
blameless.

She went into the kitchen where he was finishing a carton of
milk, drinking it down in gulps. He didn't want it. But he hated to
waste anything: food, clothing, soap, shaving cream, Kleenex.
They were so poor, after all. Humiliating, to be so poor. It was
temporary, but still. . . . How embittered they both were, to
lose that hundred-and-fifty-dollar deposit on their half of the
house! Evan finished the milk and rinsed the carton out, carefully.
He wanted to know: Was the duffel bag as full as she could get it?
And what time was it?—his watch had stopped.

For the long drive north: Evan in khaki shorts and a thin
white pullover shirt, neck stretched, sleeves shapeless from many
launderings. Fairly muscular in the shoulders and chest but legs
thin, pale; ankles white and nearly as slender as Renée's. Long
narrow nervous feet, bare toes kneading the linoleum tile. Renée
pretended not to notice. She looked smiling at him and he smiled
back. *I love you.*

Could they get as far as Lexington, Kentucky, on the first day?

Renée wore a shapeless blue shift, without sleeves. The sun
would irritate her skin but she couldn't bear the thought of
sleeves brushing against her arms. Something was wrong with the

skin of her face and arms, must be a reaction against the concentrated light of this climate. . . . Dense windless humid heat. Glowing-pale sunlight. Something to complain about in the letters to her mother, something legitimate to protest against. This relentless heat came to baffle her, as if it indicated something wrong in a general sense, beyond her own life. Insulting and dehumanizing, wasn't it? And the dependency upon air conditioning, upon machines laboring constantly to dispel the sticky heat?

The duplex they rented had an air-conditioner in the bedroom, of course. An old model that rattled. Evan became obsessed with checking it, certain that its efficiency was decreasing all the time. He telephoned the rental agency. Someone promised to send a boy over. The words were always those words. *A boy. Will send a boy over.* A few days before they left, the air-conditioning unit broke down altogether. Evan was triumphant. They argued: Renée couldn't remember why they argued. Did Evan want the old machine fixed or did Renée want to notify the agency so that a new air-conditioner could be installed before the new tenants moved in—they were due to move in immediately—or had they simply argued because they had the need to argue because of the heat because of Dr. Maynard's nausea?

Evan was Dr. Maynard, at the laboratories over in Lake City.

Impressive background!—everyone agreed. A master's degree in chemistry and a master's degree in biology. A doctorate in biology. And so young. Except for the habit of frowning, of brooding, he was so boyish it was difficult to believe he had accomplished so much. Taken on as a mere research assistant in order to be reclassified in terms of the draft, and a year later given a far better position, an extraordinary jump in salary. . . . But a young man his own age, a neurologist, had done even better.

Crossing the border, she will forget. Juniper Way and the sink that smelled and the air-conditioner and the cockroaches . . . some of them a curious brown-glinting eye-glinting egg smoothness, like an egg with tiny but sturdy legs, an egg with intelligent-staring *eyes. . . . The story of my life,* Evan giggled one night, drunk, *the wrong place the wrong time the wrong beginning of a marriage . . .* and the four small rooms the two tiny closets the scruffy back yard in which no grass grew and even weeds burnt out in June, their yellow flowers shriveling to brown wisps, elderly-looking, comic. Renée's nightmares had started before there was any cause for them. Many months before, when Dr. Maynard had not yet been working on classified projects—on "defense biology." Her dreaming dragged her one way, her conscious thinking another: a kind of argument, nastier than the arguments with her husband (which were always civilized, never really brutal: they were both too intelligent to dare to suppose either of them might be right about anything). . . . But she will forget, probably. As people do. She is in her mid-twenties, a time for living intensely, and forgetting.

Inside the men's room he is vomiting, and outside, in the car packed with luggage and a duffel bag and cartons of books and records, and Evan's old-fashioned crooknecked lamp with a base so heavy and impractical it must be made of lead, outside here in the gritty sunshine of Detroit, Renée sits studying the map, folding and unfolding one of the corners of the map, as she has been doing, idly, for hundreds of miles. The border between two nations is always indicated by broken but definite lines, to indicate that it is not quite real in any physical sense but very real in a metaphysical sense: so nature surrenders to politics, as mythology surrenders to physiology. Probably necessary. Better that way. How could love compete with nightmares? Love too would have surrendered. Perhaps it did, a few months ago, Renée waking from the misery of sleep crowded with roaches and silverfish and beetles and quick-darting lizards and the constant awareness of her husband lying beside her, unsleeping. Toward the end it was not uncommon for him to rush from the dinner table, suddenly, without explanation, and lock himself in the tiny bathroom at the rear of the house. Though he turned both faucets on loud she could still hear him. Difficult, for love to compete.

*

There was a Civil Liberties office in Jacksonville: Evan telephoned them. Renée did not eavesdrop. She did not deliberately
eavesdrop. . . . *Violating contract . . . they're trying to accuse
me of . . . insubordination . . . a year in jail . . . there are
four or five of us who want to get out.* . . . And a week of nerves,
of waiting. Evan no longer drove the five miles to the government
compound. He stayed home, waiting. Checking the air-conditioner. Sometimes silent, sometimes talking effusively, gaily. He
was already planning their new life in a new country before he
had a right to hope for it, already assuring her that he wouldn't
mind work of any type, not even work with his hands. . . . A
new life, a new country.

"We were born here," Renée said ironically.

"We aren't necessarily born anywhere," Evan said.

The Ambassador Bridge is a few blocks away. Evan, the young
husband, is now returning from the rest room of the Sunoco
station—gone only about five minutes, not bad—looking pale,
ghastly, triumphant.

Renée, the young wife, smiles at him but isn't sure he sees.

Anyway: *I love you.* Anyway: *Here we are.*

*L*ove.   Friendship.

My husband is speaking to someone in the next room. No, it is a telephone conversation. He is speaking quickly, urgently. . . . Three thirty in the morning. For a moment I can't even think what day it is. Tuesday? . . . My husband's words are no more than a murmur, inaudible at this distance. But the silences are worse, because that means . . . that means that whoever is talking with him, whoever is at the other end of the conversation, is speaking even more urgently than he.

I would like to go to the door of our bedroom; would like to open it. To stand there in the dark, barefoot, shivering, and to overhear what my husband says to Blaine when he believes he is alone. Of course it is Blaine who has called. . . . I could pretend that I'm listening to see if the baby is awake. I could pretend I am curious about who is telephoning, innocently curious; after all, it is three thirty in the morning. If I eavesdropped I might learn something. I might learn an important fact about my marriage or about myself. . . . But I lie here, motionless, afraid to move. What I must never do, must never do, what I must never do . . . I must never intentionally deceive my husband. . . . I must never behave in any way I would not want him to behave toward me.

So I lie here, motionless.

This is the third telephone call since we moved to this particular flat; the third, I mean, from Blaine. . . . Sick, is he? Lonely? Convinced he's dying? Or maybe it's money he wants. Or remorse he wishes to express. Or rage. *I know how the two of you hate me. Judith and Larry huddling together in their marriage. Safe and completed in your marriage, aren't you, in love, protected from me as if by a tough, moist membrane, an impenetrable membrane . . . Judith and Larry and now a third, a sacred third, completing a trinity no one could hope to challenge. . . .*

Blaine's voice is inside my head. Yet faint. I must be falling asleep. Will have to rehearse what should probably be said to Larry when he comes back to bed . . . will have to get the words right, the tone right . . . must not upset him any more than Blaine will already have upset him. I might say: *It was very thoughtful of you to answer the phone, to get out there so quickly and answer it.* I might also say, sleepily, warmly: *Come to bed, honey, and tell me about it in the morning . . . all right?* Or, possibly: *Why did you talk with him for so long, honey, isn't that a mistake, to encourage him. . . .* Or I might throw the covers off and start to scream: *Why won't he leave us alone! Why won't he stop!*

"Honey?"

Larry is in the room with me. I must have fallen asleep. He stumbles to the bedside and turns on the light. Larry in his pajamas, his hair rumpled, his expression vexed, apologetic, weary:

"Honey, it was Blaine."

"Yes."

". . . he sounded worse than ever."

"Yes, all right. . . . Is he still on the line? Should I talk to him?"

"No, he hung up."

"He didn't want to talk to me?"

"Well, it was like last time . . . he asked for you, of course he asked to speak to you, but I explained that it was the middle of the night. I told him you were asleep."

"And he didn't know it was three thirty in the morning. Did he. He claimed not to know."

"Honey, he was talking so hysterically, I couldn't get a word in. . . ." Larry sits on the edge of the bed; he reaches for his cigarettes, without looking at me. I pretend to be sleepier than I really am. He pretends to be calmer, even slightly amused. After all, he is The Husband. It is his privilege to be calm, amused, husbandly.

". . . oh, the usual. Accused me of not having written those letters of recommendation for him. As if I had any power. . . . Accused us both of not wanting him to come to Toronto, don't ask me why. He just kept talking, a steady stream of words, and if I tried to interrupt he shouted . . . One minute he was claiming that nobody gave a damn whether he lived or died, he could die in his bed and rot there, for weeks, and nobody would care; the next minute he was giving me that story again about his division director, you know, making advances to him. Or whatever it's called. Putting pressure on him. Trying to get him fired."

Larry manages to laugh, nervously.

"Do you think it's true?"

"What? The homosexual business? . . . How the hell do I know," Larry says wearily.

"Did he threaten to do anything? . . . To us, or to himself?"

"Oh, the usual. Unless we help him out of the mess he's in, something terrible might happen."

"Something terrible might happen."

We look at each other. A sudden impulse: shouldn't we laugh, isn't this funny? By now it's ten minutes to four and the alarm is set for seven. Isn't this funny? The situation, the conversation, The Friend back in Philadelphia threatening disaster. . . .

"He hasn't got gasoline splashed around this time, has he, and a match ready to light?"

Larry shuts his eyes. ". . . No, he didn't say anything about that. He wasn't very specific. Just sobbed something about us forgetting him, stepping on him, betraying him: the usual."

*   *   *

Friends. Friendship. Friendly evenings, friendly dinners and conversations, the sharing of warm emotions, of jokes and disappointments and triumphs. . . . Friendly discussions, late at night. Friendly misunderstandings, arguments. Friendly apologies. Friendly loves and hates. What is friendship, that it should have such power? Everyone knows about love. Romantic love, married love, adulterous love: happy love affairs, unhappy ones. Everyone knows about *love*, no one knows about *friendship*. Yet listen:

". . . it's easier to fall in love and even get married, it's much easier, in my opinion, than to establish a lasting relationship with someone . . . with a friend. . . . And you want to destroy it! Like that! As if it meant nothing to you! . . . Because you're married, because you don't give a damn about other people."

And again:

"It must be easier to break off a love affair, even a marriage, than to say good-bye to a friend. *It must be.* With friendship there's no formal beginning, so there can't be a formal ending. Everything happens and then nothing happens. But nothing comes to an end. . . . There's no moment of consummation. There's no abandonment, no ecstasy. And there's no forgiveness."

Blaine had, when we first met him, a shy, self-conscious manner, boyish and endearing. He was twenty-four. I was a year younger and my husband was thirty. Larry is rather short, not much taller than I; he's difficult for me to describe—difficult for me to see. There's nothing boyish about him and he no longer makes much effort, at least much hypocritical effort, to be endearing in the way Blaine always did. He's direct, argumentative, and yet curiously slow to form judgments . . . unlike Blaine, who always seemed to know exactly how he felt, exactly what critical attitude was proper. Blaine is a tall man, yet he probably doesn't weigh more than a hundred and forty pounds; his hair is always beautifully styled and groomed, and he has a redhead's pale, near-white complexion. He is the kind of young man who murmurs graceful, meaningless phrases like *Yes thank you* and *Yes, yes, thank you very much,* and his manner seems somehow out of keeping with his appearance: the eyes brown, darkly lashed, intelligent.

We first met him at a party. Elegantly dressed, in what must have been an expensive suit—fawn-colored, with suede trim and suede-covered buttons—and yet nervous, restless. The place was crowded; a few windows had been yanked open, but it was still smoky; I glanced around the room and saw the young man I would later be introduced to, and had the feeling that he was keenly uncomfortable, as I was. But I knew enough not to show my feelings. He was standing at the edge of a noisy conversation, holding a drink, trying to appear interested. Redheaded, curly-haired, childlike. . . . Yet he looked shrewd enough. The corners of his mouth twitched downward while others burst into hearty, vulgar laughter. He didn't seem to be enjoying his drink; he wasn't smoking. We had been invited to this party by friends of friends, and really didn't know anyone well. It would be more accurate to say that we'd been invited by acquaintances of acquaintances. At that time Larry and I had been married only two and a half years. He was finishing his graduate studies at Ann Arbor and I was working part-time as an assistant to one of the minor administrators of the library, a position that did not engage me at all —I remember hours of blank, passionless rage, a sense of incredible boredom, all the more frustrating in that I was very much in love, happily married, and imagined myself to be an attractive young woman in excellent health. Yet the unvoiced anger, the tearless rage! Unlikely as it seems to me now, I did not even tell Larry about my feelings; it simply did not occur to me. Most of the time he was vocal enough for both of us—easily angered, easily pacified. When I saw Blaine I felt a surge of interest that was both sisterly and maternal, a tinge of something I suppose must have been—perversely—a sense that here was someone rather like myself, yet someone I could handle.

That evening, Larry had just heard by way of his older sister that his father had been hospitalized—again—and that his mother, a placid, stubborn woman with whom I have never been able to talk, was threatening to file a suit for divorce. After thirty-five years of marriage! Larry's father was an alcoholic . . . he'd once worked for a real estate agency in St. Louis, had done well for a few years, and then began his long, steady decline, hospitalized and released and hospitalized again. He is still living, in fact: Larry says the old man has a tough, stubborn heart, and will keep going to spite Larry's mother. But that evening Larry was in one of his combative moods. He rarely turned against me, so he needed someone else—he needed the gregarious atmosphere of a party, a group of near-strangers. And it did not please him that, in the group he first approached, someone should be praising the antics of a local artist-in-residence, an internationally famous man, who happened to be an alcoholic who abused his wife and others in public, and who had been arrested by Ann Arbor police for drunken driving not long before . . . the usual things were being said: *He can't help it, he's a genius. He can't help it, he's so sensitive brilliant marvelous . . . isn't he? Let him do whatever he likes, he's a genius.*

Larry interrupted and began to argue, as he often does, breaking into a conversational group. Most of the time people are relieved: they turn hopefully to someone new, to a guest whom they don't know well, wondering if this person will turn out to be interesting. So Larry interrupted, Larry argued, Larry was contradicted and refuted and supported and the conversation swung along, and though the bare reporting of what he might have said—*What the hell do you know about alcoholism?—about geniuses?—* would sound rude, in fact Larry rarely strikes people as rude. He seems certain of himself. People like him, people tend to look up hopefully as he approaches. That evening, Blaine was impressed by his outspoken good sense: we learned that later. Larry struck Blaine as the only person blunt enough to speak the truth.

"Well, what good does the truth do us?" Larry used to joke.

"The truth is an irresistible force," Blaine would say. As always, when he spoke idealistically—in that shy, precise manner that made me believe, at first, that he must be revealing his innermost thoughts—he lowered his gaze. "Men have an instinct to go for it . . . they can't resist it."

Yes, we spoke of abstract, speculative matters. We became friends, and we spent many hours, even a few weekends together, discussing moral and philosophical issues, arguing about politics, comparing our childhoods, our educations, our families, our expectations, our tastes in such areas as movies and music and art and food. . . . We met at Rudy Dietz's party, six years ago this fall. Or is it seven. We met at that crowded, near-forgotten party, in one of the upstairs apartments of a big, drafty Victorian house, at the corner of State Street and Clarenton. It was miles from the university, in a poor neighborhood. When we returned last summer we happened to drive through that area, and I happened to notice that the house had evidently been razed—a new stucco apartment building in its place, the University Heights Apartments, interchangeable with a dozen similar buildings. It must have been seven years ago. That was before the mass unemployment, before the inflationary prices; then, it didn't seem that anything so old-fashioned and bourgeois as failure was possible. Certainly not anything so absurd as—economic failure! No, the mood was so optimistic as to be cheerfully cynical; young men could debate, seriously, about whether or not they would "accept" jobs that compromised their integrity.

Certainly Blaine was one of these men. And we admired him for it. We were so new at being married, so clumsily delighted with each other, that it must have been out of a desire—an instinct? —to share our happiness with someone else, someone lonely, troubled, sensitive—and yet admirable in our eyes, possibly even superior to both of us, in ways we could not have articulated.

In what did Blaine's "superiority" consist? Looking back on the
early days of our friendship, of our courtship of one another, I
believe it must have been his allusions to a family background
that included a justice of the supreme court of the state of North
Carolina . . . and someone, an uncle perhaps, who was a member
of the United States Tariff Commission. . . . Not that these
people figured in Blaine's life. Not at all. He rather scorned them,
in fact; he said his family's conservative politics were contemptible.
He was always eager to agree with Larry, when Larry pronounced
whatever political opinions he had. . . . He struck me as superior,
also, in that his manners were always exquisite. He sat correctly,
as proper as a child who is being observed, and murmured his
Thank you, yes, lowering his gaze deferentially, always compliment-
ing me on whatever I made for dinner, seeking out things in our
small, drab apartment to notice, to praise. There wasn't much.
But he worked at praise, he worked at being consciously kind.
People said of Blaine Oltman, *Isn't he thoughtful?—and so
charming.* Sometimes they said, *He's too good to be true.*

Though he was only in his mid-twenties, Blaine was in charge
of an organization called Centennial House, the southeastern
Michigan branch of a state-wide arts and sciences program. Courses
in natural sciences and "the arts"—mainly pottery, weaving, and
photography—were offered through this program for housewives
and children and retired people. Centennial House was always
in financial difficulties; Blaine was always "drafting letters" and
composing "petitions" that were models of persuasive courtesy.
He needed more state aid. He ran a campaign, all one winter, to
latch onto federal funds. And during the eighteen months of our
friendship he only broke down once, complaining bitterly, almost
sobbing, about the ignorant sons of bitches in the state legislature,
those politicians who didn't give a damn about what people like
him were trying to do. I had been in awe of him, before this
outburst; it amazed me that a man my own age should actually
be at the head of an organization, however small. But that night—
in our apartment, after dinner out and a movie—he seemed to dis-
integrate, rubbing his knuckles into his eyes, muttering, whining.

How helpless he was, and how like a small boy! I think it made Larry and me like him all the more.

After that evening, Blaine avoided us for several weeks. He didn't call. We didn't call.

Then, one rainy afternoon, I met him in the graduate library at the university, and he offered to drive me home. Neither of us alluded to his outburst. Once at our apartment, he allowed himself to be talked into staying for dinner—of course.

The three of us were relieved to be together again: and excited, and grateful. And very attentive to one another. It was no illusion —we were happier together than we were apart. Larry didn't lapse into silence, as he often did when we were alone; I never heard my voice raised petulantly, the voice of a very young woman who wondered too often whether she was being appreciated enough. That evening, Blaine drank several glasses of wine and was extra-ordinarily cheerful. He was a brother, a lover, a husband. . . .

It might have been that evening, or another soon after, that we talked until four in the morning. What about? What engrossed us so thoroughly? I can't remember. Sometimes Larry and Blaine stayed up, and I went to bed—pleased that my husband and my friend should like each other so much. I would fall asleep, contented, somewhere just inside the conversational drone of their voices. . . . At other times Blaine and I would go out to plays at the university, or chamber concerts, or gallery openings; events Larry had no interest in. Blaine even accompanied me to a few parties. One dark January day Larry collapsed at the medical-center laboratory, where he had been working for hours, and it was Blaine who drove me to the clinic to see him, and Blaine who drove me back home again, eager to be of use, as frightened by Larry's illness—a severe case of the London flu—as I was.

Dead-white with the shock of Larry's collapse. Trying to comfort me. Admitting, finally, as the two of us sat in my kitchen, that he was terrified of sickness and death, and tried never to think of such things. . . . We sat up past midnight, talking earnestly, openly. Larry was in no danger now; so we could talk as openly as possible, we could confess our most childish, irrational fears. I told Blaine that I was so deeply in love with my husband that I could hardly bear it: I hadn't known what marriage was, how violently it united people, what demands it made upon the personality. "What do you mean? I don't understand," Blaine kept saying. I confessed a strange truth: I now loved Larry so much that I believed I had become weaker, as a personality, as an individual. I was so dependent upon him, emotionally, intellectually. . . . But Blaine did not seem to understand. He kept blinking, shaking his head, trying to smile as if he suspected me of joking. *What do you mean? I don't understand. Please explain.* . . .

After the excitement of that evening we were both exhausted, oddly exhilarated, ravenously hungry. I made us both omelets, which we ate greedily. Blaine spoke awkwardly of "hoping to marry" someday. But his voice was boyish and feebly idealistic. He began telling me about a very close friendship he'd had with someone, a few years ago when he was an undergraduate at Amherst, then broke off, laughing. Well, it had "failed." Well, it was "finished." And here in Ann Arbor there was someone who had hurt him very deeply, who had betrayed him and mocked him. . . . But of course he could take it: what choice had he?

Our friendship lasted nearly two years, but we were never to be that close again. Something must have passed between us that we couldn't comprehend or control, a lowering of barriers—I remember speaking at some length, emotionally, reaching out to touch Blaine's arm or wrist, a gentle tap with my fingers, not intimate so much as conversational. We had been talking about love. Now, in trying to remember that night, I have the feeling that what I meant by "love" was entirely different from what Blaine meant—we were using the same term but we were not communicating. And from "love" we went on to talk about the possible "meaning" that life could have: the "meaning" of life itself, so passionately and naïvely discussed by two young people barely out of adolescence, that the memory of our conversation embarrasses me even now. Unless, of course, I am remembering it wrongly.

After that, Blaine alluded from time to time to my "mystical" tendency. He seemed to have forgotten his own attitude. He waved aside my protestations, as if they were meant only to be girlish or flirtatious—which they were not: they were quite serious —and even winked at Larry in my presence. *Listen to Judith! Isn't Judith charming!* If Larry complimented me on something I had prepared for dinner, Blaine was certain to compliment me even more elaborately; when other guests were there, he might even ask them whether they'd ever eaten anything quite so delicious?—so exquisitely prepared? His manner was always graceful, his voice sincere. Sometimes he wore glasses which he took off, halfway through an evening, so that he could rub the bridge of his nose, blink, and peer cozily at us, asking these fond, intimate questions I knew to be utterly mocking, yet could not defend myself against. My heart hammered with the injustice of it. "I wish you wouldn't embarrass me like that, Blaine," I would plead, and he'd turn to me as if genuinely astonished—as if my inability to accept praise were, somehow, a deficiency in me. A form of egotism, perhaps? Blaine and Larry and the others would laugh, forgiving me.

Once, Blaine even seized a long woolen scarf of mine from a shelf in the closet—wound it around his head, knotted it clumsily —waved his hands and protested *Now Blaine! Now you stop that teasing!*—in an absurdly high voice, a parody of a woman's voice. It seemed to me that I looked upon an enemy who detested me not for anything I had said or done, but simply for my existence: I was sickened by his hostility and by my defenselessness against it. Most shamefully, I was sickened by my own hurt. I knew the relationship between us had gone wrong, but I could not accept it; I believed, obscurely, that it was my fault if Blaine occasionally turned against me, and it was certainly my fault that I overreacted. He was only joking, wasn't he? This was only friendly teasing, wasn't it?

Yet it was obvious that Blaine was somehow drawn to me. Nothing so simple as sexual attraction: unbelievable as this may sound, most intense, overdetermined relationships between people, whether they are men and women, or belong to the same sex, have little to do with sexual attraction. It would be a relief to be able, magically, to reduce such mysteries to a commonplace, a biological determinism . . . but Blaine might have logically been drawn to any number of young women at that time in his life, and I to any number of men. As a woman, I loved my husband: he was, and he is now, the kind of man a woman might love without qualification. "Love"—whatever love is—belonged to him, to our marriage. It was so solid, so unshakable, that I believed with absolute confidence that nothing could threaten it. . . . But Blaine was so hilarious, in his imitation of me. That high-pitched voice, that mincing step, that brilliantly cruel parody of a woman: a Parody of Woman. I must have become abstract to him, at the same time that we were—the two of us—thrown together more and more often, by design and circumstance and peculiar accidents. If we hadn't contacted each other for a week or more, we were sure to meet at someone's house—or, if I were shopping for groceries, alone, rather tired and depressed, and possibly even thinking of Blaine, rerunning in my imagination our latest conversation, my feelings still hurt by some whimsical, cutting remark of us, he was sure to appear in the aisle before me—pushing a cart with a few frozen items tossed into it, a few cans of tuna or salmon, a single head of browning lettuce, Blaine himself surprised and smiling hopefully when he saw me, as if he truly rejoiced at seeing me, as if I meant something to him that he must, somehow, by any means possible, try to deny.

Of course I was hurt. And angry. And bewildered. At the same time, I was young for my age; my marriage to a forceful man some years my senior had made me begin to feel less certain of myself; I resisted confronting Blaine, thinking that perhaps I was imagining everything, it was simply that I worked too hard at a pointless, exhausting job, or the winter dragged on too long, through March and even into April . . . a vicious snow-and-ice storm on April 5 of that year still stands out in my mind, since it plunged nearly everyone into romantic despair. I began to think that perhaps Blaine was justified in mocking me. Perhaps I should go back to school, I should try to pit my mind against something challenging, I should enroll in a graduate program and then . . . and then . . . and then, possibly, people would take me seriously; would like me better.

Once, when I was wearing a dress that was rather large for me, since I'd lost a few pounds, Blaine drew me aside to whisper: "Is that . . . is that what I think it is?" I didn't know what he meant; I must have stared at him, bewildered. What? This dress? "But *is* it?" he asked, alarmed. I realized he meant: *Is that a maternity dress? Are you pregnant?* But he could not bring himself to say the words. So I assured him, irritably, that it was not a maternity dress; I was not pregnant; why did he profess such horror, anyway?—what business was it of his? He drew back, raising his finely shaped hands in an exaggeration of repentance. Sorry! Sorry! He hadn't meant to insult me, of course. Anyway, he assured me that he hadn't been serious.

"You take everything so personally these days," he remarked.

At the same time we were "friends." We took part in "friendly" activities: went to a poetry reading by Robert Lowell, in Hill Auditorium; went for a weekend trip down into the Smoky Mountains, when, in mid-April, it was still cold in Michigan; cheered one another up, telephoned often, relayed news and gossip, lent one another books. Blaine even showed Larry and me a series of prose poems he was writing. They were set, strangely, in the late nineteenth century: they dealt with Blaine's ancestors, or with people he imagined as his ancestors. They were written in longhand, page after page of immaculate script . . . tiny, crabbed, precise, in a way quite beautiful visually. He asked that we not comment on them. He did *not* want our opinion. No praise. No criticism. No comments at all. A few poems dealt, cautiously, with contemporary subjects—I remember one poem on the assassination of President Kennedy—but these were as obscure and painfully ironic as the others. Unless I misunderstood Blaine's poetry, it seemed to show an obsession with the ludicrous frailty of the physical life of man—as if man's ideals could be negated by the poet's insistence upon the vulnerability of his flesh, the ease with which the skull could be penetrated. And it was all a joke! . . . The most ordinary, innocent details of contemporary life were picked up, in Blaine's imagination, and set down into that ingenious prose poetry of his, revealing aspects of existence that no one would have guessed. Housewives pushing carts around the local Kroger's supermarket were participating in evil, bloody, capitalistic acts of violence . . . people who broiled or roasted or otherwise prepared meat were "disguising blood as gravy" (Blaine was a vegetarian: he occasionally ate fish, but that was all) . . . old men playing checkers in the air-polluted park near a nursing home were wrestling to see who would outlive the other, the symbolic confrontation of red and black interpreted, by the poet, as the confrontation of "life" and "death." . . .

But he dreaded our opinion of his poetry. And so we said nothing. And though he laughed, self-mocking, murmuring something about "of course it's just trash, it will never be accepted for publication," we managed to say only that we were grateful to have read it and hoped he would show us more.

A friend of Larry's stopped me somewhere to ask, in that half-anxious, half-thrilled voice I have come to recognize in others and occasionally in myself, whether the two of us were "all right" . . . ? He had heard a rumor, vaguely, dimly, an unsubstantiated rumor that. . . . The details were unclear: Larry and I were separating, or maybe we were burdened with an unwanted pregnancy, or maybe one of us insisted upon having the baby and the other insisted upon an abortion and. . . . I assured Larry's friend that there was nothing to the rumor. Nothing at all. Possibly I sounded a little upset, too emphatic. I asked who had told him this lie, but he couldn't remember. But who was it, I wanted to know. Who was lying about us?—but he couldn't remember or said he couldn't remember.

How trivial do the misrepresentations of others' lives seem to us, and how grotesquely important are our own! An ugly rumor about another person never seems, to me, to seriously affect my feelings about that person; and his protestations always seem melodramatic and unnecessary. Best to forget it. Best to ignore it, of course. But the rumors about Larry and me were so upsetting that I remember quitting work one afternoon, walking out, taking a taxi home . . . in the dismal, cramped apartment I muttered aloud, walking from room to room, rehearsing telephone conversations I would have with Blaine when I accused him of lying about us. . . . I even called Centennial House, but hung up before he came to the telephone. I considered writing him a letter; a formal, cold denunciation of him; or, possibly, a handwritten plea that would begin, *Dear Blaine, I can't understand how I have wronged you . . . have caused you to hate me. . . .* Finally, I took some sleeping pills and lay down on top of the bedspread and simply fell asleep, to be awakened by Larry's grip on my shoulder and his concerned voice, hours later.

"What's wrong with you, honey?"

"Nothing."

"Honey, are you sick?—what's wrong?"

"Nothing. Nothing."

I was confused and ashamed of what was happening. And I did not quite believe it, either. What is strangest about the entire affair—and this is true today, many years afterward—is my persistent inability to actually believe that anyone could feel such an intensity of emotion for me, both affection and hatred, over no issue at all. Erotic love was mysterious, yes, but its power seemed based upon nature itself: I could not quite understand it, but I could accept it. At least I never questioned it. But a nervous, edgy, highly charged relationship between a man and a woman not erotically involved. . . . No, it made no sense. It still makes no sense. Larry kept asking me what was wrong, why didn't I want to have Blaine over for dinner these days, why hadn't one of us telephoned Blaine, or Blaine us?—was he sick?—was he out of town?

And then Blaine would appear, often late in the evening— ten thirty, eleven o'clock—with a bottle of wine or brandy—

once, even, with a bouquet of daffodils and jonquils, for me—and all would be forgiven, forgotten. Abstract hurts always evaporated in the light of our genuine childlike pleasure in one another: a phenomenon I remember clearly. *May I come in? Don't turn me away!* Blaine was so lonely, so boyishly eager, shy, so hopeful of being liked . . . his tall, angular figure in the doorway, his expression both timid and arrogant, his dark eyes serious, solemn, almost pleading: *Allow me in. Don't turn me away.*

Sometimes he did marvelous cruel imitations of people we knew in common, and both Larry and I laughed helplessly. He wasn't shy at all, our Blaine!—but watchful, shrewd, missing nothing. Sometimes he was kindly and solicitous. Whenever I was tired or unhappy or in any way unwell, Blaine took me very seriously indeed.

"You should quit that job of yours," he often said. "You're too sensitive for it. . . . Too frail."

"She's too intelligent," Larry said.

Blaine gazed at me and smiled fondly. But he would only repeat what he had said, in his soft voice: ". . . A very delicate young lady who should take better care of her health. . . ."

In May something absurd and degrading happened: I discovered money missing from my billfold. All the bills had been taken— about forty dollars. That amount of money is still a fairly large sum to us, but in those days it was enormous. I remember the sickening sensation of that discovery . . . the disbelief . . . the physical shock of it . . . the hurt, fear, shame. I knew immediately that Blaine had taken the money, but what I felt was utter bewilderment: What should I do? . . . I stood in the bedroom, by the bureau, my empty billfold in my hand, blinking tears back; a woman who has been irreparably insulted.

"Of course he took it. Nobody else was in here."

"But I might have mislaid it . . . might have lost it somehow. . . ."

"Like hell! He was here last night and he must have slipped

into the bedroom . . . he must have taken it last night. That son of a bitch! I thought he was acting strange, he kept talking so nervously, chattering on and on about some goddamned plans of his. . . . Of course Blaine took it; who else?"

"But why would Blaine steal our money? He doesn't need money, he has a job."

"He's quitting that job."

"Yes, but . . . but he hasn't quit it yet. . . . But why did he steal from us? Aren't we his friends?"

We talked of nothing else for hours. Larry wanted to telephone Blaine immediately, but I stopped him; I kept saying, again and again, confused and shaken and disbelieving, that perhaps I had lost the forty dollars myself. . . . It might have been my fault. Larry questioned me. He tried to imagine what had happened. We went over the details of the evening, tried to remember everything. When had Blaine arrived, when had Blaine left, when had he been out of the living room and out of our sight. . . . My voice became high-pitched. Larry interrupted me; he started to shout.

"What the hell is this! What the hell does he mean, coming in here and stealing money from us?"

The argument continued for a long time. We could come to no conclusion: if I began to acquiesce to Larry's point of view, Larry would unaccountably switch to another. Was it possible that Blaine had already quit his job, or had he been fired?—was it possible that he hadn't any money at all? And was too ashamed to admit it? . . . Again, was it possible that Blaine had simply been testing us? He had taken the money, yes, and meant to return it? It makes me dizzy even now to remember the intricacies of our arguments, the tireless concentration, hour after hour of *Blaine, Blaine, Blaine.*

Maybe I had lost the money, somehow. Maybe I was to blame. No, impossible.

Maybe someone else had come into the bedroom, had taken the money. . . .

No. Impossible.

"But why would he steal our money? . . . Why us, why his friends?"

He must have been testing us. It turned out that we didn't know him well, after all: we knew his opinions on contemporary art, on contemporary poetry and films, on his own childhood, on the anemic Anglicanism he had rejected as a boy, on restaurants in the Ann Arbor area, on people he worked with, on friends of ours. . . . With no difficulty I could summon him to me, his refined, slightly edgy air, his frown that turned so swiftly into a smile, and back into a peevish frown again; his laughter, which seemed to take him by surprise, as if he were revealing a part of himself he didn't know about, and didn't trust. I can still see him, in my mind's eye. But it seemed to us that we had not known him at all, not really.

He was mentally unstable: that was the explanation.

Like hell, Larry would mutter. That would explain everything, anything. *Like hell. Mentally unstable!*

. . . or testing us? To see if we would accuse him?

But if I suddenly saw Larry's point of view, of course he no longer held it. And if Larry seemed to see the possibility of my point of view, it no longer seemed valid to me. And so. . . . One morning, Larry was going to telephone the police and report a simple case of robbery. Blaine was guilty of robbery. That was that. Simple; clear-cut. We would accuse him, we'd be witnesses, we'd go to the police station and testify against him. . . . But how could we prove it, how could we prove anything? I brought up one point, Larry retaliated by bringing up another. We shouted. One of us accused the other of trying to shield Blaine. Inevitably, one of us said *He was your friend originally!*

Thin, high laughter. Tears. Accusations, rebuttals, exclamations. And suddenly an entirely new hypothesis: offered, perhaps, in the middle of the night, one of us waking the other. . . . And then the angry dissension, the dismissal. "He was your friend originally," Larry said. "He liked you better than he liked me—obviously. Why are you shielding him?"

"Am I shielding him?"
"Am I?"

Not long afterward, the telephone rang and I answered it, half
suspecting it would be Blaine: it was. A cheerful chattery defiant
voice, unmistakably his. Larry was at the medical center. I was
alone. The rehearsed words *Blaine, we know you took that money*
were never uttered; instead, I listened weakly, sadly, helplessly, as
my friend chattered about a trip he was going to take, to visit
relatives in Washington, D.C. Shameful to admit, I actually felt
a pang of rejection: he was going away on a visit, he'd be out of
town for a while. We would miss him. We did miss him. "Judith?"
he kept saying. "Are you well? You're so quiet. Do you have a
cold?—your voice sounds so faint." Judith, Judith. Larry. How is
Larry, where is Larry, is he at the center, how are the two of you,
and thanks for dinner the other evening: a wonderful evening.
As always. As always. His voice began to wind down; I could
imagine his thin shoulders beginning to droop, as they occasionally
did when he was tired, drained by the excitement of a social evening.

I knew he had stolen the money and was daring me to accuse
him. Perhaps he was hoping I would accuse him: hoping for
something, some emotion. We might have been joined, wedded,
in a violent exchange of emotion—accusations—tears. But I refused to say anything, I murmured only a few words, not knowing
if it was courage I lacked or whether I suddenly knew Blaine too
well, too intimately, and wanted only to be free of him.

". . . Judith? Your voice sounds so faint; are you tired?"
"Not at all."
"Are you angry with me?"
"But why should I be angry?"

Our lives are narratives; they are experienced in the flesh, sometimes in flesh that comes alive only with pain, but they are
recollected as poems, lyrics, condensed, illuminated by a few
precise images. It would be dramatic of me to say that our relation-

ship with Blaine ended at that moment—that June morning. But
it would be untrue. We kept talking about the subject of Blaine
and the forty dollars . . . Blaine and the many wonderful evenings we had had with him . . . Blaine and the stray, puzzling
rumors we heard of him from time to time . . . Blaine and I,
Blaine and Larry, the three of us irreparably joined. For the first
time in our marriage we began to argue, almost routinely. We both
developed a certain attitude we could revert to, in order to argue
about that specific subject; our voices altered as if to accommodate
it, *and only it.* One Saturday I met Blaine in a laundromat near our
apartment building, where he was doing his laundry—though in
fact he lived miles away; and we managed to talk, lightly, nervously,
with an undercurrent of highly charged excitement, just like
characters in a play. I began to tremble. Blaine was obviously
trembling; he kept licking his lips. And then, abruptly, I told
him I had to leave, had to do some shopping . . . I broke the
connection between us and walked away and when I returned
to the laundromat a half hour later he was gone. I didn't tell Larry
about the meeting. . . . One day Larry happened to mention,
uneasily, that he'd run into Blaine at one of the university taverns,
an unusual place for Blaine; Larry had dropped in for a beer with
some classmates and Blaine had been there, alone, and they had
had a conversation . . . a kind of conversation. . . . Awkward,
embarrassing. Strange. Larry rubbed his hand over his face and
laughed, irritably. He said something about the vague possibility
that Blaine was innocent, after all, and we'd misjudged him . . .
but when I did not refute this statement, he said, sighing, that of
course Blaine wasn't innocent: he acted like a guilty man, you
could smell it on him.

   We saw him with Rudy Dietz and his wife, the three of them
talking animatedly in the lobby of a theater. Blaine was wearing
what must have been a new sports jacket, a lovely, impractically
cream-colored outfit; he looked taller than I remembered, and
seemed to be starting a beard. A scanty red-brown beard. . . .
The Dietzes were laughing loudly at something Blaine was telling
them, probably an anecdote. They saw us: we waved. It was not

inevitable that the five of us talk together, and so we did not. Afterward I wondered if I was hurt or relieved; Larry said nothing.

We moved to a suburb of Detroit called Oak Park, where Larry got a job as a pathologist at a Veterans Administration hospital. We left Ann Arbor, we still quarreled occasionally, we decided to have a baby . . . we told ourselves repeatedly, like children making a vow, that we would not speak of Blaine Oltman again; the subject would never come up, again. And yet: here is a memory of my opening a letter, my hands shaking, Judith a young wife and a five-months-pregnant mother, opening a letter in the foyer of her apartment building, by the row of brass-plated mailboxes, because the letter is addressed to her husband and the handwriting is that of a friend. *Dear Larry, I suppose you have forgotten me. Out of sight out of mind. Right? But I have not forgotten you & your charming wife. Am lonely. Am bewildered, that you left A.A. without saying good-bye. What went wrong? How did I fail you? Possibly you have been poisoned against me by your wife. Wouldn't be the first time. My number is the same; if you have any inclination, please call. Much has happened in my life. Disaster routine & otherwise. Yrs., Blaine.*

I gave Larry the letter, not bothering to apologize for opening it. He seemed puzzled. Irritated. Why had Blaine written to him, why not to both of us? It was an insult, he decided; he ripped the letter up.

Did this please me? He meant it to please me.

. . . And one evening Blaine telephoned. He had gotten our number from friends of friends; what was surprising was the ease with which I spoke to him. Did he want to talk to Larry? No? He didn't? He wanted to talk to me. So he talked, talked . . . a forty-five-minute monologue . . . did we know he'd left Ann Arbor and was working as a layout designer for a Philadelphia magazine . . . a temporary position . . . did we know he'd been sick, hospitalized with an infection . . . he was in debt, he'd heard we were moving to Canada, did we know that he wanted to leave the country also . . . he hated the United States . . . hated despised loathed the United States . . . he hoped to get

to Rome, maybe on a Fulbright or another grant, maybe an art
scholarship . . . he was in debt, had the gossip reached us? What
did those nosey sons of bitches say about him, back in Ann Arbor?
Well, let them talk; they hadn't anything else to do. Paltry, ordinary lives, unimaginative lives. Bourgeois. Married couples, myopic
values, fools. . . . Did I know that my husband was jealous. Yes,
jealous. Couldn't compete with other men: slow-witted, ordinary.
Did I know that Larry had been jealous all along of him, of
Blaine. Did I know that Larry had resented the friendship from
the first. Did I know that he had the power to expose us, our
marriage. . . . Based on lies, on *personae*. He wanted me, Judith,
to know that my husband, Larry, had been jealous all along . . .
week after week, month after month . . . of the sensitive relationship between us, between Blaine and me. Did I know. . . . Had
we heard about his new job? Temporary, but at least he was using
his artistic skills. A joke, actually; but at least he was working. He
wanted to leave the country. . . . He'd visited Toronto once and
it wasn't bad, awfully cold in the winter which he detested because the cold went straight through him to the marrow of his
bones and . . . and he'd just been ill . . . had lost fifteen pounds
. . . and, and . . . well, Toronto wasn't bad; maybe he'd come
to Toronto if he could get a job. Maybe. . . . Could he come
visit us? He wouldn't be a burden, wouldn't want to stay with us.
Would stay at a motel. Wanted to talk. Must talk with someone.
Must. Must talk with someone who knew him, who understood
him. . . . If Larry disapproved, maybe I could meet him somewhere: just for a few hours. For lunch. For lunch? In Detroit?
. . . Hideously unfair, that Larry should destroy our friendship.
Unfair, unfair. But typical of the bourgeois mentality. A close
relationship destroyed . . . cruelly, whimsically . . . as if it meant
nothing. . . . Married people did such things all the time, safe in
their sickening claustrophobic married love; you couldn't trust
them, you opened your heart to them and they betrayed you.
Did I remember the countless times he had driven me around,
to the clinic when Larry was sick, to movies and the library and
. . . and often he had had other things to do, in fact. He, Blaine,

had had a number of pressing engagements, often, which he'd broken. For us. And now what? . . . Married people moved away without saying good-bye; they laughed, gossiped, told lies. The Dietzes were both liars. That cow especially, slightly cross-eyed if you looked closely. No amount of eye shadow and mascara could disguise it. Hah. . . . The Dietzes were separated, did I know. Rudy claimed that he, Blaine, owed him money but it was a lie. . . . Could he come visit us? Could he? We couldn't deny him, not so cruelly and bluntly and selfishly. *We didn't dare deny him.*

After a while he began to sob. He hung up, suddenly.

I too was sobbing. Larry took the receiver from me and replaced it.

Certainly, this was the end?

Blaine left his job in Philadelphia and evidently went to Miami; we received a postcard, forwarded to us from our Oak Park address. A few scribbled lines. A valediction that looked like *Love, Blaine.* . . . Only three or four months later we received a lengthy, typed letter, filled with enthusiastic news about his move to London, the semidetached house he was renting with a friend, in a suburb of London. He sounded quite sane; I could almost hear the delightful, sweetly sardonic nuances of his voice. He was going to concentrate on his poetry. Go deeply into himself. Come to grips with his talent, which he knew was considerable: he *knew* it. . . . I replied to the letter, briefly. News of our life here in Toronto, my part-time graduate studies, the baby, Larry's work, no mention of Ann Arbor or of people we had known in common. A letter that set out facts, without passion or coyness. A recitation of the facts of our new life, which allowed for no connection with the past.

And yet. . . .

And yet he returned to the States, returned to Philadelphia. And he is there now. And he is continuing his life as we continue ours, occasionally writing to us, hastily scribbled notes of formal, cautious letters . . . requests for favors, veiled threats, appeals to our charity. He even wanted Larry to be a character witness of some kind, for him, in a legal case that evidently did not come to court. . . . These letters, occasionally; and unpredictable telephone calls, anguished, pleading. *All I want is someone to talk to. Please.* As the years pass Larry and I have come to feel, obscurely, that we are to blame for having wounded someone: for having betrayed someone. Of course, when we realize the circumstances, when we are able to articulate sanely enough our feelings about Blaine, we know that this sense of guilt is absurd. And yet we do feel it, obscurely. Shamefully.

We would forget Blaine; we would wish him happiness in his life, if only he would forget us. But he will not surrender us. He will not give us up. Larry's relationship to him puzzled me; there are aspects of it I don't understand. From time to time Larry alludes to "my" friend in Philadelphia, which suggests that he, unconsciously, is puzzled by my relationship to Blaine and will not forgive me for it. . . . The telephone may ring tonight. Or in six months. Or in a few weeks. He may telephone us as he did, not long ago, demanding that we arrange for him to get a Canadian visa . . . demanding that we forgive him . . . or he'd kill himself, he'd spill gasoline around the room of the dump he lived in and light a match and we'd have only ourselves to blame, we could enjoy his death agony from our secure smug despicable marriage and our hideout in a foreign country. . . . Traitors, we were. We betrayed him, didn't we? Traitors. Liars. Stepped on him as if he were an insect, cast him aside, tried to forget him. . . . Traitors to their country and to their closest friends.

Please let us go, Blaine, I whisper. But he doesn't hear.

*H*ello Fine Day Isn't It

—nice weather isn't it, where are you going, do you live around here, it's nice around here isn't it, well good-bye now, nice to talk with you, I have to leave now, see you around—

At first he appears to be no more than twelve or thirteen years old—there is something childish in his gangling artless body, the studious manner in which he looks from side to side before crossing even a near-deserted street; something frank and boyish in the way he walks. Perhaps it is too boyish, bouncy, as if he were trying to imitate—almost successfully—a way of behaving that had once served him well.

Approaching you, he ages rapidly. *Thirteen . . . sixteen . . . eighteen . . .* maybe *twenty?* Might he be *twenty* years old? His forehead is brick-red, newly sunburned and lined with the intensity of his emotion, he must be at least twenty years old, perhaps twenty-five, and there is something that appears to be, suddenly, adult and weary in the chirping phrases he utters, all the while grinning anxiously: *Hello fine day isn't it, nice weather isn't it, where are you going, do you live around here, it's nice around here isn't it.* . . .

Renée saw him first, but did not mention it to her husband. She thought: *I hope Evan doesn't notice that boy.* . . .

For weeks she did not see him; she forgot about him. Then, suddenly, she happened to notice him everywhere in the neighborhood—playing with younger children in the vacant lot beside the IGA store, watching a road crew laying blacktop on a section of Riverside Drive, laboriously fitting his bicycle wheel into the rack outside the branch library on Wyandotte Street. Of course he was harmless. He turned a broad cheerful sunburned face to anyone who happened to approach him, and did not seem—judging from his manner—to discriminate between children, teen-agers, or adults, or to discriminate between those who did not mind chatting with him and those who were unnerved or irritated by the ordeal. Renée noticed her husband at the end of their driveway one Thursday afternoon, late, bringing empty garbage pails back to the garage, and she saw the boy out there with him— the two of them evidently talking—or at any rate the boy must have been talking to Evan. But Evan said nothing about it later. He had not known Renée had seen him, and he said nothing. Obviously the boy was harmless and the incident not important.

The next time Renée happened to see him, it was in another context: he was far from their neighborhood, a suburb east of the city, hitchhiking along a stretch of the Drive that was rather fouled with gritty smoke at that moment—smoke from a Chrysler plant not far away—the boy vulnerable in this unfamiliar setting, in a neat, freshly ironed shirt that was a size or so too large for him. He stood with his fist raised, his thumb in the air and pointing toward home, with an awkward formality the other hitchhikers were not observing. . . . They were all young people, the half dozen of them who were hitchhiking that day, but none of them bothered to stand; they were sitting or squatting on the sidewalk, arms languidly raised or not raised at all. It was quite common for young people, high-school students or college students, to hitchhike in the city. It may have been against the law—Renée did not really know—but the police never bothered them; there was nothing dangerous about hitchhiking in this Canadian city. Renée considered slowing —pulling over to the curb and giving the poor boy a ride out to Telford, where she assumed he lived—but the Drive was only a two-lane road at this point and there was traffic close behind her. So she drove past them all. She hoped he might not notice her. . . .

Yet, strangely, he did. So seeming-vague, so amiably moronic, the boy nevertheless happened to fix his gaze directly on Renée's as she drove past at thirty miles an hour.

He appeared for the first time in the Maynards' back yard when Renée's mother was visiting in late September. It was a fine, warm, sunny day; the two women were sitting outside, on the makeshift terrace above the river. The Maynards' rented home, some fifteen miles from the center of the city, was a single-storied frame with shutters, a front veranda, a brick chimney that looked in danger of falling apart, and a small weedy terrace that overlooked the river through a cluster of still-healthy elm trees. The house needed painting, and the garage, which was at the front of the house, since houses along the river were built close to the river, was very nearly an eyesore. But Renée loved the house and had been successfully eluding her mother's tentative uncompleted sentences and questions . . . *Will you be here long do you think, will Evan be able to get the kind of job he deserves do you think.* . . . until the boy came along, and her heart sank.

God, no.

The hundred or more yards that separated the house from the river dropped slowly, all rocks and crabgrass and the remains of dandelions and thistles, a few tiny trees growing wild; it was what might be called an unimproved lawn. The previous tenants of the little house had evidently not taken care of it at all. But Renée was proud of the narrow stretch of beach—it *was* something, she believed, to have actually found a house to rent on the river—to have that view of the river, however marred by the weeds and the scrubby little trees—and so it seemed to her a kind of betrayal, that the boy should appear there, wading along the shallow shore, splashing happily, his trouser legs rolled up to his knees.

He waved at them. He called out *Hi!* He waded ashore, grinning, and grabbed onto one of the small trees as if to pull himself up the slope—though the slope was very gentle, not at all steep. Renée's mother, who had been remarking on the very nice lawns and parks in this city, all the flowers, the well-tended gardens, *Is all of Canada like this?* fell silent, seeing the boy.

His face was evenly tanned now. His grin was the same as always: wide, moist-toothed, anxious. His eyebrows were thick and curly, and sandy-hued, though his rather stiff, wiry hair was brown; someone saw to it, Renée had noticed, that his hair was trimmed neatly every two or three weeks, and shaved up along the base of the skull so that he resembled not a teen-ager, not a young adult, but an ageless creature with good intentions. Never did he wear blue jeans, never cheap soiled sweat shirts or T-shirts like the other boys. His clothes were always "adult"—the neatly ironed shirt with the baggy sleeves, the dark trousers. Most of the time he wore white socks and dark shoes, usually polished. Today he was barefoot; his feet were broad and flat, with thick toes. There seemed to be something wrong with his toenails.

Hi! hello there, didn't know you lived here, hiya, fine day isn't it, nice to see you, the river is so nice isn't it. . . .

He wiped his forehead with the back of his hand and left a smear of dirt.

Because her mother was with her, Renée was not at all frightened; she knew the boy was harmless. He wandered everywhere in the neighborhood and played with small children and so of course he must be harmless. Her emotions were confused: mainly, she felt embarrassment. She was embarrassed. The visit from her mother was difficult enough, and now. . . . She tried to behave as if nothing really unusual were happening, she made every effort to reply to the boy's mechanical lilting remarks. *Do you live here now?* he asked. *What happened to the other lady?—the other man? Where did they go? Do you like it here? It's nice here isn't it?*

He was squatting a few yards away, downhill from them. He squinted into the sun and did not seem to mind. The calves of his legs were pale but fairly muscular, and hairy. *Is this your house now? It is, huh. . . . Used to be real good friends with the lady and the man who lived here . . . real good friends. . . . Took me out on their boat all the time . . . how come you don't have a boat. . . . My name is James.*

Renée asked James if he lived nearby.

He smiled anxiously. He started to describe a cocker spaniel the other tenants of the house had had . . . he became confused, said no, that was somebody else, but they let him play with the cocker spaniel anyway. . . . He asked Renée if she had a dog. No? Why not? Was she going to get a dog? He knew of some puppies. . . .

Renée said politely that she didn't think they were going to get a dog, no.

Mrs. Brompton was staring at the boy. Alarmed, was she?— Renée could not always judge her mother. At times the older woman was quite unpredictable. But Renée spoke cheerfully to James, warmly, to neutralize her mother's hard blank stare, to let the boy know that everything was all right, he should not be so anxious, she was friendly even if other people in the area probably were not. . . . She heard her voice become mechanical as she spoke about the river being very pleasant, yes, they liked their house very much, yes, they were very happy here. . . . *Where do you live, James?*

But so direct a question seemed to baffle him. He was grinning past Renée at her mother, his forehead creased with concentration. His mouth smiled, as if independent of the rest of him. . . .

Renée noticed how the bluish-black nails of his toes, the big toes especially, had been clipped neatly across, straight across, by someone who loved him.

. . . *no dog, huh, going to be alone here, huh.* . . .

Renée wished suddenly that her husband were home.

As if he could sense her thoughts, the boy rose suddenly, lurching to his feet. He muttered something about being sorry but he had to leave now, there was a friend of his up river he had to go fishing with, had a rowboat they owned together, it was nice talking to them, he was sorry he had to go now. . . .

He stumbled back down the bank, waded into the river, without looking back. Walking away, he possessed a precision and determination somehow missing from him at other times. They watched him wade upstream, past the neighbors' beach, and out of sight. The river was shallow for about ten yards out, then it dropped abruptly, and in the center of the river—in the ships' channel—it was very deep. Today the waves were shallow and flat, there was little wind. The boy splashed through the meager waves, happily, and disappeared.

"That was—"

"Who on earth was—"

Renée and her mother had both spoken at once.

"Renée, who on earth was that?" her mother whispered. "He's dangerous. That creature is dangerous."

"He isn't dangerous," Renée said at once. ". . . He's just a boy who wanders around the neighborhood. He lives somewhere nearby, obviously everyone knows him, he's just a little slow, a little retarded. . . . Mother, I live here and I know. I've seen him playing with children. He's harmless."

"He isn't harmless. He isn't a boy."

Renée felt she hated her mother, suddenly. This heavy-breasted powdered perfumed woman, not yet old, hardly middle-aged except for the self-pitying indentations around her mouth—why did this woman want to ruin everything?

"You're not in New York City," Renée said stiffly. Then, remembering that her mother no longer lived in New York, that she had moved to Long Island after the death of Renée's father, she said, "You're not in the United States."

And certainly Mrs. Brompton was wrong.

Renée saw James waiting for her one morning outside the drugstore. He dawdled by the telephone booth, where a girl's bicycle was parked. He waved and grinned excitedly at Renée. *Hi how are you nice day. . . .* He was dressed as usual; his shoes were even polished. Though Renée was wearing sunglasses and her long dark-red hair was pulled back into a knot, the boy evidently knew her. Pleased, polite, even inclining his head slightly as if in a gallant bow, he ran through his litany of bright chirrupy phrases. Except for his curly eyebrows, the boy's face was perfectly hairless, his jaw and chin perfectly smooth. Renée wondered wildly if someone shaved him—*Does someone shave you every morning, lovingly?*—and managed to back away, smiling, smiling, while he explained why he couldn't walk with her—he was guarding a friend's bike, he said—he was a watchdog guarding it—sorry he couldn't talk longer with her—

Renée left the drugstore by its other entrance.

She forgot about James.

Evan left home most mornings at about seven-thirty and got to the hospital where he worked at eight; sometimes he did not get home again until well after six. They were not Canadian citizens —they were living here as "landed immigrants"—and he had had difficulty getting his job, which, so far as Renée could judge, had to do with assisting one of the professors of the university's medical school with research he was doing—since Evan did not speak of it often, she gathered that it must be humiliating in some way; perhaps the professor was younger than Evan, or perhaps less qualified. She didn't ask. She didn't care to know, really. The two of them were happy here. The prospect of being "happy" and of leading a simple, uncomplicated, unsoiled life was so new to them, so remarkable, that it more than compensated for other things.

So, though she had forgotten James, Renée was careful not to mention him to her husband.

One morning, shortly after Evan drove down to the hospital, the door bell was rung—yet no one was there. Renée had been leaving the door unlocked, so she thought *I'll lock the door after this*, since Telford was a fairly busy little town, and anyone might wander through.

In late October she noticed James, or a boy who resembled James, out on the sidewalk in front of the grocery store. He was talking to or being teased by several grade-school girls. They were small girls, yet flirtatious, Renée thought—daring—one of them stuck the tip of her pink tongue out at James, giggling provocatively. Renée saw the boy's reddening face, his narrowed shocked eyes, and was herself profoundly shocked. She was passing them, and her heart began to pound quickly as if she were passing something dangerous—but there was no danger, of course—neither the girls nor the boy so much as glanced at her. Heated, excited, giggling, they took no notice of her at all.

Something terrible is going to happen, Renée thought. Her thinking was not her own: she seemed to hear her mother's voice, whining and complacent. But no: she heard nothing. It was absurd. She had left all that behind, that ugly self-dramatizing panic, that entire way of life.

Nothing is going to happen at all, she thought carefully. *Nothing.*

At first he appears to be no more than twelve or thirteen years old—there is something childish in his posture, his manner, especially when he hesitates to cross the street, as if he were risking violence by so simple an action. Or as if, knowing others to be omnipotent, he were risking a complete, catastrophic punishment. . . . How easy to do something wrong, how easy to make a terrible mistake! At times, when St. Joseph's Elementary School recesses at noon, he stands in the center of the flow of children who swarm out to the variety store on Wyandotte and then it is clear he is not a child: he is thicker, wiser. His body is wise.

At other times, hitchhiking back from downtown, alone, backing along the curb, his face slack from too much eager smiling that day, he appears to be a young wizened adult—in his late twenties, maybe. It would take very little to make him smile, however, that tooth-baring grin *Hello how are you today wonderful weather isn't it looks like rain doesn't it.* . . . For weeks you won't see him; you forget him. Then you see him everywhere, as if by magic. Renée Maynard, going into the darkened garage in front of their house, had the peculiar idea one morning that James was hiding in there. The garage was very cluttered—crates, cartons, piles of lumber, trash. There were many places one could hide. She called out *James? Are you in here, James?* . . . *Are you hiding in here?*

She was reasonably certain that no one was in the garage. No one answered her, of course. But she went back in the house and locked the door. *Nothing will happen,* she thought wildly.

That day passed and nothing did happen.

Through the Looking Glass

I

Two weeks before that morning his thirty-eighth birthday had dawned, and except for a few cards and a few useless presents it had passed unnoticed. Now on this gray Monday morning, November in the flat endless Midwest that itself was like a season of the year, he rose at six to the stir and sleepy bustling of the other priests in the residence hall and was distracted by something foreign in his room. In the corner of his eye he saw something that didn't belong, some pinprick out of place on the floor behind his desk. He had had his birthday cards—mainly from female relatives, and ex-students who scrawled their perennial gratitude —in a stack on the edge of the desk and maybe one had fallen off. But when he groped about the floor, even reaching under his bed, he could find nothing. No card, not even a black button, not even a filmy ball of dust—nothing. When he straightened again he saw nothing and when he continued his dressing nothing teased him out of the corner of his eye.

Before that he hadn't thought at all about the birthday, being too busy and happily involved in his activities—he was moderator for two student organizations, he was a member of the NAACP and of the Archbishop's Committee for Fair Housing, he was a member of the National Council of Christians and Jews, in addition to teaching twelve hours a week and working on his Renaissance book and farming himself out to organizations, mostly female, who were desperate to be talked to about culture and meaning in life. And he had many friends. Everywhere he went he seemed to find, already existing, a brotherhood to which he belonged.

The damp cold of the chapel dulled his thoughts about being thirty-eight, and by breakfast time he had forgotten it. What he liked about meals was the conversation that went on about the big tables; his food sometimes grew cold while he talked. He had never much liked food, and he didn't share most of his colleagues' enthusiasm—the public liberalism of a new breed of seminarians —for social drinking, which only reminded him of his mother and her disintegration. These processes that worked upon the body, working inward, left him restless and mildly uneasy; he liked to play tennis and handball and he liked to go for long aimless walks kicking leaves about the campus, and most of all he liked to stride into his classes and feel that spark of excitement touch him as the students' eyes turned upon him, actions that led outward from himself and his long, lean, muscular body, activities that kept him alert. If he couldn't use his body as he did in athletics, then he tended, perhaps too often, to use his voice; he loved to argue, in and out of class, a friendly prattling he and the younger priests thought of as clever.

That morning he walked with his yard-long strides in and through the varying waves of students, the girls' heads covered meekly against the wind and the boys' heads, with their red ears, bypassed by Father Colton in his neat black coat and his shining black shoes. He would have liked to run the quarter mile from the residence hall to the old Hall of Languages, where he taught. The wind that chastened the young inspired him and already he felt younger than they, the hard little kernel at the center of his being the perennial twenty-five years of age he'd been when he had first begun to teach and had first attracted attention. Eight o'clock. The bell was ringing. It was part of his style to walk in after the bell rang, never before. Hurrying up the stairs, he passed students who kept up a chorus of hellos to him, so many students by now that he had to admit he couldn't remember them all. But their familiar faces and their still more familiar clothes gave him a strange sense of possession, as if he'd been here before and had known everything and everyone, had nothing to fear, he was in a sense as old as this ancient building and as permanent. When he approached his classroom the opened door framing the room was like a special invitation: only he had the right to come along and close that door.

His classes always went well. Though his students were too docile and polite to suit him, he took from them a feeling of exhilaration, a joyousness that was pure instinct: more than once, out of his vexed love and disappointment in them, he had slammed down his book and demanded, "What do you have to say? What do you think? What do you really think?" That was why, out on the walks or in the Student Union, students freed from the domain of the classroom went out of their way to talk to him. They were always asking him to be on panels discussing Christian existentialism or birth control; many gifted him with their troubles as if spilling secret treasure out onto his already cluttered desk. His friends teased him about being popular, but he did not think they were jealous. He tried not to think about other people's opinions of him at all.

That afternoon, after his three o'clock class, a woman knocked at the opened door of his office. Father Colton shared this crowded office with two other professors, one of them a good friend of his, a layman, and he had the idea—glimpsing the man's profile in the corner of his eye—that this man was staring at the woman.

But she said, "Father Colton, may I see you?" and he recognized her then as a student in his big lecture class. His friend Gormer hastily stood and pulled his chair out of the way so that the woman could pass through, and Father Colton had the confused idea that he too should stand.

With one careless gesture she indicated that he should not stand, never mind. She sat in the hardbacked chair by his desk, much too old and oddly dressed for this place. He was accustomed to boys slouching in that chair, or girls self-conscious and prone to giggling; this woman was over thirty, dressed in a dark suit that would catch no one's eye, her hair was pulled back so that there was only the bare, grim oval of her face for him to look at. "I don't understand some things," she said in a swift, cold voice. Father Colton smiled. "But what don't you understand?" he said. "Anything. All of it," she said. She was pulling something out of her purse, a crumpled blue book. Gazing up at him she had large, critical eyes that must have been gray or pale blue, her indifference blurring what he saw of her. He lit his pipe and she watched the ceremony, but without the maternal interest his girl students usually showed. Finally, exasperated, she let her hand fall onto the blue book in her lap and said, "What's wrong? Why don't you say something? Don't you want to look at my exam?"

"I've already looked at it," he said. He was patient and kindly, his mind searching about for precedent for this sort of older, harassed, unentertained student—everyone had trouble with nuns, of course, and in a way this woman looked like a nun. She looked as if she had jerked down the jacket of her suit to make it shapeless and smoothed her hair back roughly on both sides of her head, to make more definite the hard stubborn shape of her skull. "If you've been attending classes you know what you've done wrong; haven't I gone through that test?"

"I don't mean that," she said, "I mean the whole idea—the Renaissance idea of the relationship between the individual and the governing body of God, I don't understand that. Did those people really believe they fitted in somewhere? It doesn't make sense to me." She tapped nervously at the examination booklet, but Father Colton did not ask to see it. "I was wondering if there was more to it than what you say in class," she said.

Behind her his friend Gormer looked around, a polite fastidious man who was very curious about things; every other week Gormer and his wife had Father Colton over to dinner, and they had a conversational intimacy that sometimes jarred Father Colton when he wanted to be alone. Now he made himself relax and he talked casually to the woman about the philosophical backgrounds of the Renaissance. She looked dubious. "I don't ordinarily bother with such detail in my undergraduate courses," he said, wondering whether she would take that as an insult or a compliment. "The main thing to understand is that traditions do not replace one another; the old traditions continue in one form or in another and they survive for centuries."

"Did they really know all that? What you've said? All those ideas?

"Their assumptions need not have been *conscious*—"

"They must have been crazy, then."

Father Colton felt his cheeks redden. "Why crazy?"

She was stuffing the blue book back into her purse. He had a glimpse of the purse's cluttered interior; she was both severe and sloppy, this woman. Because he found her annoying he wanted to keep her here. He thought of certain people as tests sent to challenge his good will.

"No, never mind," she said. She prepared to leave. He looked again and saw that her suit was dark, thick wool, probably expensive, and on her finger she wore a ring with an odd blue stone. Her hands were long and angular and nervous, the bluish veins slightly raised like faint shy echoings of that blue stone; her nails were colorless and finely shaped. The vague half-moons of her nails made him suddenly dizzy, as if he were not looking at the surface of a thing but somehow into the distance, inside it.

"Whenever you feel uncertain about something, talk it over with your instructor. But why does this confuse you?"

"I don't believe in it."

"Do you have to believe in it, just to get through the course?"

She looked around nervously. This evasion of his gaze meant that she wasn't Catholic; even an ex-Catholic would drift into a guarded ease, faced with so friendly a priest. "I mean for myself," she said. "I don't take these courses just for credit—I'm not enrolled for a degree. I want to learn. I want to understand things clearly."

"Yes, good," Father Colton said.

"I drive down from Medford three times a week, for your course and Dr. Rich's—but that's history, that's no problem. I can believe history because it happened. But I can't believe some of the things you say."

"History hasn't necessarily happened," Father Colton said. "Not in the form it's given to us."

She paused as if shocked and saddened by his remark. Then she shook her head to get rid of it. "I only want to understand things, learn things. I'm not your students' age—I can't believe as easily as they do."

She stood. He said, a little reluctant to have her leave, "Any time you want to talk—don't hesitate to come in."

Afterward, walking restlessly out in the corridor, Father Colton thought of how grim she had been, and how he had not been able to get to her. At retreats, giving speeches, in class, he was able to *get to* his sleepiest students by being clever, clever in a kindly way. He felt he had a message to deliver and he had to deliver it. But he was the kind of priest who is always told, man to man, that he isn't like a priest at all; "You know what I mean," people said awkwardly.

After that he was aware of her in class, sitting far over to the right. There were several vacant desks around her. Her silent, dark shape was irritating, but he was pleased one day when she smiled at something he had said. "It is only man's pride that makes him think he can commit an unforgivable sin," he said. This was in oblique reference to *Dr. Faustus*, and not meant to be amusing, but she did smile; it was not often that she smiled. He looked up her name on his seating chart and found that it was Frieda Holman.

One day after class she stopped to talk with him. She was shy, edging up to him as a boy in a great white sweater backed away, hesitant and therefore a little abrupt in her manner. It was as if she were out of practice in her dealings with people. She asked him a small, reasonable question and they walked from the class-room down to his office, the woman's head slightly inclined as she listened to him talk—and how he did like to talk, when someone listened so intelligently! At his office door she said, "I've done a lot of reading in the last year but no one has ever talked with me about it. I mean . . . about religion and life and things." She wore something blond, a dress or a suit, and Father Colton had the unclear impression of something golden about her—earrings, perhaps. He was not accustomed to looking closely at people.

It happened that he began to notice her around campus—it was a small, crowded city campus—and that, at parties, he had the vague expectation she would be arriving suddenly. He teased himself with the thought that he might be falling in love with her. He did not take this thought seriously; he was too busy. But he liked the way that woman (he did not think of her as Frieda, yet) would pause and think about what he said, as if it were of profound importance. His students accepted everything, politely and enthusiastically; the wives of his colleagues—all Catholics— agreed with him before he finished what he had to say. That woman thought about things as if they might be true or not true and as if they might be important. One day when he was explaining something to her, in his office, Gormer was discussing something animatedly with a graduate student, and Father Colton felt a surge of rage at having no privacy.

"Yes, look, the Incarnation explains everything," Gormer said. He was a very religious man; Father Colton felt that if a priest were to hand him a stone and tell him it was the Body and Blood of Christ, he would gulp it down at once. "Christ is everything and we are all part of Christ. I encounter you; you are Christ. All our actions are related to Christ. We suffer, and we offer our suffering up to God. Everything relates to Christ."

If Father Colton's frowning student thought this was questionable she gave no indication; having no sense of humor, she was always polite. She had bluish shadows beneath her eyes, but her eyes were attractive just the same—had she been able to relax she might have been an attractive woman. But when he made her laugh she said, "You aren't serious," meaning that such moments did not count. Life was serious. Always she circled in, she pressed in, toward a center that was absolutely fixed. It was only after a month of their talks that she confessed what this secret was. "There's a long period before a divorce when everything is chaotic and ugly, but somehow you feel like living. You don't want to give up. You want to get through and out the other side. But after the divorce . . . nothing seems to mean anything. I know this must sound awful to you. But I'm not Catholic. . . . And you can't understand what that is, when you feel that nothing has any meaning, it's just—nothing—one day after another—"

"I can sympathize with that feeling," he said.

"But you don't know what it is."

He raised his hands in a gesture of helplessness. She frowned, staring at his hands.

"You talked about despair in class. To you people despair is a sin," she said. "I'm afraid that's another thing I can't understand."

"Despair is a condition that is sinful," Father Colton said. "It is a condition of pride."

"Pride? No, I don't understand that." Her voice was sharp. This aroused something in him, some talent for stress and tension that was rarely exercised, and he leaned forward and talked to her in a calm low voice about despair, which was a kind of *accidie*, one of the seven deadly sins because it was just sloth, inertia, sinking to the bottom of one's soul and refusing to believe in the power of God to raise one again.

"I know about despair," she said bitterly.

"It's just sloth," he insisted. "Sloth—inertia—"

"Oh, for Christ's sake," she said, with a surprised laugh. He paused, midway into another sentence, and the moment struck him as precarious and dazzling. They smiled at each other and after that single moment their smiles vanished. He said fastidiously:

"Are you in despair of God?"

"No, of reality. Of life."

"Do you live alone?"

"Yes."

"Haven't you anyone you love?"

"No, no one."

"No one who loves you?"

She hesitated. "I don't know," she said.

"Are you thinking of your ex-husband?"

"No, I never think of him."

"But—why not?"

"He could be dead, it wouldn't matter."

He wanted to protest this but, after a few seconds, he only said: "You ought not to be alone so much, then." She agreed, silently. "Do you work?—Maybe some other woman there—" But she indicated that she did not work, of course she did not work. Her sullen pride excited him. He seemed at such instants to be peering into her soul, which was prickly and dangerous. Other souls were smooth and sweet as cream, one could scoop one's finger in and taste it and pass by forever; they were saved.

"I'll try not to be alone so much," she said ironically.

He kept the word "despair" in mind and, off and on during his busy weeks, wondered if there might not be something behind it. Good-humored and healthy as he was, Father Colton had never much understood the unhappiness of others. There were priests in the residence hall who, it was whispered, were not happy in their calling; always in the great bustling world there were people who were not happy in their lives. But he had the idea that somehow they willed their unhappiness. It was their own fault. With so much given to man, so many graces and gifts, to be unhappy was to be spiteful—like Frieda Holman, who was certainly spiteful in that surprised, agitated way of grown women who find themselves with the emotions of children. She was spiteful! He would tell her that the next time he saw her.

Around Christmas he had many things to do. He volunteered for work though it kept him from his book—a study of Elizabethan drama that was already behind schedule—and he found himself invited to a number of dinners and parties, sensing that he was the center of many of these occasions and that, simply by existing, he was giving happiness to others. But he did not like to think of himself in terms of other people, because this was vanity. It made him nervous and irritable to be so weak. He had always taught himself to control every emotion, even those that appeared to admirers to be spontaneous. So when Frieda Holman missed two of his lectures he was not angry with her, or worried about her, but concerned with his own pride; he didn't like that pang of disappointment in his breast. He tramped around in the snow thinking of their last conversation—yes, he had told her she was spiteful. Was he often too careless, just as older priests were too rigid? Did they all fail?

His last lecture before vacation should have been excellent, but something went wrong. He was nervous and agitated; he wondered if the students noticed. Frieda Holman was not there. When he finished at last and the students trooped out, already dressed for the outdoors and eager to be gone, he glanced down at his rather square, coarse hands and thought suddenly that he had wanted, once, to be a writer. He had wanted to write . . . a number of short stories, nothing more. He had not thought of this for some time. The memory followed him out of the building and, looking up her name in a telephone directory, he had the vague bemused idea that she was connected with something he had wanted to write, or to create, long ago. For a while he sat with the receiver off the hook and no dime dropped—it was a public, and therefore a private, telephone—his breath skimming across the mouthpiece and making that immediate, shallow, dead sound.

Driving out to Medford Father Colton imagined: *No, you are not spiteful, but only unpracticed in joy.* Her apartment building looked so impersonal, even public, that anyone could have entered it without fear. But, knocking at last at her door—how long it had taken him to get here!—he felt a curious sensation of panic. Before he had become this charming, robust self he had been a skinny kid afraid of everything, bigger kids or the tart fires of hell, and he remembered knocking at doors to collect money for his paper route and praying that no one would answer. He remembered telephoning people and praying that no one would answer. Suddenly everything had become clear to him and he had stepped through into his new life, as if through a mirror, coming out on the other side: his priesthood had made everything possible. Everything had been explained by it—or had everything been metamorphosed? He had stepped through the mirror and come out in another world, able to deal with people because he did not quite believe in them. He believed in their "sins," however, and, yes, he did believe in them a little—they were reflections on the surface of the world he had left. Doubt, despair? They were words. He did not believe that anyone took them seriously. Evil was a word before which one looked grave; it was the lot of fallen man. "Fallen man" was another phrase. And on and on, and somehow along the way people did commit violent acts and people did fall into "despair" and even into "love," as if those words had the magic to summon up emotions in those who used them. . . . He thought: *You are not spiteful, but only unpracticed in joy.*

She opened her door but kept the chain latched cautiously, and this struck him as practiced indeed. Recognizing him, she looked alarmed—then she looked guilty. "Father Colton, I'm sorry—I haven't been well—I should have called school—"

"I thought you might not be well," he said. "I thought I'd better check."

With her face to the crack she was all eyes and hair and mouth; her alarm spread to agitate the air around them. "It's very nice of you to be concerned—I'm sorry—"

"I thought you might be . . . might be seriously ill," he said.

She stared at him. He had the idea that she was thinking, guiltily, *Might be dead, might have committed suicide;* and perhaps this would have been an annoyance to him. The silence was awkward. Then she said, "Do you want to come in?"

"Yes."

He went in with the abstract, ambitious air of Christmas that he had carried with him from the college campus, a man with a message to deliver, but her room depressed him at once. He could tell that she was sick. There was an odor of something flat and sad about the cluttered room, whose sleek pieces of modern furniture should have made it immune to sickness. So the casual disorder of clothing and water glasses and newspapers looked all the more shocking. "I've been taking some pills. I'm not really sick," she said, embarrassed. She wore a shapeless blue gown. She was barefoot. On one side of her face were faint red lines from a pillow. "It's so kind of you to come out, I don't know what to say . . . I . . . I'm a little dizzy. . . . Those pills don't help much. Sometimes doctors do that, they give you sugar or something and charge you for it, you can't trust them. . . ."

Father Colton glanced about the room, trying to locate a center. He wanted to sit down. He wanted to return to the rhythm of their best conversations, her appeal to him and his wisdom to her, but, standing as they were, he did not know how to begin. She spoke quickly and shrilly about her doctor, Dr. Flint. "I don't know him," Father Colton said.

"It's a woman," she said. "I'd never go to a man. . . . Still, I don't trust her either."

"I wish you wouldn't talk like that."

"I know what I'm talking about," she said at once. Some force nudged her into sharp little utterances—she was like a child daring the loss of love. "It's very kind of you to come here, but it isn't your problem. You shouldn't bother with me. You don't have anything to do with me and you're busy, you're writing a book—"

"I think you need help."

"That's very kind," she murmured. She was careless of how the bright winter light from the window illuminated her skin and her uncombed hair. The whites of her eyes were unclear and she looked frail and savage at the same time. "I was talking to her about you, to Dr. Flint, and she says—she says it isn't necessarily crazy—I mean religion, I mean for me—"

Father Colton laughed.

"But what are you laughing at?"

"Would you like me to call her for you?"

"Who? Call who?" She sat. She looked drugged. "I woke up and heard that knocking. . . . The problem is, if you can't sleep at night you have to take pills. Then you wake up during the night and can't remember how many you've taken. . . . How many classes did I miss?"

"Never mind the classes."

"How long have you been here? I can't remember. . . ."

"Just a few minutes."

"I thought it might be you, knocking," she said. Her voice was nervous and shrill. "I was hoping it would be you. You are the only one I can talk to. . . . I thought of your lectures and how much I learned, and out on the walk one day you told me something about yourself: that you wanted to write some stories. . . ."

"Did I tell you that?"

"Didn't you? Something about stories . . . I can't remember. My head aches."

Father Colton stared at her. He felt a heavy suffocating sweetness that was not just love but an immense gratitude for everything she said.

"I came here to get away from the other place, where I lived," she said. "I couldn't stay there any more. Someone said he was going to get married again. . . . I don't care about him but it hurt me, hearing that. I'm afraid to be alone. I don't know what to do . . . I mean, how to live. . . ."

He sat in a chair facing her. At his feet was a magazine; he pushed it away as if its glossy cover were an affront to him. The woman had begun to cry. This did not alarm him because he was accustomed to people crying in his presence; having witnessed so many tears he understood that he would never cry himself. "I was wrong about you," he said. "You are not a spiteful woman. You aren't spiteful." She turned from him, ashamed of crying. As if he were reading lines from a story he himself had written he went on, "Not everyone is strong enough to live alone. There are some people who can't do it, who shouldn't be asked to do it. Living like this you have no joy in your life."

He saw that the cords of her neck were rigid and white, as she turned from him to hide her face.

"Those pills are dangerous. Your life is dangerous like this," he said. A great pulse began to beat in him, flooding his brain with blood. But he was not afraid. All the fear and weakness between them had shifted over to her, to that frail sobbing body. As time passed and he remained there, talking gently to her, he thought about what he would do: the letters he would have to write, the preparations for another life he would have to make. He knew that he would be equal to these demands. A wistful, restrained joy rose in him. The pale winter light that flooded into the room was beautiful, with a beauty that must have been supernatural, as if angels had torn open violent rifts in the sky for the sun to shine through—and he thought of his friend Gormer's statement that day in the office, that Christ is found everywhere, and he loved Gormer for having said it and he loved the very fact of having heard it, by accident, with Frieda there—and he thought of how Frieda was Christ, in her loneliness and suffering and the terrible danger in which she lived, and how he was Christ in ministering to her, saving her. He had no doubt about the sanctity of what he was going to do. It must have formed itself in his sleep, in some secret recess of his brain, while he labored with his book or joked with friends, innocent himself of what he would be asked to do.

Later she said, "But do you love me? Do you *love* me?"

II

They were married on the third of January. He had been seeing her every day and, near the end, many people must have guessed. He must have brought back from her some of the wildness she

could not control, a love that was anguished and timid and demanding at once—and he always thought, drugged with the
memory of her and all that she needed, that he was now in reality
and his life before this had been a life of shadows; only now was
he being tested. He felt pity for the other priests. Frieda, waiting
out the long mornings and afternoons in that apartment for him
to come, seemed to him someone he had known all his life, the
very texture of her skin familiar, and the anxious glance of her
fine, sharp eyes, and all the fears she had of losing him and the
guilt she felt for taking him away from . . . his "other life."

He listed his occupation as Professor of English on the marriage
application, though this position would now be taken from him.
He listed his age as thirty-eight. Writing down that figure, with
Frieda close beside him, he had an uncanny sense of having fled
through vast spaces of time without having changed at all—still
thirty-eight, after so much—and Frieda, distracted by the official
demands now being made upon them, this filling out of forms and
this acknowledgment of their love, tapped the paper with her
forefinger and said, "I didn't think of you as any age at all."

They were to travel by train some distance to see her relatives,
all the way to Philadelphia. In the taxi she held his hand, nervously, and talked about her people. This was the first she had
spoken of them and she discussed her parents, her aunts and
uncles and cousins, describing obscure relationships between them.
. . . In the train station her voice became suddenly shrill, as if
the great empty ceiling above them were drawing it out. The
station was nearly deserted.

"Do you think I did right, not to tell them?" she said.

"I thought you should tell them, yes. But now it doesn't matter."

"You don't think it matters?" After a moment she said, "I was
wondering if I should go ahead, myself, and let them know. I
mean . . . I could go ahead first."

"By yourself?"

"And let them know."

He stared at her and saw the same brittle, frightened face she

had had on that first day, coming into his office. Her body was
rigid. When he fumbled to take her hand she said, "Please, no,"
and her lips drew back from her teeth.

"But what's wrong?"

"I don't know. I can't . . . I can't decide what to do."

"We did decide what to do."

"I don't know if I can go through with it," she said. She was
breathing quickly. "Why couldn't you have left me alone? It's
all your fault . . . no, it isn't your fault, I don't mean that. I
love you and I want to be with you, but I shouldn't have done
it, take you away from them like that. . . ."

"Frieda, what's wrong?" he said, trying to smile. "When did
all this come up?"

"Please don't touch me," she said.

He did not touch her. They remained sitting side by side for
some time. There was an announcement about the train being
late. Father Colton, who was no longer Father Colton but a man
in an ordinary suit and overcoat, listened to it and knew that it
was important, but a minute later could not remember what had
been said.

"If you go on ahead, will you call me? When should I come?"
he said.

"I'll call you right away when I get there."

"But you'll be all right?"

"Yes."

She began searching for something in her purse, something she
evidently had no hope of finding. He sat staring straight ahead,
looking at nothing, wondering what had brought him to this
drafty train station and to this particular bench, at this particular
time. He felt a little dizzy. It seemed to him that there was someone beside him, a stranger in the corner of his eye with a pale,
rigid face . . . but in the next instant he woke and turned back
to his wife and this time she allowed him to take her hand.

"If the train gets in at nine tomorrow," he said, "what time will
you call me?"

III

Months later he was still thinking it through, sifting and grop-
ing through the fragments of his life. He could not make sense of
it. He did not feel any anger toward her. He understood that she
was sick; she had never called him but he had contacted her relatives—they were real enough—and so he understood about her
sickness, but he could not understand how he had become involved with it. He worked now in Detroit, in a branch of the
post office. He worked from four o'clock in the afternoon to midnight.

Though he felt no anger for her, the thought of her over-
whelmed him. He had been too close to her. He had fallen into
sin. Barred now from the church, he liked to drift in to an
occasional Mass and watch people file docilely up to the Communion rail—and he thought of writing his old friends and writing
his superior, but he did neither. He punished himself by fasting
and this slowed down the endless rummaging in his brain. He
regretted something but he could not always remember it: not
Frieda, and not even his old life, but rather the loss of his love.
His capacity to love. He had loved Christ once but now, having
stepped through the looking glass and become Christ, he understood the sordid loneliness and sorrow of the Savior and he did not
want to share it with anyone. It seemed to him that the crowds
shuffling up to take Communion from some quick-handed priest
(he hated the young priests, who looked so righteous) must
secretly feel the same resentment he felt for Christ, that sufferer
who insists upon suffering and to hell with everyone else! That
meek, pale, holy sufferer befouled with his own blood!—*he* would
have jerked angrily away if anyone had tried to share the weight
of that cross with him, on his way up the hill. When you had gone
through it yourself you had no respect for it. This was what he
regretted knowing, but in his confusion he sometimes could not
remember it clearly.

What confusion was in his brain came out of nowhere. He did not drink. He did not want to please his body in any way, disliking its bulk and its weight and the strange otherness of its desires, dragged around after him from four to midnight every day. His sluggishness was matched by the stale lazy air of the post office after closing time; working with him were many blacks and a number of white men with backgrounds that were surprising as his . . . one of them had a Ph.D. in chemistry, another was an ex-lawyer, still another, whom everyone knew to be an alcoholic, had once been an executive with an insurance company in Detroit. Ex-husbands, ex-fathers, ex-citizens. Settled, pale, puffy faces and spreading stomachs: somehow he felt at east with these men. They asked no questions, expected nothing of him. Here was peace. Silence. Here you could listen to a few of your co-workers discuss their good luck and their bad luck at the Windsor Raceway . . . you might even plan, idly, to accompany them across the border some evening. It would be something to do, and quite harmless. Here you could flip through *Time* magazine, through the *Reader's Digest*, you could squint at messages scrawled on Kodacolor post-cards, from people who felt the cheerful obligation to send such tiny hearty messages back and forth across the country, from foreign countries, from everywhere, to loved ones back home. You could sort out acres of mail, mountains of mail, from one shadow to another. There was never any trouble. It was peace, it was a kind of paradise.

In a year or two, he thought, he might be confident enough to return to teaching—in some remote small college, perhaps. He envisioned the Midwest. Plains, prairies. Harmless distances that negated all melodrama—that swallowed up the individual. He had once been an excellent teacher and he would be an excellent teacher again. He would regain his energy and the clarity of vision he had somehow lost, and he would return to the real world, without the help of Christ, stepping back across the border, back through the looking glass, into what he imagined to be the real world. He did not need love of any kind: neither to give it nor receive it. Why should he have to depend upon anything so precarious, so absurd? . . . Gradually he would understand what had happened to him, what had been stolen from him, and then he would return to the world.

Gradually. In a year or two. There was no hurry.

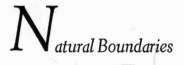

Natural Boundaries

Renée, having lived so long in apartments, inside buildings shared with others, was struck by the novelty of living in a house— though only a rented house, and very small. And since it was on the river, she found herself staring out the back windows, some- times for a half hour at a time, fascinated, transfixed by the move- ment of the river. *How quickly everything changed. . . .*

There was nothing pretty about the Maynards' frame house or the rocky back yard or the scrubby beach, and nothing pretty about the river itself: yet everything seemed to her, in this setting, in the harsh overbright light of autumn, incredibly beautiful. She wondered if her personality were being altered, subtly. On the wide choppy river were flocks of mallards . . . swimming, bob- bing with the waves . . . occasionally squawking loudly . . . one morning there had been three Canada geese out there, swimming complacently, high regal heads and bills . . . . but they had flown

away before Renée's husband got home from work, and he seemed
amused rather than interested when she spoke excitedly of them,
*how beautiful they are, and at the same time a little frightening
. . . something snakelike about the long necks and heads. . . .*

The river was continually changing. The sky was continually
changing: now clouding up, thick and gray and massive and depressing, now abruptly blue again, miraculously cleansed. And
then the storm clouds would reappear. An hour of premature
darkness . . . the promise of rain . . . then, once again, the
sky would turn blue, and the clouds were far away, blown across
the lake to the horizon, harmless. Renée liked this, the rapidity
with which the day changed. It was something new to her.

In sunny weather there were many sailboats on the river. Most
had white sails, but some were decked out with sails of blue and
white stripes, or red and white stripes, one was a bright brave
yellow . . . and there were a number of powerboats, occasionally
a large cabin cruiser from the yacht club on the American
side of the river . . . continual movement, motion. Freighters
passed all day long. From east to west, bound for Lake Erie . . .
from west to east, bound for Lake Huron. And beyond. Some of
the lakers were hardly more than decrepit barges, carrying auto-
mobiles or coal or steel . . . some of the ocean vessels, from as
far away as Japan, were handsome, gleamingly painted, their flags
and insignia illuminated at night, proudly. Home alone much of
the time, Renée stared at the slow-passing vessels, fascinated by
their rough, functional beauty, which was different from the kind
of beauty she had been taught to admire. She wondered who
worked on those boats. . . . Did the workers ever gaze at the
houses along the shore, at her house, perhaps, and wonder who
lived there?

And the coast-guard helicopters that flew back and forth along
the river—what missions had they?—why did they patrol so often?
—were they ready to arrest people crossing the border illegally, by
boat?—or were they merely wasting time, wasting fuel? The rotor
blades were certainly loud. When one of the helicopters passed
overhead, the thunderous choppy sound was deafening. Renée

supposed she would eventually come to loathe it, but in the first months she found herself unaccountably excited by it. *Had something happened? Was something wrong? Was there danger?* . . . So far as she knew there were no accidents on the river, no sailboats capsizing, no small rowboats turned over by the wash of the freighters. Practice rescue maneuvers took place once or twice a week along her stretch of the river, so she was able to watch the operation from her kitchen window, safe, knowing everyone to be safe. How orderly and logical it was, the rescue procedure: the helicopter with its enormous swordlike blades and its flashing red lights, descending slowly, almost in steps toward the boat, the roaring of its engines, the sudden dropping of the rope ladder. . . . It was an orderly, sane procedure, yet, watching it, Renée sometimes felt an accumulation of tension that was almost painful.

They were rehearsing, practicing for disaster.

She was watching the rescue maneuvers one morning in October, when the telephone rang. She continued to watch the boat and the helicopter, drifting downstream, powerful waves all around them—white-capped—and overhead the sky was battered with thick swollen-gray clouds—The telephone rang. She knew who it was; she would not answer it. From the east came one of the long rust-streaked barges with the words *Cleveland Cliffs* in white letters on its side . . . by the time it had passed, the telephone had stopped ringing.

Of course she was flattered.

But also alarmed.

He had something to do with the river, this man, this stranger. No: he had something to do with her loneliness.

She thought of him constantly though she did not love him; she did not love him. She did not even know him. Her husband worked in a hospital on the city's west side, some distance away, and Renée, though qualified to teach in public schools in the United States, was not qualified to teach in Canada . . . and she knew the futility of applying for a job, when unemployment figures were headlined nearly every evening in the newspaper. . . .

It was a bad time, economically. A very bad time. She was temporarily unemployed but believed, vaguely, that she would find something to do before long. There was no hurry. Being a woman, she thought—ironically, but sincerely—that it did not matter quite so much, her being unemployed: to Evan, it would have been like death. But she did not mind. She was a "housewife."

Still, the loneliness of the house was sometimes disturbing. That it was *lonely* because she was *alone* made sense, intellectually; yet the experience of it was somehow a surprise. The silence of the house would at times seem to her sinister . . . the sound of the wind in the oaks and poplars, usually so soothing, at times sounded threatening, like whispers not audible enough to be heard . . . so that she was almost grateful for the noisy interruptions of the coast-guard helicopters or the jet airliners passing overhead. Then the telephone. But after the first several times, the *Hello? Yes? Yes, this is Renée*, she had stopped answering it . . . *I'd like to talk with you but I can't, I can't, I can't . . . please don't call me again.*

Sometimes she told Evan that she had to get out, *she had to get out of the house*, and it didn't matter where she walked: a few blocks up to the shopping area, or down to the library, or just on an aimless walk. . . . Surprised by her, irritated, Evan had not understood; he spoke as if she had somehow betrayed him. His work was exhausting—he was a laboratory technician, assisting a chemist who had a Canada Council grant for the year, who was lovingly and bitterly attached to his work, and expected Evan to stay in the laboratory all day long and after he left, to clean things up—doubly exhausting since the research was not Evan's, and he was forced to subordinate his interest to another man's. Evan didn't speak much about this problem, though Renée had the idea he thought about it constantly, and he seemed to expect her, at the house, at home, to be fully grateful for not having to work. His hands stained with chemicals, his fingernails ridged with something dark that no amount of soap and scrubbing could get out, he laughed sardonically at Renée and said, *Surprising to hear that—you did want to come here with me, didn't you?—or were you pretending?* She did not flinch and did not exactly defend herself—she had too much dignity to "defend" herself to anyone— explaining that she loved this place, this new life, and her loneliness was a trivial and temporary thing, which she wouldn't mention again.

Just to get out of the house: she walked a dozen or more blocks to the branch library, though she had books at home, and journals of Evan's she wanted to read. . . . *To get out of the house, to escape the telephone's ringing or the fact of it not ringing, to end her absurd obsessive thoughts about that man:* so she found herself up at the library several times a week, until the librarians began to recognize her, greet her by name. There, at the round table where popular magazines were piled, Renée might fully enjoy herself, absorbed in her reading, wasting time, scanning articles on travel, though they could not afford to travel, on frozen-food storage, though they could barely afford meat, gazing at full-page advertisements in the fashion magazine . . . *STARTLING NEW LOOK FOR AUTUMN. . . . TWELVE MAKEUP "MAKE-OVERS" FROM BRITISH COLUMBIA.* . . . Other articles purported to be more serious: *WILL CA- NADIAN–U.S. RELATIONS TAKE A TURN FOR THE BETTER? . . . NEW HOPE FOR ARTHRITIS SUFFERERS: MONTREAL RESEARCHER MAKES CAUTIOUS PRE- DICTIONS. . . . THE SHIFTING MORAL PERSPECTIVE: ADULTERY IN THE MIDDLE CLASS.*

She read about adultery in the middle class.

Reading these paragraphs in their logical unexcited order, see- ing how the columns of print on glossy paper were sanely ar- ranged to divide advertisements, to bracket recipes and occasional cartoons, she could see how superficial a subject it was. The mere fact that the word "adultery" might be used in this way, the lead article in the November *Woman's Journal*, with graphs and statistics and quotations and small excited headlines, and all of it to sell copies of the magazine, to sell, sell, sell . . . allowed Renée to see how ordinary it was, how unthreatening. What had it to do with her?—what had it to do with this man Karl?—certainly she was superior to it all, saved from it, from *it*, by the fact of being able to read about it. Still, she felt nervous, not wanting anyone to stroll past her as she sat at the table . . . nervous as if she were already betraying her husband.

The Telford branch library was hardly more than one large room—the floors always polished, the librarians chattering quietly behind the desk, no rude noises, no upsets. Not many people came in during the day, and few sat down, as Renée did, to read. After three fifteen, students came in and things got noisy, so Renée usually left by then. . . . No, the very sanity of her surroundings would prevent her from making any mistakes: what was *passion*, what was *love*, what were emotions of any kind, in this setting?

The danger was back at her house, where she was alone.

She had met Karl Davies at a poetry reading two weeks before.

He was one of the area poets, one of six people reading poems at a special program at the city's art gallery. Renée had received a flier in the mail, sent to occupant, *no admission charge, everyone welcome* . . . and had known at once that she would go. It was certainly not a desperate act; she wasn't that lonely, really. And Evan was home in the evenings.

Long ago, Renée had come to terms with a part of herself. She was one of those people who admired worth in others, especially artistic worth, she was one of the followers, a member of an audience, grateful enough, yet sometimes rather baffled by the division of humanity into those "with talent" and those "without." She wondered if perhaps she were smaller-souled than artists, somehow less concentrated, less passionate. Yet she was more easily content; she was not a competitor, only an admirer. She wanted to admire. She considered it mature of herself, to have come to terms with her own lack of originality, and to be eager to admire it in others.

Why, that night, a feeling of resentment?—jealousy?

The reading was held in one of the gallery's wings. Folding chairs had been set up on the parquet floor, and about fifty people had come out. There was an emphasis on casualness: informality. Each of the poets read without strain, low-keyed, standing at a podium, leafing through papers without much concern for performing. Renée did not know if she cared for that; she wanted to idolize someone, after all. . . . Four men, two women. They were not remarkable people physically, though attractive enough, likable enough; one was especially nervous and ended his selections abruptly . . . Renée had the idea he was a little drunk. . . . Karl Davies read last. The program must have been arranged in order to allow him to read last, since he was the best speaker— probably the best poet, though the poetry was so obscure that Renée could hardly judge. What she could understand was striking, some of it banal, but much of it was lost to her . . . though she didn't mind, she didn't mind not understanding, as she usually did not understand music or art in any rational way. Karl Davies's voice was rather raw, seemingly untrained, yet very effective—very dramatic. He was about thirty-five years old, with black curly hair, thick eyebrows that nearly met over the bridge of his nose . . . a powerful, pushing manner and bearing. He read some of the poems too rapidly, but his voice rang upon certain words, images, and Renée knew she would remember them. *Yes, he's good, that man is really good.* She sensed that the audience admired him very much, it was a performance well done, well done. . . .

Coffee was served in an adjoining room. Renée noticed Karl Davies with a small group of people—friends of his, probably, one of them a woman who linked her arm through his, his wife?— yes, his wife—Renée could see her wedding band. Karl seemed still rather unusual, though he was shorter than Renée had imagined, and the way he spoke, laughed, tapped at his friends' arms showed that he too had been nervous. Though away from the podium he struck her, still, as being an extraordinary man. . . . Two of his children were there: a small boy, a girl of about seven. They were restless, dodging in and out of the crowd. The boy had Karl's dark curly hair and his mother's roundish, high-colored face. Renée, fascinated, stood alone and watched the Davieses and their friends . . . now being joined by one of the women poets, a tall lanky girl in trousers, with a curtain of straight bronze-brown hair . . . all of them laughing loudly, cheerfully. When Karl happened to glance over at her Renée did not even respond to his vague smile, since she had imagined she was invisible: she had become especially invisible, since moving to Canada.

He came over to her; he introduced himself. His manner was aggressive, overbearing, and whatever they said—she must have managed to congratulate him on his poetry, he must have asked her the usual rapid-fire questions *Are you new to the city? American? What does your husband do? Like it here?*—was afterward lost to her. She was intimidated by him. It had really startled her, his singling her out like this . . . she was quick to laugh, embarrassed and girlish and honored and at the same time disturbed . . . thinking that something was wrong, must be wrong. Around them people were milling, holding coffee cups and doughnuts. Karl was telling her about an informal group of people who liked poetry, some of them poets, some not, some associated with the university, some not . . . they just enjoyed each other's company, since the city wasn't exactly a center of culture, as he said sardonically. Renée liked the city and had not compared it to any other city; she was grateful just to be here. But she stammered an agreement and he seemed to be left with the impression that she would join them sometime.

. . . A *fairly good turnout tonight, surprising,* Karl muttered.

Renée, twenty-six years old, with dark-red hair sometimes worn loose on her shoulders and sometimes drawn back into a knot, had the look, she supposed, of a university student: one of those tall, startled-looking, quite often very attractive girls whose bearing— both submissive and striking—make them popular with men of a certain type. Never extravagantly dressed, never ostentatiously "pretty," their appeal is almost intellectual: even their beauty, if they are beautiful, is an arrangement of facial bones, strong elegant cheekbones, strong graceful body. Renée's complexion was milky pale and freckled. Her forehead was rather wide, so she wore bangs to disguise it; her red-blond eyebrows were scant and light, making her eyes appear larger than they were. Her nose was small and ordinary. Her mouth was ordinary. She was convinced that her appearance was an ordinary one, and most of the time she didn't bother to exaggerate her good features—to outline her eyes in black or to paint her eyelids green or blue, as many of the girls here tonight had—so it always surprised her, it truly flattered her, when men approached her; *it must be for herself, herself alone.* Tonight Renée did feel pretty; she was flushed, excited. Karl spoke enthusiastically to her about a recent provincial grant that had come their way—"their" referring to his circle of poet-friends, she assumed—that would subsidize readings in local high schools and in several institutions, a home for the blind, a home for elderly people, a halfway house for young people near the university, and as he spoke he leaned toward her, urgent, yet still casual, with his mannered informality, so that she lost the thread of his conversation and began to feel, uneasily, that this man had somehow recognized her . . . there was a kind of agreement between them. . . . But she must have been imagining it. Only near the end of their conversation did he say something odd, meant to be amusing: *I can tell you're married, you couldn't not be married . . . right? . . . How do you like my son Jamie, the brat crawling under the table there, see him, about to surface by that lady's legs? . . . that's how I looked at his age.*

Later, Renée wished she had drawn closer to Mrs. Davies, after Karl excused himself and returned to her and his friends . . . she wished she had made an effort to see what the woman looked like, up close. *Evie,* her name was; Renée had overheard it. *Evie.* She was a pretty woman in her mid-thirties, though rather flush-faced—her cheeks reddened with the pleasure of conversation, of laughter—blond, the hair too severe, too short, for her plump face. She wore scarlet slacks and a silkish scarlet and green blouse. . . . The kind of woman everyone liked, and Renée herself would probably have liked her; she knew suddenly that she would never meet her. Renée watched the group, watched Karl with them, sliding his arm around his wife's shoulders . . . and, without glancing back at Renée, he drifted with the group across the room, to meet someone else. Renée stared after them, her cup still in her hand, the coffee cold, thinking that it did not matter; it really did not matter. . . . *You couldn't not be married.*

He had nothing to do with her loneliness, or with the river out there, nothing to do with the infinitely changing sky and the waves that were now fierce and white-capped, now flattened, shallow, washing up on the beach. Yet when he telephoned her the first time, a few days after the reading, she stumbled with the telephone across the kitchen, as far as the cord would let her, to stare wildly out the window. She hardly heard what he was saying; she hardly heard her own hesitant, confused replies, *No I don't think so. No, really.* . . . It was a shock, though she had been thinking of him. She had even endured a puzzling and possibly humiliating dream about him, which she could not quite remember. *No, Karl, really . . . I . . . I don't think so.* . . . She laughed at her own timidity. He laughed also, nervously. She had the idea he was extremely nervous. . . . He forced himself to speak more casually, asking her fairly routine questions about how she and her husband liked living where they did: any discrimination against them, as Americans? . . . he hoped not, he liked Americans, he identified with them, for some reason . . . not with the government, of course, but with Americans . . . that is, the Americans he ran into, here and in Toronto. They were rather like himself, he thought. Did she agree? . . . Renée didn't know; she told him *Yes.* He was overbearing even when seemingly deferential. It must always be easier to agree with him, she thought. Always easier to agree. . . . Then he asked her what she did all day long: she hadn't a baby, eh? Somehow he knew she hadn't. Her body, her stance, the way she'd been standing there . . . something about the tilt of the pelvis, he knew, he could tell . . . she was certainly someone's wife, but not a young mother, was that right? . . . Renée was too confused to be offended; she stared out at the river, not seeing it, aware of one of the barges edging into the corner of her vision, aware of something happening, something mysterious and alarming . . . she stared out there, as if Karl were there.

Finally she told him, embarrassed, that she had to hang up.

Of course, of course, he said philosophically.

Yet he telephoned again that day, so late in the afternoon that Renée kept listening for the sound of Evan's car—their drive was gravel, and noisy—and felt how, if she heard it, she would put the receiver back at once. It would be an automatic reflex. . . . Karl apologized for bothering her. He knew it was rude, he knew it was absurd. His excuse, he explained, was to inform her of a foreign-film series shown every Friday evening at the university . . . he thought she might like it, the film being shown next was an early Bergman movie, was he correct, wouldn't she enjoy that? . . . Then he laughed, he said that his excuse really was . . . his real excuse was . . . that he was at Leon's, did she know where that was? . . . no? . . . A tavern, a fish-and-chips place, really a kind of dive . . . right on the river, adjoining a marina, he had the idea it wasn't far from where she lived. . . . Where did she live on the Drive, exactly?

Renée said she would talk to him another time . . . her husband would be home in a few minutes, and. . . .

Hey, I know I'm bothering you, upsetting you, Karl said. But he was cheerful. Behind him were muffled noises: occasionally someone laughed. *I realize that. The thing is . . . the odd thing is. . . . I'm writing a poem for you, having a hard time with it, very frustrating, most of my stuff as you may have noticed is short and blunt and not exactly, you know, idealistic. . . . All I would like is your address, Renée, so that if I ever finish it I could mail it to you.*

When she did not reply, he laughed agreeably. He said he'd read it at the next poetry reading, then; hopefully she'd be there. . . . He mentioned a place, a date, a time. Hopefully she'd be there.

Renée could not remember what she said. She had the idea she said *Yes.*

*

But he must have discovered her address, since she received a letter from him the following week.

She seemed to hear, reading the five-page letter, his highly charged, nervous, yet casual voice: his handwriting was heavy, mostly block letters, he had used a felt-tip pen and had made whimsical slashes and curls and question marks and explanation points in the margins, as if he were writing to himself, daydreaming, a long lyric monologue. The letter began *Dear Renée (Maynard)* and was signed *Yours, Karl (Davies)*.

He began by apologizing again, underlining the word *Sorry!* several times. He told her he'd been born in Blenheim, in Ontario; that he'd traveled mainly in the northeastern part of the United States, and in New York State; that he'd lived in this city most of his adult life . . . and though he mocked it, like everyone else, he really liked it here and had no interest in moving. . . . What he wanted to know was why *she* had come here. Why. Did it mean anything to her, had it meant anything to her. Only an accident, probably? He supposed so; only an accident. . . . But embarrassing as it was to him (and in parenthesis he said *It's good to be embarrassed, good for my ego, let the worst happen I deserve it*) he had the strange idea that, years ago, probably when he'd driven around summers with some friends, down into New York, years ago he must have seen her. . . . She had mentioned she was from New York City originally; he hadn't gone there, but perhaps . . . was it possible . . . was it possible he'd seen her somewhere else? . . . He was not superstitious, he said; he disliked people who believed in astrology, omens, dreams, that kind of thing. . . . But, embarrassing as it was, he had to confess to her that seeing her face had reminded him of someone: a sense of *déjà vu*, very powerful, upsetting. And he was certain he had dreamed about her the night before the reading. She had appeared to him along with the word *separation* and somehow, magically, she had erased that word . . . had caused it to vanish. He had not seen her face clearly, and yet somehow he had absorbed it. . . . It had been a disturbing dream, and he had remembered it when he woke. Now he apologized for having written so much, for probably embarrassing her and wasting her time, but he was curious . . . she didn't have to reply, of course . . . he was curious about whether she had dreamed about him or seemed to recognize him or. . . .

Renée let the letter fall on the kitchen table, her head spinning. . . . She did not usually remember her dreams; she shied away from thinking of them. That jumble of emotions, memories, visual fragments. . . . No, she had never taken any interest in them, she believed in a way that it was risky, to try to recollect too much, poking and probing into that part of one's consciousness. There was something in the dream life that was not human, not recognizable. What was "human" was tempered with a cold, relentless, sinister objectivity, as if viewed from an angle not experienced during the day; though confused and baffling, the dream world struck her as hideously truthful. Yet she did not remember dreams when she woke, only the aftermath of emotions stirred by them, and she never made any effort to recall them.

When Karl telephoned again, one morning a few days later, she thanked him for the letter but told him no, she hadn't dreamed of him, no, she was sorry, and it wasn't likely that he had ever met her . . . and though she hoped to attend the next poetry reading she didn't feel she could talk to him much more, like this, because. . . .

Right, he said at once. *I agree.*

She stopped answering the telephone.

She read clinical articles about "adultery"—scanning the quotations—women's remarks, *Mrs. S., Mrs. K.,* allegedly housewives responding honestly to the interviewers' prying questions, *Mrs. Y. of Toronto, Mrs. M. of.* . . . She had the idea that the entire article was fiction; that the interviewer, a sociologist, had made everything up. For the view of marriage, love, family life, and of adultery itself advanced by the essay was peculiarly passionless: as if these events happened so easily, so mechanically! . . . No, she could not believe. With one part of her mind she respected the statistics, of course. But she could not believe it was that easy; that these women, if they were "real," would not pay emotionally for their cheerful lightweight adventures.

IS TRADITIONAL MORALITY DYING?—DEAD?—OR IN HIBERNATION?

She stopped reading the articles, and now that the weather was colder, rainier, she stayed in the house, she occupied herself with repainting one of the bedrooms: there was much to do, since the house was in poor repair. One day someone knocked at the door. She knew it was Karl; she felt a rush of certainty that was physical, a charge that went through her entire body. A rapping at the door . . . at the front door. . . . She knew it was Karl, and that she would let him in.

No, she would not let him in.

She had not gone to the October poetry reading; she had refused to think about it. At the same time she had been thinking, not quite consciously, that he would therefore come to her . . . he *must* therefore come to her. But now that he had come and was knocking on the door, she would not let him in.

She was trembling. Panicked. . . . Found herself in the tiny bathroom, the door closed, even locked. He could not get her. Let him knock on the door, let him pound on it . . . he could not get to her, she was safe. The young woman who watched her in the mirror was almost white-faced, the blood drawn out of her cheeks especially. Grotesque. Ugly. *If he should see her like this—!* She was wearing old clothes, paint-smeared. A smudge of yellow on her chin. Sallow-pale complexion, not pretty. She was not pretty now. She trembled, wondering if she would be sick to her stomach, wondering at the bravery other women possessed or said they possessed or were said to possess, that adultery should be so easy for them, life itself so easy.

She knew now that they lied.

One day, downtown, she was heading for the parking lot near the river, when she saw a man who resembled Karl. He was leaving Cole's, walking quickly. Alone. Karl himself, Karl Davies. It was a

Saturday, streets were crowded, Renée had been walking near the buildings, on the inside of the sidewalk—she always gravitated inward, away from the curb—and Karl took the outside of the walk, not seeing her. They were going to pass within a few yards of each other. He wore sunglasses with metallic frames and lenses of a dark, greenish-beige, and was dressed as he had been at the poetry reading, in an open-collared blue shirt, a baggy colorless sweater, work trousers, canvas shoes. He was scanning the sidewalk, scanning faces absentmindedly; he seemed to glance at Renée, his eyes moving quickly and curiously behind the beige lenses.

Her hair was drawn back into a knot; she wore an old olive-green trench coat; her face felt very exposed.

. . . He glanced at her, he had seemed to glance at her. Yet he kept on walking. Evidently he had not seen her.

Renée kept on walking.

She knew he had seen her; he had looked right at her. Yet he had not recognized her. . . . Clutching a yellow and black bag from the store, Karl Davies on a Saturday, early afternoon, an attractive man of medium height, with black curly hair. . . . No, not really attractive. His face was bumpy in the white-glaring air. His hair was not black, really brown. And he had not recognized her.

Hello, Renée thought. *Hello, good-bye.*

After months of drought, rains were falling farther north, along the river. The river was rising. There might be floods: floods were excitedly predicted. Renée raked debris off the beach, a scarf tied tight around her head. If the telephone rang back at the house, she could not hear it. If it didn't ring, she could not hear the silence.

"Hello," she would tell him. "I can't talk. Good-bye."

The river made a natural border. Across its choppy, rather ugly waters was the United States, looking like any dismal manufacturing city at this point—smokestacks, billowing black smoke, ragged puffs of white smoke, occasionally small figures that must have been human. "Renée Maynard" raked the beach and laughed to herself, thinking of how she must tell Evan about her experience, someday. How "Karl Davies" and "Renée Maynard" had almost come into existence, had almost confronted each other, yet had not. For some reason they had not. They had not even met. So "Renée" raked the beach, deftly, impatiently, and did not care at all about the flood warnings: let the river rise, let it flood. They were not going to leave their new home. She was not going to leave her life. "Renée" thought of how Renée would always be safe, no matter what.

D_{reams}

I

Several years ago in an eastern city there lived a woman who was afraid. She could not have said exactly what she feared, sometimes it was the fear of fear itself, a state of mind that was ludicrous but terrifying because it was so open. Anything could fill it. She was an intelligent woman in her late twenties who did not really take herself seriously, and so she thought of this strange emptiness as a puzzling joke: but it was not funny. She carried herself around like a vessel, ready to be filled with anything. To keep out fear she had to be filled always with new ideas, new books, the constant assurance of friends.

The city was so crowded that the very jostle of the crowds kept her occupied. To preserve oneself in such confusion demanded a constant surveillance. So she was filled with thinking, a kind of shrewd thinking. At these times she was not a "woman"—she was just a person in a city, manipulating herself in stores and restaurants and waiting for buses. She did not drive. The very idea of driving a car was too "open"—that is, anything could happen, just as anything can happen in a dream when one is driving a vehicle or flying or simply moving along at a bizarre dreamlike speed. So she never learned to drive, and anyway her father had once pronounced her unfit to drive. She respected his judgment. He had been giving her lessons when she was sixteen and had become angry at some small blunder of hers, so she was fated not to drive. It was too much trouble to go against fate, far easier to give into it, and therefore the waiting for buses in good weather and the jockeying for taxis in bad weather.

Imagine a woman of about twenty-seven, with short dark hair and a fair, smooth, slightly puzzled face—eyes large and dark— the whole face not beautiful but in the right light, seen with the right affection, striking enough. She had to wait for these little islands in her life, in which she was viewed in precisely the right light, with the right kind of affection. Time stopped when this happened, and then time moved on again. She was from a small upstate New York city, with a last name that was so important in that city—Brownell—that just to leave the city was a kind of death, because of course her name meant nothing anywhere else. But she had left. Whatever her life was to be, she knew it was not to be discovered in upstate New York.

Because she never had to worry about money she did odd casual things—she taught night courses in poetry at a university extension, she worked as a kind of secretary for a welfare program, she went to Europe with friends. She had a number of friends. They thought of her as a poet, because she wrote poetry and had had several poems published. And so she became a "poet" and people respected her, able at last to categorize that halting gentleness about her, that hesitation in her talk—which was always intelligent talk—the result really of fear but which they took to be a sign of her poetic sensibility. She went to parties and was to be seen talking with groups of men, hesitant, sincere, keen, her dark eyes intelligent and a little haunted at the same time, as if she were afraid of what might happen when the talking had to stop—in short, therefore, an ordinary intelligent woman who happened not to be married, in a society which defined women in terms of their relationship to men.

She was engaged for a while to a man who was studying for an advanced degree in history, but nothing came of it. She lived alone, in an apartment far better than his, and their relationship dragged out over two, three years, another familiar predicament but impossible, really, for her to change. She was aware that she should break off with him, sum up their futile romance with the right kind of joke, but she was so afraid of the emptiness of being without him that she put it off until the man himself decided against her, which was not surprising but which did hurt. She had been afraid of being hurt, and she was hurt, and she lived through it and got a job with a local branch of a federal welfare program, at low pay. Back home women in her family did this sort of thing, for nothing, and it was part of the style of their lives, but to Margo the work had to be serious whether the pay was serious or not.

She was still living alone. At a reception for people on the program she met a psychologist, a man of about thirty-five. She was able to pick him out of the crowd just as he was able to pick her out; it might have had something to do with their clothes, which were good, or their reserved, patient confidence in themselves. For though Margo was a frightened woman she never showed it. Her black hair was puffed out about her face and she stood a little apart from the conversations, as if about to leave, and it was one of her good days—as mysterious as her bad days—when she felt in control of herself, her center of gravity firm within her. His name was David Harris. She saw that the reception bored him and gradually she became afraid, not of his leaving, but of her vulnerability to his leaving. There was something fussy, something nervous and distracted about him; he was a man who believed himself not appreciated at the moment. She said, to get ahead of him, dismissing him politely, "I really have to talk to these people, here—"

indicating her employers, who had been glancing at her. But he went along with her over to them. He was very serious, joining in their conversation about a special project, a class for slum children who were doing poorly in school though they were supposed to be brilliant, according to tests—and Margo knew enough about the project to understand the defensive ironies that surrounded it, for everyone here was afraid of failure and wanted to be protected from it. So they were ironic. David Harris was ironic. Listening to him, Margo thought that she had met this man before, or many men like him before—this careful, intelligent irony, this fear of enthusiasm that was in itself a kind of charm, all so innocent! And yet she was attracted to him.

Though she was unmarried and lived alone she was not easily attracted to men, that is, not seriously. This was part of her fear. She went out casually with men who were friends of hers, and the friends of friends, and she was always relieved to know that this casualness protected her from anything violent. She wanted to be married in a vague, abstract way, because it was the next thing for her to do, and yet the steps leading to it were so dangerous and confusing that she clung to her friends and kept herself occupied. Back home, she would have been married by now. That was part of one's style of living, back home, if one's name was Brownell. But she lived in a great, busy city, by her own choice. Since her engagement had ended she had not seriously cared for anyone, and that was good, and now that she met David Harris she felt the panicky sensations of a hard, strong attraction, which she did not want but which she could not control.

He called her the next day. He had things to talk about—could they meet? Could they have dinner? Margo was the kind of woman, always well dressed and at home in her clothes, casual with even the best clothes, who seemed never surprised and always a little hesitant. With nothing before her except an evening alone she was yet able to hesitate, sincerely, as if she were afraid of leaving her apartment; it was not a trick of hers. Later he was to tease her about this reluctance, which he thought to be coyness, but she had not meant it as a trick and had, in a way, not wanted to see him. She knew that he would disturb her and she was afraid of being disturbed. But it was something she was fated to do, and so he came over.

She gave him a drink. He talked. Alone with her, and covertly appreciative of the apartment and its furnishings, he talked more freely than he had the day before. He had attended excellent schools, but he had not wanted to go on for his M.D. He had tired of school. He had tired desperately of preparing for life, always preparing, and therefore putting life itself off. And he had never married. "You haven't married, either," he said, more statement than question. His familiarity annoyed her, because she saw that it was a gesture, just part of his manner. Just so did he talk to certain women, and to other women—more aggressive, glamorous women—he talked in another manner. Margo was quiet, letting him talk. She felt strangely dependent upon his talk. They seemed to be old friends; it must have been that their types were friends. Her emotions were stirred by him, by his vague unfocused anger, and she thought that he was another of these men who need a woman, a certain kind of woman, just to tell them they are a certain kind of man—not the kind they are, but another kind. They needed to believe in that ideal and they needed a woman to support them in their illusion.

"I think it's possible to live without any plans, just to live from year to year," Margo said. She heard herself turning into the ideal of a woman this man probably desired—upper middle class but now emancipated, "good," civilized. "You only need to have faith in what you are," she said, noticing how his expression rejected this but going on with it anyway. With a woman she could have made herself understood easily, but with a man there was this perpetual provocative business, this saying of things she half meant or had never considered before, dragging out from the back of her mind things other women had said. There was always the point, even with the most intelligent man, when frankness would not work. If there was one thing men feared it was frankness, really.

They began to see each other often. They began to fall in love. She recognized all this and knew that it was more serious, this time, because there was so much to dissuade her from him—his combativeness, his dissatisfaction. He was kind to her in a pointless ceremonial way: in restaurants; helping her with her coat. In other ways he was combative and she had to give in. If he mentioned a friend of his who took religion seriously, and who was therefore neurotic, it did no good for Margo to point out gently that perhaps the friend was not simply neurotic, perhaps it was a matter of faith . . . ? But no, no, his superior intelligence was like a hand pushing against her, saying no, no, listen to me, I think, I *know*, and she gave in to it and was afraid at the easiness with which she gave in. She was happiest at a distance from him, knowing how distances enhance, able to think about the condition of being in love as if it were a condition belonging to another self.

Seeing so many wretched people, hearing their perpetual stories, he was cynical of weakness and yet certainly dependent upon it. She knew he liked her to say, "I was afraid you'd had an accident" when he was late—and he was often late—not because this meant she loved him but because she was dependent on him, she *had been afraid* of something. In their long, long talks, she could hear through the persistent, dogmatic monologue that was his most familiar style of conversation certain notes of discord, of his own fear, which was hidden from him. His image was the strong, stubborn, tough professional man. Her image, served up to him, was the slender, delicate, but very intelligent young woman. It was an image close enough to Margo herself to assuage her guilt. But she did feel guilt. For it was always with men to whom she must lie, even slightly, that she felt most stimulated—with those men whom she liked casually and who were no more than friends, she was always peaceful and frank and in a way she hated this self, which was her real self. She wanted to be pushed and prodded and distorted out of it, modeled into a woman superior to herself, and it was only through the demands of a superior man that this might happen.

Their life together became filled with little jokes, little innuendos. She became the "Upstate Lady," as he put it, when something he said shocked her. She did not tell him of her fear of vulgarity, her real loathing of it, but he sensed it and this was an important victory, for he could bring her down and—once she was deeply dependent upon him—almost shatter her with a sudden vulgar remark, which was his way of "being realistic." He was "Dr. Harris" when he lapsed into jargon, speaking of malformed egos, manic behavior, schizoid patterns; he sometimes spoke of the "neurosis of the artist," as a kind of joke. (He had been told about her poetry, though he had never seen any of it.) Another joke was Margo's famous incompetence: she was supposed to be unable to do anything that required mechanical ability, like opening tin cans, maneuvering a key successfully in a lock. This was based upon nothing much, so far as she could see, but she enjoyed the joke.

And another topic that was woven into their lives: their concern for his work. The pattern was his feeling of personal inferiority, which was countered by Margo's insistence upon his superiority; his spells of depression, brought on by the hopeless cases he treated, which were countered by Margo's good nature and Margo's encouragement. This pattern gradually strengthened. And there was the half-serious, half-ironic jealousy of his, based on nothing at all, that she had had other lovers and that, beneath her veneer of propriety, she was a passionate woman—as if this were somehow a matter of scandal. And her retort to this, depending upon her mood, that he was conventional despite everything, that he did after all want a girl who was "good" and not one, like Margo, who was an adult and who behaved like an adult.

"But I don't bother with good girls, as you call them," he said. "I don't have time. I'm bored with them."

"What is it you're bored with, in them?" Margo asked.

Secret patterns, known only to Margo: based upon fear. How, on their trip to Mexico, she listened carefully to his Spanish and made sure that hers was inferior; how, at concerts, she listened carefully to his remarks and did not contradict them; how, with friends, she refrained from making any gestures toward him that were wifely, maternal, tender, because he disliked any public demonstration of their being in love, though everyone knew they were in love. Above all, her care never to mention marriage in any way, never to mention children, houses, gardens, "back home," married friends, engaged friends. He was a tall, lean, rangy man who liked very much the comforts of domesticity, liked the quiet of her apartment and the laziness of their weekends together, but who believed that he hated the very idea of domesticity.

The most bitter pattern: her fear of losing him, woven into the very fabric of their life.

Only in the form of someone else did she dare speak of herself, and then guardedly. They liked to go for walks, even in bad weather. It was part of their stoical inclinations, or their sense of martyrdom, and on these long walks—back and forth along the boulevard, past the great hulking art museum and the science museum and the war monument, past the high-rise apartment buildings and the oaks and elms that lined the boulevard, she in her excellent tweed coat or suit and he in his trench coat, a handsome couple—on these walks she spoke cautiously of other, lesser people, either men or women, who were terrified of life. Of loneliness, of being unloved, of having no "place." "It was the experience of my friend Esther that every man who loved her, who believed he loved her, withdrew in a kind of panic when she began to love him in return. You might do a study of this peculiar American problem."

"Is it a problem only men have?" David asked, seriously.

"Only men."

"I doubt that," he said. He was grave, a little annoyed; she realized later that he always defended other men, even when he had no idea these men represented himself. He defended men on principle, against women. And he would say, overwhelming her with his quiet, frank, clinical knowledge, "Well, women fling upon men this terrible hunger, this need, it's like a mouth opening suddenly and sucking everything in—you can see how it would terrify a man. You can understand that."

She did not know, at these times, whether he was speaking to her as a superior woman or whether he was warning her.

During the first year they had many happy times, but Margo tended to remember only the uneasy times. Surely, she thought, by herself in the apartment and waiting for him to return, surely there must be something that holds us together, in spite of these arguments. (For they did argue, the arguments were spun out of nothing.) There must be something there. Some core of intimacy, of casual, humorous understanding, of friendship, of irony, something. A respect for each other's intelligence. She would fall listlessly into arguing with him, the argument disguised at first as an exchange of open, reasonable remarks, then blossoming into bitterness, his bludgeoning of her with words, his *I think, I know, I've seen*—and she would wait for him to come back, reliving these arguments, waiting alone in her apartment which was much too large for a single woman. There were times when she wanted to fall asleep to escape the thought of him, the memory of him, to get away somewhere inside herself far from the tension of their life together. (They were living together, in a way.) She believed that, inside her, was a core of being that was Margo Brownell and had no relationship to anyone else. No dependence, no love. This "Margo Brownell" was a pure self who had not yet met David Harris, or anyone. It was a purity that had nothing to do with experience. It was the same "Margo Brownell" she had been as a child, the same "Margo Brownell" she would be in forty years. If I think this way, she thought, I must be optimistic in spite of everything.

When they were happy together, she was sometimes caught up by a sudden sense of panic. This was insane, it was ugly and poisonous, and she did not understand it. But it was based on the fear that, if he left her, these happy moments would rise up to challenge the rest of her life. (In the same way, memories of her childhood rose up to challenge the tense, uncertain present of her adulthood. She had had a happy childhood.) It was probable that they had more happy moments together than they would have had were they married, or were they simply seeing each other casually, because they knew each other and yet were always a little guarded. They were eager to please, or to displease. Margo chose her

clothes with him in mind, and he did not take her for granted.
When he was late, or rude, it was deliberate, which meant they
were still in a combative zone, not husband and wife, and not
friends: they did not take each other for granted.

When she was alone she began to recall his words, which she
only half heard in his presence as if she were afraid to hear them.
It seemed even that her sight botched in his presence. It was
strange, the power he had over her. So she began thinking and
rethinking of things he had said, unplanned unrelated remarks
about anything—the traffic, their friends. She thought about him
all the time. The two of them were alone too much, but he
preferred it that way; he did not like the company of other people.
He hated parties, pretending boredom, he was afraid of parties
perhaps, afraid of being second-rate. His conversational style was
ironic, but the best style at parties was generally enthusiastic.
Margo understood that this intelligent man's irony was a disguise
for serious attitudes and emotions, but she did not tell anyone
this . . . she never defended him. She was afraid of him. The
fear that had been so diffuse in her was now concentrated in this
man she loved, but who had a tremendous power over her. She
was terrified of losing him.

Her terror rose to a pitch of nausea one night. They had been
talking late, it was Friday night and he was tired and exhilarated
from a week of hard work, and so they sat and talked and he told
her a secret: his feeling of strength. "Talking with those people
I feel very strong. I don't feel like myself. I think I become the
person they imagine I am. And I have the idea that with a word
I can change their lives, I can control them, the women especially.
They are yearning for a word of affection from me, the women
are yearning for me to touch them—you understand—and I have
this peculiar sensation of strength, as if I were a god. It's absurd
to talk about it, but it's true. . . . The women especially, they
would let me do anything to them, in a sense they belong to me
as soon as they come into the office. But it's all nonsense, of
course."

Once he asked her, oddly, whether she ever thought of other

men as lovers; oh, men on the street, men she met at work. She said no, not really. He said, but didn't women feel that way, most women? She said she didn't think so. Not women who were in love, anyway. But this wasn't the answer he wanted, his expression showed that she had retreated coyly and neatly into a wifely answer; it wasn't what he had wanted at all. She was hurt and bewildered, not knowing why she was hurt. Her brightness was a disguise for her deep, mysterious hurt, but it was the hurt he somehow knew about and resented, as if she had no right to it. He kept asking her, "But isn't that how women feel?"; he kept after her. It led to a serious argument about a mutual friend of theirs, a bachelor who by tradition "liked" Margo, another myth. The subject of the argument was nothing; the argument itself was everything. "If you're going to take such offense you should protect yourself better," he said angrily. "You should kick me out, then. You should live alone."

He was bitter and sullen, as if she had been the one to say this and not he. And she was too alarmed to reply. The next morning, conscious of something precarious between them, he suggested they go somewhere for a few days—get away from the city, from this sunny, tidy apartment. She agreed. They went on an aimless trip, in his car, up toward Maine. It was on this trip, in the second year of her knowing him, that her dreams began.

II

Her memory of her family's house, on High Street, was a memory she cherished. David told her teasingly that happy childhoods were unfortunate, because nothing in life can match them —all adults are disappointing versions of one's parents. She had said that theories in textbooks did not apply to her. She believed this. When she was unhappy she liked to let her mind drift back to that big old house, an excellent house on an excellent street, and she remembered her room upstairs in the front of the house, overlooking the long curved front walk that the mailman climbed

every day. The room was painted pink, with light pink curtains.
Dotted swiss curtains. Her closet door had had a mirror on its
outside. And the floor, even, was a pale speckled pink. The ceiling
was white. Her life had been shaped magically by that room,
Margo thought, the pinkness, the neatness, the girlish whimsy
of the bed and its fluffy bedspread, her stuffed animals, all clean
proper animals. . . . Down the hall, her brother's room had been
quite different: vaguely nautical in tone, light blue and dark
blue. And their parents' room had been quite different indeed:
as big a room as her living room in the apartment, with pale-
yellow silk wallpaper and excellent pieces of antique furniture.

Why did David say it was bad for her to remember that house?

On the first night of their trip they stayed in a motel near the
ocean. He wanted to go for a walk and she kept looking for a
sweater, she was certain she had packed it, and after a moment—
it had not really been more than a moment—he became impatient
and said he would go alone, never mind. She obviously didn't
want to go. So he went out, alone. She was stunned but somehow
not surprised, not really surprised. She took a sleeping pill and
lay down and fell asleep, not daring to wait for him to return,
knowing he would make it a point to stay out for a long time
though the weather was unpleasant. . . . And she had this dream:

She was herself, alone. Very alone. She was walking somewhere.
Not quite a city, not the country. Nothing from her present life.
A dull day. A sense of danger. Overhead, nothing; on either side,
windowless buildings which were meant, in her dream, to be
warehouses. (She understood that the dream was not functioning
properly.) She walked along in a kind of panic, alone. Something
was going to happen. She saw, materializing ahead, what was supposed to be her family's house. She waited for it to become whole.
But it wasn't her house, not really. Something was wrong with it.
It was small, shabby. Windows were boarded up. There was no
hill before the house; the house was right by the road. She walked
up to the house, her heart pounding, and put out her hand to
open the door. The door fell away. She went inside, knowing
that something would happen—and yet here she was inside. She

went along the downstairs corridor, and up the stairs (now the house was large again) and along the upstairs corridor to her room: but the room was not the same. She was dismayed, frightened. This was not her room! It was the room a friend of hers, a very sick girl, had had in college: just an ugly rented room. A black woman who should have been dressed as a maid was standing at the window, fixing something. Margo remembered her suddenly. She had been fired for a reason, for a secret, when Margo had been very young. Now Margo came forward, eager to see and yet afraid of what the woman would show her. She wanted to see what the woman was doing. Then the woman turned with a hideous grinning face, all teeth, and held up her hands for Margo to see what was in them—but Margo somehow didn't see it, or couldn't see it. She stumbled backward. She began to scream and the scream mingled with the black woman's laughter.

She woke. She was breathing heavily, as if she were trying to scream in silence. The bedclothes were damp with her perspiration.

When David came back she told him that she had had a nightmare. He held her guiltily in his arms and comforted her. He told her to tell him the dream. "I can't get it out of my mind," she said. She was so nervous that her teeth chattered. He embraced her tightly, warmly. He told her to tell him the dream. "It was about my room at home," she said reluctantly, for she had the idea that he would not really listen, "my room with the . . . I've told you about it. . . . It was in the front of the house. . . ."

"What's wrong?"

She lay rigid in his arms. She could not remember the room.

"Margo? What's wrong?"

"Nothing."

"Why did you stop?"

She could "remember" the room as having pink walls, a pink floor. She could "name" the furniture. But it was not a true memory. It had nothing to do with her experience, her emotion, certainly not the love she had always had for that room. The love was emptied out of it. The room was an empty room. She had forgotten it, she could not get to it again, past that ugly distorting false dream that was like a screen held up to block out reality. Her mouth went dry with the panic of being unable to get back to the room, to its reality. "Please hold me. Take care of me," she whispered. She was like a child, docile in his arms. He held her and she went to sleep again.

The second dream did not come until some weeks later, when she was nearly over her fear of having another bad dream. This was a dream based upon a certain memory, her father spanking her for playing down in the street. It was not a bad memory, though it involved punishment; Margo liked to bring it up laughingly as a sign of her having been naughty, a tomboy, but really she liked it for the casual intimacy of her father and herself. He had spanked her so hard that his watch had broken! That was the truth. But it had been a spanking of love. This was the important fact.

And yet she dreamed:

An amusement area, near an ocean. (Based on their recent drive to Maine.) Distances unclear, foggy. Silent crowds. A boardwalk. Margo thought suddenly of the street before her family's house, and the thought was magically imposed upon the boardwalk. Really, the two places had nothing in common. It was a foolish, awkward dream. The dream had not done its work at all—she was vexed, frustrated, she wanted to cry. Why couldn't she be back in that street, in front of her house? Why was she here instead? She wanted to scream. Suddenly, across the way, her father appeared in his winter overcoat. The dream had not completed his face, but it was her father. His nose was missing. Then it grew a little, it was a small nose. She wished it would grow to normal size but nothing happened. She was angry and frightened, having to look at her father like that. He had not yet seen her. She began crossing the boardwalk to him, but her legs were stiff and rigid. People bumped into her. Strangers. She began to cry. Someone bumped into her and pushed right on past, without pausing. Her father did not notice. Part of his face was missing— part of his cheek. But there was nothing beneath, no ugly bone or tissue or teeth. It was just a blur, not yet filled in. She began screaming to him to help her, come help her! He was a distance away. The boardwalk was wet and steep, and crowded. Why didn't he come help her! She was only a child! She screamed at him and her heart shattered. . . .

She woke up twisted in the bedclothes, her mouth again shaped into a silent scream. David lay beside her, breathing heavily. It was about five in the morning, back in the city. Margo lay gripped with the terror of the dream, unable to shake herself from it. She stared at David's sleeping face and for a moment did not recognize him—did not recognize the room—did not know what day it was. She was damp again, from perspiration. She wanted to cry aloud in anguish, for anyone to hear: I'm so afraid, help me not to be afraid! I can't live with such fear! She felt as if she were shackled, bound in chains. She could not think of the dream because a heavy sensation of panic returned to her, a sickening feeling. She put it out of her mind. She did not think about it and she did not tell David.

Later that day, when David was at work and she was having lunch with a friend, a woman, she tested herself: "I've had some strange dreams lately." She spoke apologetically, though the woman expressed interest. "Other people's dreams are so boring," Margo said. "It was based on this incident . . . with my father. . . ." But she could not really remember the incident. While her friend waited, sympathetically, Margo sat in a paralysis and tried to remember. She remembered a child playing in the street, a very small child; she remembered an adult running, catching the child, spanking him. But the child was not necessarily herself, not necessarily a girl. The adult was not necessarily her father. She had a reasonable feeling that the event had happened, but not to her. It was someone else's memory. It was lost. "Dreams are so ugly," she said, where a moment before she had said they were boring. She sounded a little vicious. She would not go on. Her friend waited to be told this mysterious dream, but Margo did not care about the dream—what was valuable was the memory behind it, which was now lost. It had been blocked out by the dream, which had slipped between it and Margo.

She told David nothing about this.

With David, much the same life as before. Just as she did not
dare to show him her poetry, so she did not dare to unload upon
him the crazy business of her nightmares. It was a world that had
nothing to do with him and he would certainly be scornful of it.
(An incidental note, emphasizing his unconscious scorn: his mention of some acquaintances of theirs, a married couple now planning divorce. A certain satisfaction in his voice, "You see how it
is" implied. I see how it is, Margo thought angrily. I understand.)
His thirty-seventh birthday. Vague aimless complaints, obviously
a fear of growing old—without accomplishing anything. They went
out to an expensive restaurant, talked seriously. This fear of
growing old without accomplishments (he meant writing a book,
he'd been planning to write a book half his life) hurt her deeply,
because she understood that she, as a woman, represented no
"accomplishment" to him. Margo would have abandoned her
poetry, any pretense of poetry, given it up forever with no regret
if she could have had this man promised to her: but no. He was
not promised to anyone, he was quite free. She was not free but he
was free. His freedom, in fact, assured her bondage. Her "poetry"
(which meant her having a secret, invulnerable core that was herself) was all she had left, would have left, if he abandoned her
. . . so she held onto her pretense of poetry. Didn't he imagine
she would like to accomplish something too, a book of her own?
If not a book, a few excellent poems? And, if neither of them
accomplished anything, if they turned out to be ordinary well-
educated intelligent people, did that matter? Weren't they in
love?

Her third dream. Based on an experience that had been unpleasant at the time, but shaded over by Margo's love of fancy,
her exaggeration. This was the first time a man had behaved to
her as a man, and she had been to him a young girl, a Young Girl.
She had been fifteen. A man, really a boy, of about nineteen
had met her in a drugstore, talked to her. She knew him, re-
motely. He had a certain reputation. He was "cute." He'd dropped
out of high school, he had a car, he wore a corduroy jacket and
jeans. He talked her into meeting him in front of the movie

house on Sunday. She agreed, reluctantly, she went on Sunday and he was there, they sat through the movie; afterward he drove her out somewhere in his car. Then they had a skirmish, an argument, the boy insulted and angry and Margo frightened, trying to push him away. There had been a stale, ugly taste in her mouth. . . . Recounting the incident in later years, she had embellished it with a certain raw charm, her "first experience" with a man; her innocence; her stupidity. It had become a kind of depersonalized anecdote.

Margo seemed awake in the dream. Everything was clear, vivid. She was much too alert, too awake to really be asleep. And so she was not on guard for the terrible openness of a dream. She was on a city sidewalk, calling, "David?" in a calm, expectant voice. For it seemed to her that he was nearby, perhaps hiding. It seemed to her that if she were to stare hard enough he would materialize out of the air, given substance by her desire. How badly she wanted him! But in this strange setting her desire did not work. She came forward on the sidewalk, waiting, and checked within her was that blossom of fear that was always ready; she said, "David?" to put it off. For she understood that she was setting against this name a memory that was older than she, a vision of a dark, violent force that ruled all the world and that had no concern for this woman who cried out, "David?" in a voice of love. She walked forward. It was much too still, too "open." The terror began inside her. It was a blossoming terror, taking up too much room in her body, forcing her out of shape. Someone appeared before her—a boy of about nineteen. He was familiar to her. She ran to him and embraced him. She pushed herself against him, pushing her body against his. But he was motionless as a statue. He was rigid, frozen. She cried out, clutching at him, and his face was a vague angry face with its gaze set somewhere past her, beyond her. The terror was forcing her body slowly out of shape and she woke in the instant before she would have died. . . .

It was afternoon. She was alone, David was at work. Or he was over at his apartment, "looking through papers." He had never given up his own apartment, and he had never really entered hers, and he had never talked of their getting an apartment together, one that would have been their own. She hated him for that, for his caution, but it was a useless hatred. So she lay alone now thinking of the dream she had just had, not wondering what it meant—she did not want to know what it meant—but wondering at the terrible power of dreams, their almost physical power. She was exhausted. She did not dare to think of the dream itself or of the memory behind it, she did not dare to test herself. It was better to lie still. The dream had not been too terrible; it could have been worse. There was this tremendous ungovernable power of a dream, strength enough to destroy her. And so she was grateful that it had not been worse.

What was strange was that the power, rising in her brain when she slept, was a power that belonged to her. But she could not control it.

Her apprehension these days, in her daylight life, was that she would show her weakness in front of David. She would begin to cry, or tremble violently, and that would be an insult to him. She had to keep on with their quiet, sane, rational talks, their being reasonable to each other, fair to each other, and never show the depth of her anguish. This was not all the time, of course. But their peaceful times were, to her, stepping-stones to the times of nervousness, tension, which David seemed to control. Margo's need for this man was so great that she could go neither backward nor forward. She said once, bitterly, "It would be better if we hadn't met," and he said, "Isn't that cowardly?" It was cowardly, yes, and anyway she couldn't go backward to a time that was innocent of him. They were too involved. And she could not imagine a future time when she would be free of this degrading love. It was degrading because she could recognize, calmly, that she was in love with a man who was able to love her only mildly. He loved her as he was capable of loving any woman—that is, mildly. He was fond of her and attached to her. His passion was only physical.

And yet he was jealous. He would have been jealous of the boy who had become a statue in Margo's dream, and he was jealous of phantom men in Margo's life. Men who were not quite there. Nameless men. In August after their trip to Maine, that peculiar haunted trip, they sat outside in his car one night arguing. They were parked before Margo's apartment building, they had just come from a party. David said, "But if you want to learn to drive a car I can teach you. Why do you want to take lessons?" She said, "To get my license. It's absurd that I've never tried." He said, "But I could teach you," in a dogged, stubborn way, though she knew quite well that he would have said he was busy, he wasn't patient enough, if she had asked him to teach her how to drive in the first place. She tried to be amused by this knowledge. But, listening to him argue, listening to him repeat the same point— "But why now, after so many years?"—she realized there was nothing amusing about it. Why now, after so many years? Why now? He wanted to make her old, worn-out, ludicrous. Why now? She thought suddenly of her father, who had declared her forever unfit to drive, and it occurred to her that she really hated her father, and when David was like this she hated him too. Of course she loved her father and she loved David, but there was hatred as well, a tiny poisonous spot of hatred.

"Why now, after so long? And why a professional teacher? You could get any number of people to teach you—that man you spent most of the evening with tonight, that what's-his-name—you found him very interesting."

"Who?"

"You certainly know who I mean." And he sat back, exhausted. He smiled at her as if she had won an important round. "You are the kind of woman, I'm beginning to see, who has to be married. Otherwise—"

"Otherwise what?" she said coldly.

"Otherwise, you are too free."

She laughed, dizzily. She had had too much to drink. This conversation was out of focus, it must be her fault for having drunk too much. And why did something freeze in her at his mention of marriage? She was afraid to let herself feel what she wanted; she was afraid to feel anything. "I'm going to go up now," she said, sliding over to the door. "It might be better if you didn't come up tonight."

He laughed, moving after her. They both got out onto the sidewalk. "Are you kicking me out, Margo? When we mean so much to each other?" He said this in a grave, mocking voice. He also had had too much to drink.

And so she began to think, in the following days, *I must change my life.* Marriage would not change it. Marriage with David would be no different from their life now, this heavy bondage of her love for him, her dependence upon him. She wanted to be free. She wanted to be as free as he was. And a few days after their argument in the car, she had this dream:

An urban setting. Streets, sidewalks, fronts of buildings—her life now. No people. She was anxious for him, saying again, "David? David?" But he was not present, or he was hiding. Yet there was the promise of him so she came forward, her body soft and vulnerable, and the setting changed at once to her own room, her own bed, the very setting in which she lay asleep and somehow knew herself asleep, and she willed him desperately into being by crying "David!" Her voice was harsh. He appeared. It was the David of that first night many months ago. She had not known him then. She had known they would be lovers, but she had not really known him, and something about the set of his mouth frightened her—was he the kind of man who made himself want a woman, as a kind of goal to be accomplished? He came to her. The setting was her room, but it was mixed up with the street, the sidewalk, a gray gritty world of buildings and no people. Both worlds were together, as in a film. He came to her and they embraced. She put her arms around him hungrily. Her body was so soft that he might bruise it, but still she pushed against him and said, "Come to me, David. Come to me." And he lay above her, clumsy and warm, his embrace soft as a woman's embrace but very heavy, his breath hot upon her, and she begged him to come to her, but there was nothing—there was no flesh of his to enter hers, nothing. She cried out to him bitterly. He was nothing.

He could say nothing. She thrust him from her to look at his face and to accuse him, her yearning turned now to an angry strength, and she saw—

She woke. Her body was alert and tingling, on guard. It was very strange. David lay beside her, turned from her, and she blinked in the darkness and thought that she had awakened but the night was much darker than her dream had been; in her dream she had seen his face clearly but now she could see nothing, even if she were to lean over him or if she were to snap on the light. Because she could never see him that clearly, not when she was awake. And she knew now that she did not love him any longer. It was as if she had thrust him from her and he had not the strength, now, to fall back heavily and greedily upon her. Her body rejected him. It was alert for someone else, not him, or for the adventure of someone else, or for the adventure of being alone. . . . She did not love him any longer, she was free.

This was a secret she kept to herself for a while, wondering how to tell him. There was a kind of happiness in her now, with her tension gone, her caution gone. He did not quite notice. What had been her love for him passed over into interest in him, a vague worry for him, because she could see that his hair was thin with the years of dissatisfaction—with his work; with himself—and the years of his not having "accomplished" anything. He was a well-dressed, handsome man with a dissatisfied mouth; no one could change that mouth. It was no one's duty to change it. She was fond of him, but she did not love him any longer. And whenever she cast her mind back to the first time they had made love, in her room, her bed, she could remember not the real man and the real experience, but the dream that had supplanted it, and it was the dream experience that was real: the "reality" was blocked out and gone.

And so it was all over.

She said to him one day, "It would be good for us to go away for a while. I want to go to Italy by myself."

His eyes narrowed suspiciously. He did not know if she was teasing, or if this was a calculated way of prodding him into a declaration of something permanent. In another moment he would say, "What's wrong with us the way we are?"—but he must have sensed that she did not mean this. She meant something else entirely.

"You're kicking me out?" he said.

"I want things to change."

"Change? By going away? Can't we both go away?"

"Then it wouldn't be a change," she said. It was experimental, her lack of concern. She was testing herself and him; her very words, uttered so casually, were encouraging. She and David were walking through a small park adjacent to the art museum, and she found herself appreciating the scenery, the day, the hulking marble statuary, as if this setting had no meaning except to be appreciated. It was with an effort that she turned to her lover, as if she were already looking at him across a vast distance, trying to imagine what he must feel. For he must feel something. She herself had once felt something.

"If you go to Italy I'll go with you," he said.

She thought of him embracing her. Flabbily, clumsily, he lay upon her and tried to weigh her down, a heavy, inert man with nothing to him—nothing. It had been an illusion, a dream of her own, his vigorous manhood. She had had to thrust him away, finally—she had had to free herself of him.

Of course that had not been the real David. And yet that dream image had canceled out the real David—who stood now beside her, frowning.

"If you go to Italy I might as well go with you. Why not?"

"You don't want to go to Italy, David."

"I'm tired of this country too. I'll leave, I'll go with you."

"I'm not tired of this country; that isn't why I'm leaving," she said.

"But what will you do, alone?"

"Don't worry, please."

"I'll come with you."

"No."

"Yes, I'll come with you."

But by September they were already abstract to each other, like friends who have shared an intense experience, but now cannot quite remember what it was that so passionately united them. They said good-bye, they kissed good-bye. It was a formal leave-taking: Margo knew she would never see him again.

Customs

Citizen of what country? he would ask and she would say *United States. Born where?* he would ask. And she would reply. And he would ask possibly another question or two . . . *purpose of your visit here today . . . what is your destination . . . how long will you be in the United States . . .* and then he would wave her on. There had never been any trouble before.

She was not worried. She had nothing to hide. Guilty of nothing, smuggling nothing across the border. Wanting to cheat no one. Not worth it, in Renée's opinion, the petty smuggling people did —buying eyeglasses over in Detroit, wearing them back—wearing clothing they had bought and would not declare; anyway, she was crossing the border into the United States and it was obvious that she was bringing nothing over. The seat beside her was bare, the back seat of the car bare.

There were several sentry boxes, but only two were open. Red lights burning above the others. Cars backed up, considerably. Two cars ahead of Renée was a station wagon packed with children —couldn't all belong to the same family—must be an outing of some kind. The customs official asked the driver a few questions, then waved him on. In the lane to Renée's left, however, a group of teen-agers were less fortunate. White boys, all of them long-haired, one of them without a shirt. Pallid skin, not very attractive. The customs officer made out a pink slip for them, tucked it under the windshield wiper, and sent them over to the side to be examined. The driver had trouble starting the car; must be embarrassing for him.

The car just ahead of Renée's, a late-model Buick, was detained for quite a while: Renée could see the driver and his companion from the rear, couldn't judge if they were white or black. A man, a woman. The customs officer took papers from the driver and examined them and handed them back. Evidently he wasn't quite satisfied; the driver got out, went back to open the trunk. A tall, angular white man in his thirties, suit too large for him, face set in annoyance, opposition: lines beside his mouth so severe, they looked like ink lines drawn on the flesh. The car had Ontario license plates. The man unlocked the trunk and swung it up and the customs officer did no more than glance inside—from where Renée was, the trunk of the car looked empty except for a spare tire—and released the man.

And now Renée.

"Citizen of what country?"

"United States."

"Born where?"

"New York."

He was speaking rather perfunctorily to her. A man of moderate height, probably in his early forties, with a small graying moustache and slightly pitted skin. A uniform of blue. White shirt. Regulation necktie. Leather belt, holster, pistol. He wore glasses; he struck Renée as really being a kind of clerk or accountant, no one to fear. She answered his questions formally and rather coolly. *Bringing any goods, merchandise, or gifts? Any citrus fruits? Any plants?* No. No, no. She had nothing to hide. Whenever she and Evan crossed the border back into the States, Evan was always driving, and he answered most of the questions. In Renée's opinion he did not answer them wisely: there was always an edge to his voice, an abrasive sound. He hated the customs routine. He hated being questioned, by anyone. And so he could not accept the procedure as a formality that really meant nothing. The officer usually asked to see his draft card and, once it was examined, waved them on. But Renée was alone today. She managed to answer the man's questions without showing any annoyance; really, she felt very little. It was only a routine, after all.

"Where in New York?"

"New York—New York City."

"New York *City?*"

He raised his eyebrows and might have been about to smile, to make a joke. *Didn't think anyone was born there.* Or, possibly: *Wouldn't want to live there, eh?* But he didn't smile. He stared at her and asked what the purpose of her visit was and she answered easily, immediately, that she was going to the library on the Wayne State campus—Wayne State University, she said carefully. He walked around the front of the car and checked the license plates. His expression altered, subtly. Renée felt a flicker of irritation. Of course the man was playing a role, going through a routine series of questions, and yet he seemed to be pretending . . . to be acting a part, for her benefit.

"I see there's Ontario plates on the car, miss," he said. "Didn't you say you were an American citizen?"

"Yes."

"Residing in Canada, then?"

"Yes," Renée said. "Residing in Canada."

He leaned forward. Peered into the car. Past her head, squinting. Though he must have seen nothing, his expression did not change; he was pretending to be suspicious now. He asked for her birth certificate. Proof of citizenship. Identification. While Renée fumbled in her purse, extracted her billfold, she was aware of her own excitement: not quite nervousness, just excitement. She was

annoyed, yes. But not angry, as Evan would be. Not really angry.
. . . She handed the man her identification, managing the smile.
Surely this was all . . . ? And now he would wave her on . . . ?

"I said your birth certificate, miss," the man said, handing the
card back. "That's no good; that's not identification."

She had handed him her landed-immigrant's card.

"But I . . . I . . . I don't have my birth certificate," she said,
guiltily, "it's at home, it's . . . I thought this card was sufficient;
isn't it sufficient? I thought . . . I mean. . . . In order to get
this card I had to have my birth certificate and other papers and
. . . and . . . it's stamped by the Canadian government. . . .
It's hard to get this card, it's hard to get this status. . . ."

He was staring at her now. Looking directly at her. Her voice
faltered, faded. He began to smile. Not even rudely, but rather
politely, he informed her that Canadian identification was worthless over here. "That's for *them*," he said, jerking his head back
toward the tunnel. "I need to see your birth certificate or a passport. You got them with you?"

"I don't have a passport," Renée said. Her voice had become
childlike; she was still trying to smile. "My birth certificate is
. . . is back at the house. . . . I'm only going to stay in Detroit
a few hours."

He waved this aside as if it were an obvious lie. Or, worse, as if
it were irrelevant. He asked her how long she'd been residing in
Canada. She replied. He asked her whose car this was. She told
him. Could he see the registration. Yes, of course. Yes. . . . Her
husband, eh. Who was her husband, was he an American citizen
also? Was he a draft dodger, eh? No? Not a draft dodger? But living
in Canada. Residents over there for a year and a half? And did
her husband work there? He did. And did she? No. Well—yes.
She did? It was not a real job, not a salaried job; part-time office
work . . . not a real job. But did she get paid for it? She did?
Then it was a real job, wasn't it?

Renée managed to smile at the man, just the subtlest ironic
smile. "But this isn't relevant, is it? Sir? I'm not bringing any
merchandise over, I'm not going to stay more than a few hours—"

"What did you say the purpose of your visit was?" he interrupted.

Renée paused. For a moment she could not remember. Then she said, giving as much detail as possible, suddenly anxious to tell the entire truth: ". . . I'm going to a study center . . . an institute . . . it's called the Community Rehabilitation Center . . . it's funded by the American Friends Service Committee . . . an organization . . . a social-welfare organization. . . ." This seemed to convince him: she gave him information he obviously couldn't absorb, details, names, addresses. The weekend before, she and Evan had met a young couple at a party in Windsor; they were not married but lived together, with a few other people, in a community-owned building somewhere just south of the Wayne State campus, all of them Americans, none of them born in the area. They were connected with a social-welfare program at the university and had talked excitedly of its workshops and weekend seminars, had invited Renée over to visit the center, to look at their library—which they were slowly accumulating—and to do volunteer work for them some day, if she had time. Renée had been very pleased with the invitation. She was interested in social-welfare work; she hoped to return to graduate school in social work or in psychology, when they could afford it.

Renée explained herself so thoroughly, with such a schoolgirlish voice, that the customs official nodded vaguely, as if not listening; already he was glancing behind her, at the considerable line of cars waiting to come through. And. . . . And in that moment. . . . He must have been about to wave her through; but for some inexplicable reason—for no reason at all—he suddenly said: "Okay, over to the side." He scribbled something down on a pad, ripped the pink slip off, and stuck it under her windshield wiper.

Renée was shocked—as if someone had spat into her face.

She drove across the way, to where a half-dozen cars were parked against a curb, awaiting inspection. Too surprised to be angry. She was certain the man had forgotten all about the birth certificate . . . had known from her landed-immigrant's card who she was . . . had known she was no danger, no threat to the city. . . .

And yet, whimsically, he had decided to have her inspected. Absurd, her surprise; she should not mind so much. Only a routine, after all. There was nothing to be frightened of. It was an ordinary weekday, sunny, hazy, fairly warm; she was no more than a half-hour's drive from home, should they decide to send her back. . . . But the upset she felt was because of something else, wasn't it. . . . She didn't want to quite admit to herself how she'd tried to placate that son of a bitch, she had tried to charm him, yes she had, no denying it, she'd tried very very hard and it had not worked. Humiliated, wasn't she. But of course she was alone and no one knew, no one had heard. . . . Alone, safe. Blushing. But unobserved. Thank God Evan hadn't been in the car; he would have gotten into a vicious argument, might have been sent back or arrested, if the customs officials had the power to arrest anyone. Renée wasn't sure exactly what powers they did have. . . . Anyway, Evan would never know. In fact he didn't know she was going to visit the center that afternoon; she had not told him about her plans.

A young man in a uniform snapped at her—"Can't you read, miss?"—and she looked up to see a large sign, white with black letters. SHUT OFF IGNITION. WAIT IN CAR FOR INSPECTION.

So she waited. She would not become angry; she knew better. . . . A book of maps in the glove compartment: she leafed through it, idly. State after state after state. Pale pink, pale orange, pale green, violet, blue. The provinces of Canada a uniform pale yellow. States, provinces, territories. Bodies of water. . . . Unfortunately, there was nothing to read. She leafed through the book, came to the end, discovered she was trembling.

All around her was commotion. Car doors slamming. A police radio in a squad car parked a short distance away . . . a radio in a car nearby, blaring music. . . . People were walking back and forth. Some were in uniform, others were obviously travelers. A boy in a denim outfit, with straggly Christly hair, was perched on a counter of some kind, smoking; propped up beside him was a sign *California please*. Touching, wasn't it. Hopeless. Idiotic.

. . . Renée wondered what to do. People were getting out of their cars and walking with their pink slips into an office, were milling around, were asking one another what to do, and she was afraid to get out and ask, and miserable to be so diffident; might sit here all day, possibly, while others were inspected before her. It was getting hot now. Midday sun. Noisy radios, noisy people. . . . Two cars down, a low-slung mud-caked car was being inspected quite thoroughly. The boys Renée had noticed before were standing, watching, their arms folded and their expressions blank. The bare-chested boy had a dead-white face, really ghastly. How he hated! . . . standing with his thin arms folded, watching the customs officials. . . . He must have been about eighteen. Renée would have liked to catch his eye, establish a kind of rapport with him . . . a connection . . . one victim to another, perhaps. But he ignored her. A portly man in a uniform and a cap was examining the car, using a flashlight. Under the front seat; under the back seat. The boys' luggage was on the curb, a single suitcase and two duffel bags. Now the hood was opened . . . now the trunk. . . . But still the inspector was not satisfied. Renée stopped looking when he squatted down to pry the first of the hub caps off.

She passed the time by reading a sign just in front of her. Federal and state regulations. Statutes. Penalties for possession of the following: a long list of items, in smaller letters. The words "Firearms" and "Narcotics" were in boldface. At the bottom, the words "Felony," "Confiscation," "Prison." . . . Now the car beside her was being inspected. A couple got out, a black man and a woman. They went to stand beneath the shed roof, out of the way. Rather haughty, they were. The man wore a sports jacket of creamy white and trousers with large checks, almost too large. Beige, black, white. A trim, sporty outfit. He was probably in his thirties, small-bodied, with absurdly stylish sunglasses: wide batwing frames in black, lenses in blue. The woman with him was younger. Attractive, though pouting. What thick, pursed lips! . . . the color of grapes, dark grapes. Dyed hair, a glossy dark red, in fact the same shade as Renée's hair; but Renée's hair was not so glossy these days. The black woman's hair was short and sprightly and the ends turned up and her bangs were lavish and very shiny. . . . Ah, must be a wig. Of course. Some inexpensive synthetic material; too glossy and too perfect. While her companion stared off into the sky the black woman watched attentively as their car was being searched. From time to time her lips moved. What was she saying? . . . what was she wanting to say? Renée tried to catch her eye. But no. She was watching the white man and missing nothing.

Something had begun to bother Renée. Something vague, peripheral. . . . A memory, a warning, a . . . What? Couldn't remember. It was hot in the car, sun beating through the side window, a relief when she was told to get out from behind the wheel; she got out gracefully, smoothing down her skirt. Yes? Any questions? The inspector was a man Evan's age. About thirty. Short-trimmed dark hair, sunglasses with wire frames. Her height. No, he had no questions for her, hardly glanced at her, was more interested in the interior of the car. Renée smoothed her dress again, touched her hair. Fortunately she had worn an attractive dress, dark blue, plain, with a silver pendant on a thin chain . . . her hair brushed back into a bun . . . stockings, even, and her usual sandals. But they were good sandals, good leather. Hand-tooled. Wisps of hair had come loose, on her forehead, around her ears. Renée brushed at them absentmindedly, watching the inspector's back. Perspiration had begun to show through his jacket. And she too, Renée too, was perspiring. Nervous, foolishly nervous. Nothing could happen and nothing would happen. She knew that. She was a citizen of the United States and not a criminal, not a smuggler, she had no hidden merchandise or narcotics or. . . . Nothing to hide, absolutely nothing at all. But something alarmed her. What was it? What? . . . Possibly the lack of communication. No one was saying much. There was noise on all sides, the police radio yammering on and on, someone shouting orders at someone else, yet the young man who was inspecting her car didn't so much as glance at her, didn't smile in embarrassment, though he must have been well aware of the absurdity of what he was doing. *Only doing my job,* he might mutter. But perhaps he didn't dare say such things; he might be overheard, might lose his job.

Glove compartment. The book of maps: he flipped through it, as if expecting to find something slipped between the pages. Other papers in the glove compartment. A candy wrapper. Kleenex. The manual for the car. He used a flashlight though he must have been able to see perfectly well that there was nothing else in the glove compartment. . . . Renée expected him to turn to her, to smile sheepishly; but when he did turn in her direction his expression was empty, blank, like the boys'. He asked whether there was anything under the seats? A bottle maybe? Anything? A *bottle?* Renée told him no, of course not, no, she didn't even . . . didn't even drink. But he cared not at all for her protest; he glanced down at her feet, at her sandals, and continued his search. Squatting, grunting, in order to look under the front seat. *The bastard.* . . . And yet, he reminded her of an acquaintance of hers and Evan's, a part-time student at the university who also drove a cab, a new friend of theirs, an ex-American who had become a Canadian citizen. It had taken five years; but now he was a Canadian citizen. A very nice man, very nice. Not quite a friend, perhaps, since they didn't know him well. But friendly, congenial. . . . The customs official was slighter than Gerry, but had the same build, skin tone. Strange, that the two men should be so different. Gerry had been telling them, a cheerful drunken anecdote, about how he had become a Canadian citizen and the very next day read of a new movement in the country, *Canadian Birthright,* wasn't it ironic, yes, but amusing and he could take it in stride, he was tough, cheerful, hadn't surrendered yet, wasn't it ironic that the day after he became a legal citizen, sloughing off the U.S. and taking on Canada, he should discover that there might be such a thing as a born Canadian, as opposed to a "legal" Canadian, and that a movement was beginning . . . at least some angry native Canadians were trying to begin a movement . . . and. . . .

"What's this," the officer muttered. He had found a crumpled-up cigarette package on the floor of the back seat. His flashlight under his arm, he began to pull it apart; carefully, fastidiously, he shredded the cellophane and the paper wrapper, while Renée stared in disbelief. Why, he was utterly serious about what he was doing. Serious! . . . The flashlight began to slip; he stuck it in his belt, flashlight on the right, holstered buttoned-down pistol on the left. Renée began to feel faint. What was happening? What had gone wrong? The man glanced at her, unsmiling. Maybe she was tricking him, eh? He had shredded the cigarette package thoroughly; had found nothing; maybe she was laughing at him . . . ? Renée was trembling now; she was very frightened. Something was wrong, something was terribly wrong. Couldn't quite articulate it. A memory, a warning. Couldn't remember. Couldn't free herself of the paralysis of the moment, the eerie knowledge that something was wrong, out of focus, out of control. Why didn't he speak to her? . . . Bantering, even cruel joking, even an exchange of insults . . . she would have preferred that, would have preferred anything, to his grim silence.

She tried to smile at him. She was a white woman, after all. And neatly dressed. Neatly groomed. Thank God she was white and not black. . . . Tried to smile, her lips dried, painful, and she heard him say *Open the trunk* and for an instant did not know what he meant . . . but she moved, came awake, opened her purse and fumbled in it, searching for the key to the trunk. Of course she had it. She had it. Tried to apologize, explaining: ". . . I do have the key but it slipped off the key ring . . . it's in my purse somewhere . . . it's in here . . . somewhere. . . . Anyway there's nothing in the trunk, there's nothing in the trunk." He waited patiently; might have been listening. She was very nervous now. Couldn't seem to see right. ". . . I do have the key. I'm sure I have it. I. . . ." He told her to empty the contents of her purse on the seat of the car; she obeyed, mechanically. Billfold . . . comb with broken handle (my God, it wasn't very clean) . . . more wads of Kleenex . . . hairpins . . . a tube of lipstick . . . notes, shopping lists, titles of books, things she must do and must buy . . . addresses . . . a pair of earrings she'd taken off in a theater some weeks ago, and forgotten. . . . "Let's see that.

Them," the man said. She handed him the earrings. He examined them; he must have taken thirty seconds, simply standing there, examining them, though there was nothing to see—only a pair of imitation-jade earrings, slightly tarnished clip-on earrings, obviously cheap. . . . At that moment there was a commotion at the far end of the inspection shed: some black men, raised voices, a childish high-pitched whine. *What the hell? What the hell?* Renée's inspector glanced up, alert. Other officers moved forward. A policeman in a uniform that looked like a riding outfit appeared, swinging his legs out of the squad car, a slender cigar clamped between his teeth. . . .

The voices died down at once; the moment passed.

Renée found the key. She opened the trunk. Thank God, she could get it open; sometimes she couldn't. . . . Nothing inside, only the old spare tire; and some seeds, a scattering of sycamore seeds. Must have blown in the trunk somehow, one day in the spring, when Evan had had it open. Sycamore seeds in their winged cases. Obviously they were only seeds. . . . The customs inspector picked one of them up and stared at it; he even adjusted his sunglasses in order to see it better.

Renée waited. And now, suddenly, she remembered: she might be searched bodily. If they required it. A matron might take her somewhere and ask her to remove her clothing and. . . . She felt faint, sick. She was trembling and obviously guilty, wasn't she, white-faced, ghastly, as guilty as everyone else. Only a few days before, she'd listened to a girl ahead of her in line in a grocery store telling the cashier about her eighteen-year-old sister and her friends being searched, examined, going through customs into the United States, and she had hardly bothered to listen to the bitter, ugly little tale, since it had nothing to do with her. A physical examination, a bodily search. No, it had nothing to do with Renée. . . . Now, the customs officer glanced at her, as if deliberating her fate: should she live, should she die. Or should he toss the sycamore seed back, shrug his shoulders, slam the trunk door down, gallantly, manage a professional wry laugh, and wave her through . . . ?

He waved her through.

. . . A stop sign a block away; Renée was confused because traffic was rerouted, coming from odd angles. She felt light-headed. Couldn't seem to remember why she was here, in Detroit. Bulldozers, a wrecking crane, an air hammer. The inspection was over, she was safe, nothing had happened . . . nothing had happened. . . . Sickened, weak. The pit of her belly. Sick. Evan would never know, no one would know. She need tell him nothing. . . . But why was she here? Why? Pathetic, wasn't she, driving over to an address she'd scribbled down on a slip of paper . . . not knowing why she had started out . . . not ready to admit the eagerness that had leapt in her, meeting those people. Might they be friends? Eventually . . . ? It was possible, possible. They might be friends. It might turn out well. Possible. Pathetic but possible. Evan had not cared for them, but. . . . She waited at the stop sign, trying to make sense of the traffic pattern. She knew where she wanted to go, but how to get there?

*T*he Transformation of Vincent Scoville

Alone much of the time, Vincent had never really been lonely.
He supposed himself intellectually superior to most people, and
perhaps physically superior as well—he was handsome in a lop-
sided lazy way, with large greeny-gray eyes that could be made to
express comic horror or contempt, exaggerated to create an impression; his hair was deep red, a nodding mass of curls, Byronic,
cupidlike, utterly charming—which made the razorish effect of
his wit all the more surprising. He did not take himself seriously,
of course, and had created a public *persona* years ago, as an undergraduate in Toronto, which had been refined and heightened
during his eight-year stay in New York City. The Scovilles were
of what is called "an historic house"—wealthy landowners in
Nottingham in the eighteenth century, fashionably impoverished
by the early twentieth century, and now scattered throughout
the Commonwealth without much interest in or knowledge of one

another. Vincent imagined himself as a stage aristocrat: it was a pleasant role that allowed him to express his genuine enthusiasm for culture, especially poetry and music; it allowed him to play down his considerable intelligence, and it kept people at a distance.

He had enjoyed being alone, being solitary, and had not known how abnormal he was, until he came to Hilberry College to teach, in the autumn of his twenty-ninth year. Here, everyone was married; everyone had children. Everyone was *normal*, like people in advertisements aimed for an only moderately sophisticated audience—suntanned men in shirt sleeves, grinning freckled children, wives who continued to have babies as if it were still the fifties. In New York, where Vincent had earned his graduate degrees and had taught introductory courses, everyone was "solitary" in a cheerful, almost communal way; even married couples seemed lonely. Privacy was protected, cherished, at times worshiped: like Franz Kafka, Vincent had weighed the joys of marriage against the incontestable joys of privacy—and of course privacy had won. But he had been forced to leave New York, he had been forced to humble himself by accepting a teaching position at a small, nearly unknown college in southeastern Ontario, in an industrial city his friends had never heard of. They said good-bye to him solemnly, knowing they would never see him again. And he was nearing his thirtieth birthday—the New York phase of his life was obviously over. What was most embarrassing was the fact that Vincent was shamefully grateful for the teaching position at Hilberry.

His area of specialization was Edwardian literature, though he also taught basic courses and courses in contemporary theater; he had always been a very successful, popular young teacher, and had he not tried to establish himself at so competitive a university— Columbia—he would have had no need to send out nearly two hundred letters of application, to colleges and universities in Canada and the States, to Leadville State Teachers College in Montana, to Prince Rupert College of Technology, to Cal-Southern Methodist in Lamesa, California, near the Anza-Borrego desert; and to Hilberry College in Telford, Ontario.

What surprised Vincent was his discovery that, at Hilberry, everyone was so aggressively normal; and at the same time so cynical. Nearly everyone he met at the college felt superior to it, and of course to the city. Many individuals, whom Vincent assessed as decidedly mediocre, even felt superior to the nation, to Canada itself. Amazing! Not even in New York had Vincent encountered this universal lighthearted cynicism, which could be inspired as much by the climate, the weather, as by matters of genuine significance. The mayor of the city spoke disdainfully of the president of the college; the president of the college spoke disdainfully of the politicians, both local and provincial; the deans of the college were critical of their faculty and of the politicians; everyone was critical of the "news media," which of course distorted everything. Vincent's colleagues in the English Department were critical of the politicians, the college's administrators, their students, even the departmental secretaries, but most of all of one another. "You won't find much intellectual stimulation *here*," Vincent was told several times.

One of the department's scholars, Dr. Basil May, told Vincent irritably that Dr. Barth, who had hired Vincent, "could not recognize genuine scholarly achievement from scissors-and-paste collages" and was, moreover, "teetering on the brink of senility." He went on to name his colleagues, all of them strangers to Vincent, listing their flimsy accomplishments one by one, reserving his wittiest contempt for the numerous poets on the staff. "No, you won't find much intellectual stimulation *here*," May said. On the other hand, Jake Hanley, a Canadian and American literature specialist, spoke contemptuously of May himself: "Once a popular classroom teacher, now a failure. He had an exhibitionist mania of some kind, went to a psychoanalyst for treatment, evidently got cured and now he's a flop, and intensely jealous of the rest of us." An impeccably dressed black man in his thirties took Vincent aside to tell him that the department's standards were shockingly low—he himself worked almost constantly on an immense, ambitious bibliographical project—but the poets got all the credit, they were skillful in matters of public relations, and though two of them did not have Ph.D. degrees they had actually been given tenure the year before. He gave Vincent offprints of articles he had published in *Augustan Studies*: "The Decline of the Enjambed Couplet in the Early Eighteenth Century" and "The Return of the Enjambed Couplet in the Late Eighteenth Century." His name was Frank Ambrose and Vincent rather liked him, would have enjoyed seeing more of him, but for some reason their friendship simply did not develop—it was possible that Frank was too busy with his project, or that he had been offended by seeing Vincent talking to one of the poets.

Ron Blass was the department's chief poet. He had a twelve-page bibliography and even a book to his credit, and he was a very popular teacher on the undergraduate level; he was always "scribbling a poem" in his notebook, always inviting Vincent to have coffee with him and then remembering, at the last minute, that a student was waiting in his office. He struck Vincent as a very nice person, though absurdly out of date in his early-sixties gear—black pullover sweaters, leather belts with wide buckles, blue jeans, boots, a medallion on a chain, even a small beard. He often said, "We must get together sometime," and "My wife would love to meet you," but nothing came of it—no further invitation. Vincent tried not to mind. But even Ron could be critical at times. He shook his head over the news that one of the medieval specialists had received a Canada Council grant, saying that research of that kind was entirely wasteful; money should be given to the creative arts, "to living, breathing people." He had the departmental secretaries type his poems and send them out to magazines, and occasionally they made mistakes. He showed Vincent a sheath of poems "filled with typographical errors"—said in disgust that he might as well type them himself. "Sometimes I think things really are deteriorating here," Ron said sadly.

Then there was Perry Sandeen, another young instructor, with whom Vincent shared an office. Though he was twenty-eight years old and the father of three small children, Perry behaved and even looked like a boy of fifteen. He was always cheerful, always bubbling with little remarks—"How's it going, Vince?"—never quite listening to Vincent's replies, since he was rummaging through the drawers of his desk or leafing through stacks of student papers, muttering to himself. His face was bland, bright, engagingly plain: he seemed to Vincent the most normal of them all. He chattered about baseball, football, hockey. He telephoned his wife during the day, asked her to put the baby on the telephone, and gurgled and chirruped, not minding if Vincent overheard. *He's normal, he's a very nice, kind, normal person*, Vincent thought carefully. And yet he was reminded, at times, of no one so much as the babbling self-absorbed psychotics of the New York streets and parks, who spent their days quarreling with invisible companions or relieving old battles.

But Perry was new to the college, like Vincent; he too required companionship. So Vincent made every effort to be friendly. He suppressed his wit, his sarcasm, his impatience, he disguised what he felt to be his essential *charm*, and tried to talk on Perry's level about hockey, about physically attractive female students, about the weather. There must be some secret to Perry, Vincent thought. That constant cheerfulness! That boyish imbecilic normality! Perry's hair was trimmed short and his glasses were mended with adhesive tape; he brought his lunch in a paper bag, even brought a thermos of coffee—or was it chocolate milk? He had published one article so far, on a prairie poet of the nineteenth century named Herbert Hockings Peterson, whose work Vincent didn't know; his Ph.D. degree was from Edmonton. "How's it going, Vince?" "How's the world treating you, Vince?" "We'll have to get together sometime—Valerie would love to meet you, I've told her all about you."

One day while Vincent was trying to prepare a lecture on Tennyson, Perry rushed in, talking to himself, sighing, giggling at something in his mail, groaning at departmental memos which he read aloud; he rummaged through his desk and through his bookshelves; he sat on his desk chair and leaned back, so that the chair was on two legs, and then let it crash back to the floor, crying happily: "Time for a break, Vince?" Vincent simply stared at him. Who was this? Who were these people? They were all mad. He would never adjust, never become one of them; he would be lonely the rest of his life, in exile here at Hilberry College. It was his fate. The essential Vincent Scoville—intelligent, playful, even at times a little theatrical and frivolous, in the New York style—would slowly die.

It looked for a while as if Vincent might be taken up by the Hanleys, Jake and Cynthia. Cynthia was not simply a "faculty wife"; she took courses in pottery and sculpting, and had a cousin who lived in New York—"a wonderful wild exuberant life," she told Vincent gaily, using her eyes on Vincent in a way he believed must mean something; she did not appear to use her eyes like this with other men, certainly not with Jake. He was stocky, balding, good-naturedly contemptuous of people not within earshot—and yet kindly, for he seemed to sense Vincent's unhappiness, beneath his constant civil smile, and kept patting him on the shoulder and mumbling something about Vincent "eventually getting used to it." Jake was fairly intelligent, but he seemed to drift away from intelligent subjects, and to fasten onto departmental or college gossip—a professor in the Philosophy Department had been caught with a student in his office—*not* a girl—the secretary of the department had told Jake in confidence that some very interesting documents had been typed up recently, on Dr. Barth's own typewriter, and sent directly to the dean—she had come across discarded, crumpled first drafts—of course all this was secret, highly secret—Frank Ambrose had applied for a special leave of absence so that he could conclude his bibliography of whoever he was working on—Lord Warburton?—Lord Lewesbury?—but the application had been turned down; he was threatening to go to the faculty association, charging racism. "And that uppity little nigger has been promoted faster than the rest of us, all along," Jake said. The remark, crudely put, was somehow not exactly crude— Vincent labored to interpret it in Hilberry style, as disparaging in a fond, almost familial manner. *They are really kind, decent, very normal people,* Vincent thought. It was somehow very natural, very "normal," for Mrs. Hanley to try so hard to be eccentric—

peasant blouses with ruffled sleeves, full-skirted orange and green hostess gowns, strands of wooden beads, carved, totemistic earrings that swung back and forth with a dramatic intensity of their own. Even her awkward flirtation with Vincent was sweet, appealing, quite natural. She made comments about his "Byronic profile"—she alluded to departmental gossip about the evident success of his teaching, these first few weeks—she confided in him that Jake, practically alone, with only Dr. Barth supporting him, had argued *and argued* last spring that he, Vincent, be offered the position he held; others in the department, notably a "rival poet" (it was disclosed that Jake Hanley wrote poetry) had strongly favored another candidate, from British Columbia. Gradually it was disclosed that the "rival poet" was none other than Ron Blass—who had seemed so friendly to Vincent! Vincent was absurdly hurt.

The Hanleys invited Vincent to a large cocktail party in September, and then again to dinner the following week; then to accompany them to a concert; but something must have gone wrong—Vincent believed it was his exasperation with Cynthia Hanley's fawning and yet impersonal manner—did she flirt with every bachelor?—was it simply a ritual, something to do?—a way of exciting her lethargic husband's jealousy?—and the friendship ended abruptly; they never contacted him again. He did not know whether to be disappointed or relieved. His private life seemed rather empty, it was true, and apart from his teaching he hadn't much contact with people, but was it worth it, finally, assuaging his loneliness with the Hanleys? Jake had a habit of rigorously clearing his throat several times in rapid succession, especially when he was excited in conversation—in fact, Vincent had heard one of the graduate students imitating him in the common room, one day—a habit that was really intolerable. And so. . . . Therefore. . . . It was really just as well that. . . .

Through the Hanleys, however, he had met an interesting young woman. Since an unhappy love affair some years ago, about which Vincent did not allow himself to think, he approached women shyly and cautiously: he was evidently considered an attractive man, and this sometimes raised expectations in women which he had no intention of fulfilling. His single serious, long-term love affair had developed into a long-term engagement, which had ended disastrously . . . but he did not want to think about it, did not want to drag the unfortunate and ludicrous past with him, into southeastern Ontario. So, optimistically, he telephoned the young woman, who was an assistant professor of clinical psychology. Her name was Sondra, which he had mistaken for "Sandra," only the first of a number of mistakes.

Vincent was nervous, of course; but he had the good taste to disguise it. He would never have dreamed of making any companion of his aware of whatever state his mind happened to be in—he considered it tactless to be emotional in any unpleasant way, uncivilized, rather vulgarly "American." But Sondra was extremely nervous. Not only did she keep brushing her long, jet-black hair out of her eyes, and smiling a queer smile that involved only the lower part of her face, but she kept referring to her state, as if it were intriguing as an end in itself: "God, but I'm neurotic. . . . God, look at my hands shake. . . . This is the fifth cigarette. . . . Jesus, I must be reacting to you on some fantastic subconscious level. . . . How about you? How do you feel? How do you feel, I mean, *emotionally*? . . . in a basic sense?"

Vincent had encountered women like this in New York, many years ago; in recent years their kind had disappeared. There were new affectations, new fashions. He tried to ignore her jabs at intimacy, and the desperate smiles that appeared and disappeared, while keeping up a fairly routine conversation that should not have upset anyone. How did she like teaching at Hilberry . . . ? Where had she received her graduate degree . . . ? Did she enjoy traveling . . . ? What about books . . . films . . . music . . . hobbies . . . ? She countered by asking him a few conventional questions, but obviously was not interested in his replies, and as he spoke of being favorably impressed with his students—so much more courteous and literate than he had expected, saner, more dependable, less obvious use of drugs, less flamboyant costumes and behavior—Sondra stared deeply into his eyes as if

reading the inner man. In telling her about one of his pleasant
experiences with his first-year group, he noticed that he was talking to himself; she was not really listening at all.

"Cynthia told me you were a Pisces," she said, nodding. "Ah
yes."

Vincent decided he did not care for the woman, he suspected
she did not care for him, yet the evening could not end so
abruptly; it was only twenty minutes after nine.

And so back to her apartment.

". . . I suppose Cynthia has acquainted you with . . . filled
you in on. . . . It seems the bastard was involved with two girls
at the same time . . . not one but *two*. . . . Each ignorant of the
other's existence, needless to say. Both well acquainted with the
intimate details of *my* existence, however. Oh, he told them everything! Everything! And he lied, he exaggerated. . . . Private life
. . . quirks . . . habits . . . mannerisms," Sondra murmured.
She shook her head. They were seated side by side; Vincent was
trying to make sense of her monologue, trying to see where he
fitted in. Sondra was a little drunk. "Thank God I was able to see
how Jerry needs to debase women . . . *that* kept me sane, that
insight. It kept me sane throughout the winter! . . . Because there
are men, you know, walking around as if they were whole, who
are *not whole*, but *half*, half men walking around as if they were
whole, *half men pretending to be whole*. Walking around! Victim-
izing people! . . . He needs to debase women because of a
terrifying fear of castration at their hands, Jerry needs to debase
them, I mean us, because . . . of this fear. Based on his relationship with his mother, of course. It always is. We were married
only two years but I learned so much . . . so much wisdom . . .
truths about human nature through suffering . . . there's no other
way, no shortcut to wisdom, to maturity," she said, beginning to
cry. "The son of a bitch is in Vancouver now. Letters I send
come back unopened—*Addressee Unknown*—how do you like that!
The day of the divorce he left town, and now it's *Addressee Unknown!* All because of this infantile regressive terror of his . . .
terror of castration at the hands of the mother . . . simply proof

of his immaturity, the bastard! He owes me five hundred in alimony, and do you know what? He had a friend write saying he had drowned, drowned in a sailing accident, an obvious bare-faced lie, and I'm going to take that letter to the Legal Aid Center. . . ."

She brushed hair out of her eyes. She made a move as if to sink into Vincent's embrace, but he was sitting stiffly, not quite looking at her.

". . . so miserable, so unhappy, so neurotic I could die . . . could just lie down and die," she panted. ". . . lying filthy sons of bitches. . . . Men taking advantage . . . but I got my Ph.D., didn't I, nobody can take that away from me. . . . *Addressee Unknown!* We'll see who's unknown! Two can play that game as well as one. . . . Where are you going?"

"I must leave," Vincent said.

"But wait! Wait!" she cried. "Wait, we haven't even. . . ."

"I must leave," Vincent said, standing. He could not see how it might be possible to reconstruct this scene, to reimagine it as amusing rather than pathetic, as "comic" rather than simply depressing; he drew himself up to his fullest height, gave an aristocratic shrug, tried to smile. Sondra jumped to her feet, still crying. She tried to take his hands, tried to maneuver him into taking her hands, seizing them. At the restaurant—a pretentious French restaurant—she had had too much wine, too many cock-tails; the dinner had cost Vincent far more than he had dreamed; and now it was ending in a kind of squabble, an intimate exchange between two strangers.

". . . haven't even . . . haven't even. . . ."

"Good-bye," Vincent said. "Good night."

She made a halfhearted attempt to unzip her dress; she brushed her gleaming black hair out of her eyes, framing her face with her hair, staring at him; but it was useless. "Haven't even become acquainted," she said accusingly.

Afterward, Vincent was so upset he could not sleep. He tried to read and could not read. *Love,* he thought. *Where is it? Where was it? How had people fallen in love in the past?* He could not read, could not even sit still. In his bathroom mirror a ghastly pale creature gazed at him, sexless, stricken, utterly alone. "Love," it said aloud. "Marriage. Friendship. . . . Friends, friendship. Marriage. Love. Normality: normal people. Where . . . ?"

Deranged by Sondra's tears and the late hour and the several drinks he had had since returning to his own apartment, Vincent even considered writing to his former fiancée. Her name was Florence; she was now studying at the University of London. Frail, honey-haired, with lovely brown eyes . . . an I.Q. of 180 . . . more than a match for Vincent. She could not bear to be contradicted: it enraged her. Vincent had always enjoyed her sarcasm when it was directed at other people, but when she turned it on him. . . . Frightening, really. Terrifying. But she was a marvelous young woman, and so intelligent, so well suited for him. . . . They had finally become engaged: Vincent was, of course, really quite conventional. He was formal, ritualistic, old-fashioned. He wanted an engagement, and he wanted marriage, and he wanted . . . wanted. . . .

"I want to be one of them," he whispered.

But he decided not to write. No. Impossible. Florence would only leap back into the fray, too eagerly, she would accuse him of whatever terrible textbook things she had discovered: narcissism, repressed homosexuality, selfishness, egotism, the inability to bear contradictions. No, it was impossible. "I want to be like everyone else," Vincent said. "How . . . ?"

It happened that, in November, his life was changed irreparably. The woman's name was Violet Kipling-Horne.

Dr. Barth told him one morning that he should see Mr. Bell, of the library's rare-book division. "It seems there is a need for a scholar of your talents," Dr. Barth said. He was a white-haired, small man, with a tendency to mumble; much of the time no one knew what he was saying. "Yes? My talents?" Vincent said. He did not know whether to be intimidated or pleased. After some minutes of speaking with Mr. Bell, of listening to Mr. Bell's long, convoluted, confusing sentences, Vincent gradually began to real-

ize that he had been singled out for something quite special. Or
was he? ". . . for some years now we have all been awaiting . . .
with expectations . . . the unsealing of the Melrose gift . . . as
you can imagine. Nineteen forty-nine . . . 1921 . . . and of
course the present day. Very valuable letters donated to this college . . . tax-free gift . . . generosity. I assume you're familiar
with the circumstances and the fact that the letters exist . . .
Dr. Barth has said that the English Department has awaited the
unsealing anxiously . . . though not, of course," he said impas-
sively, smiling at Vincent, "not wishing the donor to die . . . to
pass away . . . according to the directions in the will, the pecu-
liarity of the . . . the legal stipulations in the will. And so. That
brings us to today. President Swanson is most, most eager, as you
can imagine . . . most eager for the letters to be studied, to be
given the publicity in the scholarly and academic world they
deserve, and of course Hilberry College will . . . the college itself
will necessarily come in for its fair share of publicity, which I
think you will agree, judging from the outrageous editorials the
local paper sees fit to print, is very badly needed. And so, and so
this brings us to today."

Vincent smiled. "Evidently I have been selected to . . . ?"

"Yes, and it's a considerable honor," Mr. Bell said. He rather
resembled Dr. Barth: small, with a little paunch, thinning white
hair and an agreeable elfin charm that at times slipped into den-
sity, obscurity, a thickness like lard . . . but most of the time,
Vincent believed, was genuinely charming. A tall man, Vincent
made every effort to be generous. He could not believe the disturbing hypothesis, recently brought forth by a psychologist, that
all men detest men who are taller than they, and the very shortest
men in any society feel murderous (though of course unconscious)
rage toward the rest. This could not be. Vincent hated psycho-
analytic generalizations, he hated scientism of any kind. Yet, as
Mr. Bell continued to talk, he had an uneasy sensation of being
somehow isolated . . . assessed . . . by an enemy in the guise
of an old cheerful librarian. ". . . haven't had a chance to read
the letters very thoroughly myself," Mr. Bell said, "but of course I

am not a scholar or historian, like yourself; it isn't my place to be assessing the Kipling-Horne papers. The young lady, as you probably know, was the favorite niece of Rudyard Kipling, so it is said . . . even helped him with some of his manuscripts, I believe . . . went out to India to visit him, with her family . . . I think. That sort of thing. You're probably quite familiar with the whole era. The bequest came to us through the generosity of Mrs. Frederick Melrose of Toronto, who died recently . . . a special gift made to Hilberry College . . . in honor, I believe, of Mrs. Melrose's admiration for President Swanson. Very, very generous of her, a very great honor. It seems that these letters were the possession of her husband, Frederick Melrose, the well-known Toronto attorney and philanthropist . . . no, the name isn't familiar? . . . well, he died many years ago and the letters naturally were willed to his widow; and eventually she died, of course, and so . . . and so we have them, *we have them now.* I don't need to tell you, Dr. Scoville, how excited President Swanson is. These letters are the first real literary gifts the college has ever received. We've been awaiting their unsealing for years, though of course Dr. Swanson hasn't been hoping for the death of Mrs. Melrose. It's a very complicated thing, as it usually is, legal matters, wills, estates, situations of that nature. Now Dr. Swanson, whom you may have met . . . no? . . . is a fine, fine man. One of the few decent people in administration, I might as well tell you, and it's a pity, how he has had to suffer such attacks by the city newspapers . . . the student paper . . . many members of his faculty . . . even a few of the younger deans. . . . Even, as you probably know, an occasional attack by members of the board of governors, who should of course be more loyal to him. And so . . . well, I won't exhaust you with needless details . . . and so it falls upon you, Dr. Scoville, to be equal to the honor. It is quite an honor, I believe. You've been selected out of the entire English Department to work on these valuable holdings. . . ."

Vincent tried to explain: "That's very generous of you, but in fact it's probably because of my area of specialization. Dr. Barth no doubt chose me because. . . ."

"It's quite an honor," Mr. Bell repeated.

"Yes, I realize that," Vincent said quietly.

"An honor, an honor that must be lived up to. Why, these holdings are so valuable that you won't even be able to examine them for another week or ten days. They were specially weather-proofed, you know, and treated in a delicate series of chemical air baths . . . for the prevention of aging, rot, mildew, destruction by pests . . . termites, rodents . . . that sort of thing. The acquisition of such rare materials necessitates severe measures, and so you can imagine how enthusiastic Dr. Swanson is, and how eagerly he will look forward to your report."

"I realize that," Vincent said slowly.

My God. This cannot be.

Vincent was in the Octagonal Room on the fourth floor of the library, alone in an immense, expensively appointed meeting room, at the head of an enormous mahogany table. He had been studying the Kipling-Horne letters for several hours. He had made his way through the young woman's spidery handwriting . . . had doubled back . . . reread . . . had sighed, scratched himself rather in the way Perry Sandeen scratched himself, unknowingly . . . and had come to the inescapable conclusion that these letters were worthless.

Utterly worthless.

He groaned aloud, theatrically. How had it happened that. . . . How . . . ? Why . . . ? But of course: Basil May and the one or two other people who might have been considered "experts" had declined the task. They had been approached, no doubt, many years ago. They had wisely declined. They had declined the honor. *And so it falls upon you . . . to be equal to it.*

Vincent reread the five letters.

He had had difficulty with Miss Kipling's handwriting at first: thin, flowery, ornate, the "artistic" calligraphy young ladies had learned at that time, on certain social levels. Of course, those young ladies had learned so elegant a calligraphy in order to disguise the fact that they really had nothing to say. Vincent had done his doctoral dissertation—a hefty six hundred pages—on the minor works of Virginia Woolf; he had studied the letters that had passed between Miss Stephen and her sister and other relatives, and innumerable members of their world, many of whom wrote in Miss Kipling's style. Sprightly breathless phrases . . . dashes, exclamation marks . . . underscorings of banalities.

My dearest,
   I am writing this atop a lovely fresh-green hill overlooking Ovingdean—thinking of our last meeting—my mind & heart entirely enraptured—enchanted—tho' stricken with dread from time to time that we should be *found out.* Dearest, I can almost imagine you here—can almost imagine you able to hear the birds —the cattle lowing in the village (they are being herded through the street at this very moment!)—can feel the pressure of your hand against mine. I am unable to concentrate—feel giddy & helpless. My cousin is climbing the hill to me—I must close— *with love.*
                                        As always, your
                                                          Violet

   It had taken Vincent nearly an hour to decipher this, the first time through; the second time he read it swiftly, as if looking for small ironies, little clues that might indicate the whole thing was a joke. But no. No. Violet Kipling had been eighteen years old, according to his calculations, in June of 1921—poorly educated, of course—hardly more than a child. Her letters to Frederick Melrose were a child's letters. . . . *This cannot be,* Vincent thought calmly, even as he was scanning the second letter, which had been written the next day, dashed off while tea was being prepared downstairs and Violet was dreading at any moment the interruption of her mother's voice. *My thoughts are only of you, dearest, tho' the world would mock me for my unwillingness to hide my feelings.* . . . A brief note, one page only.
   The third letter was dated June 30, 1921. It was longer, written after the lovers had evidently met in London. Miss Kipling's handwriting was more flowery—perhaps hysterical?—than usual. Idiotic swirls and convolutions and exaggerated dashes: Vincent winced, as if he were being forced to peer into someone's soul. How the

girl was revealing herself!—not simply her emotions, but her intellectual shallowness as well. *I torment myself with doubting your words—I know, I know that I am perverse—but your being has so imprinted itself upon my soul—I will never be myself again*—After this several lines were blotted out heavily, as if Violet had shaken ink drops on the stationery and smeared them together. Vincent wondered what the girl had written there. But the fourth letter, dated September 1, was not much different from the others. Three pages of earnest, breathless declarations of love, again the contemplation of their most recent meeting, and Violet's confession that she was "unable to concentrate" on anything else. The letter was sent from Brighton and concluded with some chatty, pointless gossip about her relatives and a curate name Fifield who had married a very domineering woman . . . reminiscent of Jane Austen, whom Violet had certainly read. The last letter was dated October 15, sent from London. Nothing seemed to have changed: Violet declared she would love Frederick forever. She thought only of him, she yearned only to be with him once again. . . . *It is raining here & terribly melancholy—but such is the state of my soul—I hardly know if I share in that melancholy or am giddy & joyous in spite of all.*

Vincent sighed and pushed the letters away.

Worthless.

He would have been embarrassed, perhaps even a little disturbed, to have spent hours scrutinizing a young girl's love letters —a girl now dead, as her lover was dead—had he not felt so miserable himself. His digestion had always been quirky, precarious; he was not so healthy as he appeared. Occasionally he even wondered if he was entirely sane . . . but perhaps everyone wondered that? And who could judge? Vincent was supposed to prepare a preliminary report on the "Kipling-Horne Collection," to be submitted to Dr. Barth before being sent up to the president's office. After that, he was to prepare a thorough bibliography of the holdings, listing the contents of each letter in as much detail as possible; he was to contact other libraries, museums, and special collections in North America and England, to see what other "papers" of Miss Kipling's might be available for scholarly analysis; it went without saying, of course, that he should relate the letters to some significant aspect of Rudyard Kipling's literary career.

Maybe Melrose and the girl hadn't even been lovers . . . ? Maybe Violet had simply written the letters, recording her girlish infatuation, her fantasies . . . ? If Melrose had replied, the replies were never alluded to. And how had the two of them met, unless Violet were chaperoned? A mystery, a worthless mystery. Fantasy within fantasy. "Love." Vincent seized his curly hair in both hands and pulled at it until pain awakened him. He must resist this madness. He would, he must. He would begin by. . . . He would refuse to. . . .

A young man of integrity, Vincent wrote an honest report of less than half a page, summing up the entire collection. He wondered if the worthlessness of the letters would speak for itself . . . ? But Dr. Barth was not a subtle man. So he concluded his report with the statement the Kipling-Horne letters had no value, literary or historical.

Dr. Barth telephoned him in his office. While Perry Sandeen giggled and clucked and sighed over a group of first-year papers he was correcting, Vincent listened to Dr. Barth's slow, ponderous, blunt remarks. Vincent's report would not do. It simply would not do. It could hardly be sent along to President Swanson . . . perhaps it was only a first draft? Vincent tried to defend himself but was interrupted. He stared blindly at Perry, at the watercolors and finger paintings of Perry's children taped to the wall behind him. Dr. Barth suggested he study the letters again, more carefully this time. It was a most important task. The acquisition of the Kipling letters was a very important event in the history of Hilberry College . . . didn't Vincent realize that?

After he hung up, he seemed to fall forward on his desk. Perry cried, "What's wrong, Vince? Hey, what is it?"

Vincent's forehead was pressed against the desk top. "Don't ask," he said.

"It isn't the—it's too early for—It isn't the announcements of contracts and promotions and—They didn't fire you, Vince, did they?"

"Don't ask," Vincent whispered.

So Vincent returned to the Octagonal Room.

The Kipling papers were always brought to him by the same woman, a secretary-librarian in the Rare Book and Special Collections Division. She was grave, unsmiling, rather fearful that Vincent would hurt the papers somehow—though he assured her he didn't smoke, wouldn't drink coffee or eat—would barely *touch* the letters, in fact. "They're insured for a large amount of money," the woman told him, "but if anything happened to them . . . it would be an irreparable loss. I just don't know how Dr. Swanson would take it." When it was time to leave for the day, Vincent went to get the woman so that she could carry the letters back to the vault. The Octagonal Room was luxurious: floor-to-ceiling windows, comfortable leather chairs, a thick rug. Such surroundings should have pleased Vincent, who did like luxury; but the unnatural silence of the place began to disturb him.

He spent hours laboriously copying out phrases, isolating key images or symbols, "motifs," patterns . . . trying to imagine a chronology of events. By this time he had read every book the library had on Kipling and his era, and though he had not come across any mention of Violet-Kipling or Frederick Melrose, there had existed, evidently, a very minor poet named Jonathan Melrose, of interest to Lytton Strachey scholars. . . . Perhaps Jonathan and Frederick were related? Or even the same person, somehow? In the meantime, of course, he had directed the library to send to England for more materials.

His preliminary report had been sent along to the president, a revised report of some two pages, with wide margins. Vincent bit his lips while typing it out; he bit himself unknowingly, and tasted blood. He was certain that Dr. Barth or Dr. Swanson would recognize the hysterical vacuity of the report; but it was evidently accepted, and a few days later Vincent received a letter from the president himself, filled with encouragement and congratulations. Dr. Swanson even speculated on the possibility of "there being established at our college a center for the study of the papers of Violet Kipling and her circle. . . . Perhaps, someday, Kipling scholars from all over the world might come to Hilberry to work in quiet surroundings, alongside Hilberry scholars." And of course he, Dr. Scoville, would be the "nucleus" of such scholarly activity.

After the Christmas break, the weather turned foul in Telford. There were days of overcast, low-hanging skies, and snowflakes that fell wetly, darkening with soot, never a genuine snowfall that cleared the air and left the sky a healthy, gleaming blue. Vincent pretended to work on the letters, though of course there was little for him to do. He grew secretive about his private life: he declined Perry's invitations for coffee, avoided Sondra when he accidentally ran into her on campus, he found it difficult even to mumble a few vague optimistic words to Dr. Barth, who sometimes cornered him in the common room to ask about the "papers." One day an idea occurred to him. He interrupted Ron Blass's cheerful monologue of complaints—Ron was unhappy with a number of people, most of them strangers to Vincent—and asked Ron whether he had heard of the library's holdings, its collection of rare works . . . ? Did Ron know about the "Rudyard Kipling" letters . . . ? Did he know how valuable . . . what an opportunity existed . . . ? But even before he finished his questions, Ron began to shake his head. Tears of sympathy and pity appeared in his eyes; though perhaps Vincent imagined this. Thinking it over, afterward, Vincent wondered if perhaps the tears had been his own.

"Jesus, am I glad I have tenure," Ron sighed. He was still shaking his head. "And of course I'm a poet, a creative writer . . . I'm not expected to do, to be, scholarly . . . you know. Like yourself. Yes, word has gotten around, I think it was an innocent breach of confidence, one of the secretaries, probably . . . it's awfully difficult to keep things secret here. But, yes, it's generally known that you've been stuck with Swanson's monomania. I might have warned you, except. . . . Well, frankly, it *is* something of an honor. They might have asked any of the younger instructors, they might have seized upon anyone without tenure. . . . Your office mate Perry Sandeen, you know, is *very, very* ambitious. Didn't you know? And even Jake Hanley, though he does have tenure, is only an assistant professor and seems stuck on that level . . . *very* bitter, needless to say *very* jealous of those of us on a higher level. I think he might have accepted the assignment, frankly, if he'd been asked. But his specialty isn't English literature . . . and he's an awfully mediocre man, people say. Students say. And then there's. . . ."

But Vincent had stopped listening. He thought: *At least I have my teaching, my students. They are real; they will keep me sane.*

He made one more attempt to interest another faculty member in the letters, but his approach was an ungainly one, and doomed at the outset. There was a woman writer named Stella Burkhardt in the department who taught composition and creative writing; remarks were made about her height—she must have been six feet tall —and her abnormal shyness—she was always ducking around corners to avoid people—but in general she seemed to be respected. At least people did not dismiss her as contemptuously as they dismissed the poets. Vincent learned that Stella Burkhardt had become famous in the area a few years ago—"famous" through having been featured in the Sunday supplement of the Toronto *Globe and Mail*. Her single publication was a book of stories, *Sketches of an Ontario Girlhood*, which was said to have been generously received by Canadian critics, though Vincent could never discover anyone who had read it. Everyone said of Stella, "She's very talented" or "She's very hard-working," but no one knew her well. She was unmarried, probably in her late thirties though she looked younger, like a haggard schoolgirl, in flat-heeled shoes and clothes of neutral colors.

Vincent did not dare approach her head on, she was so evasive; so he courted her through notes left in her mailbox. Might they meet . . . ? Might they have lunch together, or at least coffee . . . ? He had read her book and liked it very much (it was true that he had read it: he had even bought a copy from the college book store) . . . he very much admired creative writers . . . perhaps they could talk sometime . . . ? He was sure they had many interests in common. . . .

She always turned him down. Her notes were terse, her handwriting small and tight. She was too busy with her classes, too busy with her writing. Vincent read these notes and blushed angrily. Did this awful woman imagine he was pursuing her? Vincent Scoville pursuing *her?*

One day Perry Sandeen shook his finger at him and made a clucking noise, the kind he made over the telephone when talking to his children.

". . . hilarious rumor . . . obviously exaggerated. . . . You and Stella Burkhardt, eh? People say you've fallen in love with her . . . you leave notes for her and she rips them up. . . . Vince, it isn't possible, is it? *Why don't you give all that scholarship a rest?* One of these weekends maybe you could drop in . . . Valerie would love to meet you . . . just relax and have a nice family dinner . . . how about it?"

"I'm not pursuing anyone," Vincent said angrily. "I'm not in love. Who the hell is making up such rumors? . . . Why should I give scholarship a rest? Who has been talking about me?"

Perry giggled and made a playful gesture, protecting his head with his arms.

"Who has been talking about me? *Me?*" Vincent asked.

At least he had his teaching. His classes went well, though not so well as they had in the fall; but of course everyone was gradually slowing, energies always sagged in the dark of winter, that was to be expected. . . . But at least he had his teaching, Vincent thought grimly. That would keep him sane.

One day in March he received an engraved invitation to a luncheon, sent from the president's office.

It was to be held in honor of Elizabeth Melrose of Blenheim. Evidently she was the daughter of Rhoda Simmings Melrose, the widow of Frederick Melrose, who had emigrated to Canada just before World War II; she was the only living descendant of Violet's lover. Vincent's initial pleasure at being invited to the luncheon faded as he tried to fit himself into the context . . . tried to fit the two lovers into the context. . . . A luncheon to be held in Telford, Ontario, in March of this year, in honor of a woman who was related to a man to whom a young woman wrote five letters in the year 1921 . . . a young woman said to be the "favorite" niece of Rudyard Kipling. It had all come about because of someone's whimsical donation to Hilberry College. It had all come about because. . . . He did not know why. He knew why, in a giddy, depressing way, but he did not know why *he* was involved. What was truly depressing about the situation was the fact that Violet Kipling had evidently never seen Frederick Melrose after October, 1921; according to photostated materials Vincent had received, from England, the young woman had become engaged to another man before the year was out . . . had married him, had borne him five sons and one daughter, with never another thought of or letter to Frederick Melrose. And what had it to do with Rudyard Kipling? Vincent had always detested Kipling; before coming to Hilberry, he had not even read Kipling. He tugged at his curls, trying to figure out why he was so inextricably bound up with these people. Almost, now, he no longer minded being lonely; he seemed to walk about, everywhere, accompanied by Violet's breathless simpering voice, and Frederick's silent, imperious presence. . . .

The luncheon was held in one of the College Center's smaller banquet rooms. The table was tastefully set: white linen, actual silverware, a small bouquet of yellow roses. Vincent had bought a new suit for the occasion, not trusting the lived-in, casual appearance of his other outfits. He even wore a wide tie and a vest that gave him a rather Edwardian look.

The president of Hilberry College, Dr. Swanson, introduced the luncheon guests to Miss Melrose, one by one. Vincent awaited his turn nervously. He was impressed with Dr. Swanson's stature, his almost military bearing: a man in his sixties, totally bald, with a brisk, even athletic manner, and a surprising suntan. Did he use a sunlamp? His eyes were pale blue. His smile was quick, perfectly controlled. Elizabeth Melrose turned out to be a stately woman of indeterminate age, with a heavily made-up but peevish face. She wore a wine-colored wool suit and an old-fashioned hat with a veil; her handshake was surprisingly strong.

Vincent was introduced by Dr. Swanson as "the young scholar who is working on your father's letters." He had the idea that Miss Melrose approved of him, though she did no more than smile perfunctorily. Dr. Swanson's gaze met his, man to man, before moving on to the next guest. Vincent's nervousness was unnecessary, since everything went quite well. The event was covered by the local newspaper: a woman reporter took down Dr. Swanson's introductory remarks, and a young photographer in a sweater and blue jeans took photographs of Dr. Swanson and Miss Melrose, as Miss Melrose handed the packet of letters to Dr. Swanson. A number of photographs were taken. Vincent wondered why other people were not included—Mr. Bell of the Rare Book and Special Collections Division, for instance, or Dr. Barth, who was looking rather wistful; it was not out of the question to think that perhaps even Vincent himself might be asked. . . . But the photographs were only of Dr. Swanson and Miss Melrose. "This certainly is an historic occasion," Dr. Swanson said several times, smiling at Miss Melrose. "We of Hilberry College are . . . honored . . . deeply honored. . . . Never quite anything like it, in our history. . . . Scholarly academic competition . . . reputation, don't you know; so very, very generous of your parents. . . ."

The luncheon itself went quickly. Vincent hardly tasted his food, he was so strangely exhilarated. There was Dr. Swanson himself . . . brusque, attractive for a man of his age . . . perhaps a little pompous . . . of course he had to suffer a great deal of criticism, like everyone in high office. He reminded Vincent of an old soldier, a hearty old warrior. Miss Melrose was eating rapidly and without looking up, as if accustomed to eating alone; she nodded whenever Dr. Swanson spoke to her, but in general the conversation was confined to Dr. Swanson and one or two of his aides. In fact, the conversation was confined to Dr. Swanson himself. It was an exuberant, meandering monologue that touched upon the "Kipling gift" from time to time, but careened off into subjects that might have been related—Vincent could not be certain, he was having trouble following Dr. Swanson's shifts and transitions and leaps—now the latest outrage in Ottawa, the most recent "poor showing" of a local M.P., now the inconvenience of the city's decision to lay a storm sewer near Dr. Swanson's residence . . . now the uncommonly disappointing weather . . . was it as disagreeable in Blenheim, he wondered? Miss Melrose said that it was. Dr. Swanson nodded gravely, his pale, almost colorless blue eyes meeting Vincent's gaze for a split second. "I think it not unlikely that many things are deteriorating," he said, "not the least of them the respect for tradition one could take for granted in the past . . . the sense of sacrifice for one's community, country, church . . . don't you know; that sort of thing." Everyone at the table agreed. "The Anglican Church in recent years. . . . Shocking."

"That's so," Mr. Bell said.

"It's incredible . . . beyond one's wildest fears. But they are all around us, you know, the 'reformers' . . . *levelers*, I have always called them." He went onto speak animatedly, and with occasional smirks and knowing, paternal smiles, of various difficulties inherent in the office of president of a college, or in any high office, any position of responsibility in which one's life energy was entirely dedicated to an ideal; always there were enemies, always resentful small-souled people, "critics" they called themselves, but Dr. Swanson saw them for what they were. . . . *Anarchists.* Vincent listened in fascination, no longer eating. He felt almost childishly pleased at being here, though of course he knew Dr. Swanson was . . . it was quite likely that Dr. Swanson was not so intelligent an individual as, say, the president of Columbia University, or of the University of Toronto; but of course Telford was not New York City or Toronto; it was prudent to keep that in mind. And he was pleased at the small number of people who had been invited to the luncheon—aside from Dr. Swanson and the guest of honor, there were only six or seven—no one else from the English Department except Dr. Barth. Evidently Dr. Swanson had wanted the luncheon to be a very special event. . . . Still, though Vincent felt better about it than he had imagined he would, it was getting late: nearly two o'clock: and Dr. Swanson was still talking. He was now deep into an anecdote concerning his days as a young dean . . . something to do with military service as well . . . "distinguished" . . . "citation" . . . "long-range goals." Miss Melrose had finished eating; she alone at the table showed signs of impatience. She glanced at her wristwatch from time to time. She even stifled a yawn. Finally, she put her napkin forcefully down, and told Dr. Swanson that she had to be leaving.

"Yes, yes," he said hurriedly, "and it has been such an honor. . . . Most privileged, indeed. . . . We will have to arrange similar events in the future, perhaps . . . ceremonies. . . . The dedication, perhaps, of the Kipling Center, with you, Miss Melrose, as guest of honor . . . scholars and distinguished academics from all over Canada . . . that sort of thing. If it should come to pass. . . . You have met Dr. Scoville, have you not? Dr. Scoville has been entrusted with your late mother's gift to the college, and I needn't tell you that it has been a. . . ."

But Miss Melrose did not even glance at Vincent. She stood so abruptly that Dr. Swanson did not have a chance to help her with her chair. "Dr. Swanson," she said irritably, "I'm here today because my mother would have wished it. There is no other reason, I assure you. My mother would have wished me to attend this luncheon, to be photographed with you, to continue this vulgar and pointless farce to the very end. Don't interrupt, please. I know full well what that old woman would have wished, and senility has nothing to do with it: she was not senile when she discovered the letters, or when she made out her will. A martyr, Dr. Swanson. She was a martyr. She would have us all be martyrs. I, like yourself, am an educator; I am a teacher of Canadian history, have been so for nearly thirty years, in the Blenheim public schools; I am hardly a fool. My mother deliberately seized upon those letters, many years ago, to make my father's life a living hell . . . letters from a silly little girl . . . a girl he could not even remember when questioned about her. She made his life miserable, she reaped many a harvest from those letters! I don't say that my father did not deserve it—my father's reputa-

tion is not to be considered here—I don't say, even, that anyone does not deserve *anything* that happens to him. I don't say
that. I believe in free will, in the individual's responsibility for
himself. But my mother brought up the ridiculous subject of Violet
Kipling whenever it suited her, as a way of inducing hysterics, and
her final act of bequeathing the letters to this college is typical . . .
completely in line with the woman's sense of martyrdom, her absurd jealousy, her persecution fantasies and exaggerations, which I
had to live with, Dr. Swanson, I assure you, for many, many years.
I found such behavior offensive, and told her so. Nevertheless, I did
attend your luncheon, I posed for your photographs, I did what my
mother would have wished. But I am hardly a martyr, Dr. Swanson,
and I very much doubt that this occasion will ever be repeated.
You may do with the letters exactly as you wish, but please do not
involve me any further."

After Miss Melrose left, there were some awkward moments. Dr.
Swanson looked about and cleared his throat, as if preparing to
speak; but he did not speak. Then Dr. Barth said cautiously that he
had a very important meeting at two thirty . . . might he be excused? And the dean asked to be excused, since he too had a very
important meeting. Before Vincent quite knew what was happening, all the others, more adroit than he, had slipped away—all had
meetings at two-thirty, extremely important meetings. Only Dr.
Swanson and Vincent remained. When Vincent tried to explain
that he had a conference with a student at two-thirty, and must
leave, Dr. Swanson interrupted him—he jabbed his forefinger at
Vincent and said heatedly that he, Vincent, had a very responsible
position . . . a young man hardly out of graduate school . . . did
he understand the situation, its gravity?

Vincent's smile had become painful; he ached to be out of here.
Away, somewhere, anywhere . . . away from these people, away
from what was happening so inexorably. . . .

Dr. Swanson began to reminisce. His days as a schoolboy . . . as
a student . . . in the armed service . . . his professional life as a
young man . . . his work with Hilberry College . . . "wresting
power away from those who would misuse it" . . . his constant

vigilance. The importance of . . . the need for . . . the dangers of failing to. . . .

Vincent found himself nodding after a while. It was painless: it seemed in a way the polite thing to do. He had not noticed that Dr. Swanson had had a bit to drink—perhaps the old man had been drinking before the luncheon? But it was so, it was so. Drunk. Or if not drunk, exhibiting the characteristics one associates with drunkenness . . . or with neurological disorders of some kind. . . . Vincent's upbringing had been conventional enough; he knew how to be grave and agreeable and courteous; no matter that part of him wanted to jump up and shriek *Let me go, you insane old fool!* He remained seated. ". . . Dr. Barth has put in many years of service with us . . . many, many years. But at times I begin to doubt . . . to doubt his judgment. And his ability to control his faculty. Very, very important thing for an administrator, don't you know; controlling your faculty. Otherwise. . . . Otherwise strife and anarchy. . . . You seem to possess, Dr. Scofield, an astonishingly mature personality for one so young. . . . Remarkable. Very valuable. You can't imagine. . . . Dean Eddington's day is nearly finished, I fear. Fine man, fine background. But increasingly absentminded of late . . . so the rumors assure me . . . absentminded, garrulous, frightfully out of touch with his faculty. You would not guess, would you, that we attended Cambridge at the same time? . . . Ah, the marvelous tradition there . . . the quiet, the respect for tradition . . . the bells tolling so often during the day, at the oddest times. Stays in one's memory over the years. Amazing."

Dr. Swanson asked Vincent to sit closer, and though Vincent protested that he really must leave—he had a meeting at three o'clock—Dr. Swanson even pulled out the chair Miss Melrose had been seated in—indicated that Vincent should sit a little closer; there was a great deal he must learn. And so for the next two and a half hours, Vincent sat beside Dr. Swanson. Now and then Dr. Swanson would ask him his opinion on something—the new dean of the law school, the plans for the new conference center, the Prime Minister's education policy—but it was never necessary for Vincent to actually reply, since Dr. Swanson always cut him off after a few words. "Ah, *there's* where you go wrong! *There's* the error in your thinking!" Gleefully, his tanned face brought close to Vincent's, Dr. Swanson explained where he had slipped up, where "even a young man of your youth" had gone wrong. As it neared five o'clock, however, Dr. Swanson became increasingly wistful. He was on the subject of the deterioration of the Anglican Church, in both Canada and England, and could not seem to get onto another subject. ". . . the terror is, young man, the terror of it is . . . and I tell you this in absolute confidence, since there is no one . . . no one else . . . no one to whom I can speak . . . *no one*. The terror of it is, simply, that . . . unfathomable as it is . . . I seem to be losing my faith. I seem to be in grave, grave danger of losing my faith. Ah, how I need trusted friends, friends to whom I can speak my heart, people who are not always plotting and calculating and spreading rumors. . . . I seem to be losing my faith, and what will remain?"

"Your faith?" Vincent said groggily.

"My faith! The faith of my fathers!" Dr. Swanson said. His face seemed to shrivel suddenly; it took on infantile qualities. But when he wept it was noiselessly, and he did no more than squeeze Vincent's arm. He did not rest his face on Vincent's shoulder, as Vincent halfway feared, nor did he throw himself into Vincent's arms—he wept rather gracefully, like an old soldier. ". . . belief in a God of goodness . . . absolute good, goodness . . . wisdom . . . justice, don't you know. My belief in the One True God and the Trinity and . . . and Christ Himself . . . and the forgiveness of sins. I am losing it, losing it. I tell you I am losing it! . . . Woke up one morning to a vision of devils . . . devils . . . swarming everywhere, out of control . . . crawling in the very vestments of Our Lord . . . hiding in His pockets, hiding in His armpit, even! The Lord of Hosts, mind you! . . . and all the devils swarming around Him . . . and Him indifferent, or taking their side. . . . Oh, it was horrible! Horrible! I am a bachelor, Vincent, and live alone and . . . and I told not a living soul about this vision . . . yet it stays with me constantly. . . . How will it end, Vincent? How do you think it will end?"

". . . end?"

"Western civilization, Vincent," Dr. Swanson said softly. Tears ran down both his cheeks. "How do you think it will end?"

Winter continued: there was a blizzard in the last week of March, and yet another blizzard in the first week of April. His colleagues complained bitterly, but Vincent found the weather oddly stimulating.

By now he had begun to discover the essential intricacies of the Kipling letters: a certain voice . . . a certain repetition of key images, motifs . . . curiously enough, rather similar to image clusters to be found in Kipling's "The Peacock's Tail," written at about the time the letters were written. Through new acquisitions and through interlibrary loans, Vincent had assembled quite a number of books, monographs, offprints, and other material. He spent most of his time in the library; he was relieved when the teaching year ended. The final weeks of the semester had been particularly exhausting. . . . Reading, rereading the letters . . . arranging them into different patterns . . . taking laborious notes . . . working out the prospectus for a monograph of his own, which would necessitate a year's leave of absence . . . work in the British Museum and in special collections in England: all this took time, and his teaching was a distraction. He had hypothesized several chronological sequences, several "explanations" of the letters, several ways in which they touched upon, helped to illumine, or had actually dealt with certain materials Kipling dealt with . . . but of course his research had only begun. The entire project would take years.

"You handled yourself very nicely at that luncheon for Miss Melrose," Dr. Barth said to Vincent one day, having met him by accident. "I heard the old boy trapped you afterward, eh? Obviously he'd been drinking."

"He didn't trap me," Vincent said carefully. "I wouldn't say, precisely, that Dr. Swanson had *trapped* me."

Dr. Barth eyed him with interest. "Yes? Is that so? . . . What sort of things did he say to you? Did he talk about the college? Did he happen to mention me?"

"I really don't remember," Vincent said.

Dr. Barth was silent. Then he said: "Well. You seem to have gotten along very nicely with him . . . I've received a memo since. . . . It's to everyone's credit, of course. We're pleased that you have adjusted so well to Hilberry. And the research is evidently going well, I hear? You're working very industriously?"

"I think so, yes," Vincent said. He managed a smile: it felt real enough, natural enough. Perhaps it was real.

He had even acquired a photograph of Violet Kipling-Horne.

It had been taken in the forties, and showed a woman considerably older than eighteen—of course—no longer the sweet, dimpled, breathless, giddy girl of the Melrose affair, but a mature woman. Square-jawed, with an immense bosom that looked muscular, a generally thick, even stout body . . . rather heavy eyebrows . . . a measured smile. Her hair was parted in the center, neatly. *I torment myself with doubting your words—I know I am perverse —but your being has so imprinted itself upon my soul—*

No. But he taped the photograph to his wall anyway, beside the window.

The woman in the photograph smiled sternly at Vincent and he sometimes smiled back. He could not have said why, exactly, something about her presence pleased him . . . soothed him . . . allowed him to know that all was well; nor could he have said why Perry Sandeen so angered him one day, when Perry pointed out that the woman was a little cross-eyed. "That's a lie," Vincent said coldly.

"Hey, she isn't a relative or something, is she? You don't look alike.—Yeah, Vince, she's a little cross-eyed, look here—"

"Get away," Vincent said at once.

"But—"

"She isn't cross-eyed," Vincent said furiously. "*You*—you're— You're the one—Jealous—You're jealous of—"

"But Vince—"

"*Get away*," he whispered.

Perry backed off and Vincent was alone again and all was well.

The Golden Madonna

She led him into a room with a high paneled ceiling, talking all the while, questioning him closely. *How long would he be in London? —why was he alone, hadn't he mentioned he would bring a friend?* Alexander tried to answer her questions politely but heard his voice go vague and flat. He resented being here, with his aunt. He was forty-five minutes late because the streets in this part of the city were so strangely marked, changing names every block; the humiliation of having been lost several times was still with him. "Weren't you going to bring a friend with you . . . ?" Marthe asked.

"She decided not to come."

"I'm sorry. . . ."

Though she looked at him as if hoping for an explanation, he said nothing. He was still nervous and irritable from having been lost half a dozen times. And he resented being here, visiting his aunt Marthe, whom he didn't know at all and had not even seen for six or seven years. Frankly, he hardly recognized her. While she

chattered and fussed over him he recalled, painfully, his girl back at
the hotel, Marian, saying *She's your aunt, I don't want to meet her
after all, go alone, leave me alone* . . . lying across the bed with
her long slender legs pressed together. He told his aunt about
Marian not feeling well enough at the last minute—they had had
lunch in an Indian restaurant on Wardour Street, and Marian's
stomach was delicate—and he himself didn't feel well when he
traveled—

She interrupted him. "Oh, but you look so healthy, you look so
handsome, Alexander! You're thin, but you've always been thin
. . . and boys your age are all so terribly thin now. . . ." She
squeezed his hands; she leaned close to him as if she were near-
sighted. Her perfume was flowery. He wanted to step back, in irritated embarrassment. Except for her eyes, which were dark and
slightly protruding, heavily lashed, like his father's eyes but more
attractive, he might not have even recognized her.

"How long did you say you were going to be in London?" she
asked.

"Only a few more days," Alexander said quickly. In fact, he and
Marian had no plans to leave. They would do what they wanted
to do. "We're going to rent a car and drive up into the Highlands,"
he said. "We like . . . we like to be on our own. . . ."

"I'm sorry I won't get to meet her," Marthe said.

He sat somewhere, still a little confused. Though he had left his
hotel near Russell Square nearly an hour earlier, he had gotten lost
several times; he found himself rushing through the underground
on his long anxious legs, bumping into people, apologizing, then
resigning himself to being late as he rose on escalators behind
tightly jammed double lines of tourists. Like himself, they looked
around with alert but glazed eyes. Marthe asked him whether he'd
had any trouble finding her flat, and he said no, then he realized
how late he was and how out of breath and wild-haired, so he made
a joke out of it and described the uniformed man with a broom in
the South Kensington station who had given him directions, a complicated set of directions, and though Alexander hadn't been able
to understand every word he kept nodding, nodding . . . experi-

encing from time to time that sensation of rising, incomprehensible panic that he had felt several times since leaving New York. "Then I kept seeing myself in the same advertisement on the wall," he said, "a kind of curved, concave metallic advertisement for cigarettes . . . once at the St. James stop, once at South Kensington, and finally up here at Sloane Square. . . ." His aunt smiled at this anecdote, as if willing to laugh but not able to see why it was funny. She might have thought that his long, frizzy brown hair and the denim jeans and tight-fitting denim jacket he wore were not funny, any more than his parents did. He remembered her from years ago, staring at him and assessing him, strangely, and he fell silent. His face hardened with resentment.

This woman, his father's sister, was forty-eight or forty-nine years old. He knew that: his father was fifty-one. But she looked much younger. She wore her frosted blond hair in a stiff, complex style, which seemed to spring weightlessly from her forehead, falling nearly to her shoulders; the ends were turned up, bouncing and fluttering as she spoke. She was girlish, animated. Her face was smooth and unlined and her mouth was too perfect, outlined in red, a blatant impossible red. It was difficult for Alexander to take such a face seriously, after the faces of the girls he knew—pale, fierce, naked faces, absolutely honest. He was calculating rapidly how soon he could leave, maybe pleading the excuse of not feeling well—he had already mentioned the Indian restaurant, deliberately, cleverly—and of worrying about Marian back at the hotel.

A porcelain-smooth face, a smiling charming too-red mouth, and earrings that swung free of her hair occasionally and gleamed in the light, his aunt Marthe Loeper, Marthe Resnick, at one time Marthe Fromm of White Plains . . . he forced himself to agree with her, to smile and nod agreeably, but he did resent being here and it was a mystery to him why he had bothered to come over at all. Just to please his mother, whom he didn't usually bother pleasing, and now he had to puzzle through a complicated question-and-answer period with a woman he hardly knew. Marthe had not been back to the United States for a half dozen years, and before that she'd visited them only a few times; no one had ever met her husbands. Alexander had learned, over the years, without having much interest in the information, that her first husband had been a minor diplomat, and her second husband, Loeper, was a novelist; she must have been divorced from him, or separated, because she made no mention of him and Alexander did not ask.

He found himself sitting on a low, awkwardly low sofa, so close to the floor that his knees rose almost to the height of his face. He finally turned his legs sideways, in exasperation. "Aren't you comfortable? You aren't comfortable," Marthe said. He assured her he was fine. She got to her feet, though, and hovered over him, adjusting pillows, murmuring something about how she hoped he wasn't disappointed in the weather, it had been dark and raining for the last week, day after day, and perhaps he had read in the paper of icebergs drifting down from the North Pole, and of how June 21 was colder this year than December 21 had been. . . . "But I don't want to complain," she said. "I like living here very much."

She poured him sherry, which he didn't much want; but he accepted it. There was a bowl of cashews squarely before him, obviously meant for him, and Marthe went to get a small basket of fruit from somewhere—absentmindedly setting it before him, as if he might want to eat a pear or a greenish-yellow apple or some large purple grapes. She returned to her seat across from him, leaning forward, as if addressing herself to someone else, someone not Alexander at all; he was not accustomed to being treated so well by people his aunt's age. "You don't look comfortable," she said again. "You don't look happy. . . . Are you worried about the girl?"

"No, no," Alexander said quickly. He blushed. "No. I'm very happy to be here."

"Tell me about your father. Is he hard-working as ever? How is he?"

"The same," Alexander said flatly.

His aunt smiled. He saw there, in that smile, a subtle ironic look. She clasped her ringed fingers together around her knees, nodding slowly to encourage him. He went on, "Exactly the same. I haven't been out to the house for a while, because he and I don't get along

—he thinks I'm hopeless, a failure—and I can't be bothered to defend myself to *him*. When I quit medical school he wouldn't speak to me for a month. So. So, he's the same, as far as I know or care."

Marthe watched him, smiling gravely, thoughtfully. He half expected her to say *go on, tell me more*. There was something tense between them, she was keyed-up, as if the dwarfish furniture they sat on and the bowl of fruit and the warm, sluggish light cast over the room from a single lamp with a carved pedestal were props for a stage, things to be used, touched, to establish some basis of reality they might both believe in. Her dress was long, falling to her ankles; it was made of a coarse, costly-looking material, gold and silver and golden-green threads, and Alexander could see small raised figures on it that might have been dragons. . . . He felt a little sorry now that he had deliberately worn this denim outfit; he did have something better back at the hotel. He shifted his legs, embarrassed, and began to tell his aunt about his father's latest hobby: karate. The old man was taking karate lessons. "There's a shopping mall behind our house—do you remember the woods we used to have?—all razed, for a damn shopping mall—and there's a karate training center there," he said, smiling sardonically, "for men like my father. Hard-working, fifty pounds overweight, troubled and confused and instructed by their doctors to take up hobbies, stop smoking, discover their bodies. . . . He used to come home from his karate lessons looking pretty humiliated. I suppose it was good for him—the humiliation."

His aunt laughed. Alexander, warmed by the sherry, was beginning to speak in his usual manner: dry, witty, ironic, fluent. He went on to tell Marthe an anecdote about the morning his father had discovered—right there on the train, headed into the city—the article in the *Wall Street Journal* that announced that one of his twenty-year accounts, with some computer corporation out in Minneapolis, had switched to another law firm. "The reason they gave was that my father's generation was *out of phase*," Alexander laughed.

Marthe shook her head at this, as if pretending to disapprove of him.

"Your father must have been very upset by that," she said. "Especially reading it that way. . . ."

Alexander shrugged.

"Your father does have some feelings," Marthe said slowly. She spoke dubiously, deliberately, staring at Alexander with mock-sympathetic eyes. He noticed that her body was plump, shapely, her bust rounded and almost too large for that sheathlike dress; she wore shoes with thin old-fashioned heels. There was something dramatic, musical, about her and about this setting. It did not seem quite real.

For some time his aunt kept questioning him about home, about his mother especially. But he began to feel relaxed; he didn't mind, really. Then the telephone rang. She answered it in another room, and he was left alone for quite a while. . . . He was irritated, a little hurt. When she came back, she apologized breathlessly but did not explain. Then she sat back down again, without mentioning dinner.

After a while he glanced at his wristwatch: he saw in amazement that it was already after ten o'clock.

But she was eager to hear about what Alexander referred to as his "trouble with the police," so he launched into an anecdote about that, about a police raid on a house in Cambridge he had lived in. She kept pouring them both sherry; he knew he was getting drunk. *Go on, tell me more,* she seemed always to be saying, urging. She was a very attractive woman, with her intense, sympathetic stare, her habit of nodding and smiling at him. She leaned forward, clasping her hands again. "You've certainly had adventures for someone your age," she said, amazed. "Things are so different today. . . . I hate to show my age, Alex, but I had the vague idea you were still in school. *High school.* Isn't that awful? But even with that moustache you look so young. . . ."

Alexander laughed, embarrassed. He finished his glass of sherry.

Then the telephone rang again. Marthe made a movement as if to stand—*no, don't answer it*—and then sank back, catching his eye. She smiled. Again, she did not explain, and only shook her head as if to assure him, no, she was not going to answer it this time. Alexander waited, tensely. The phone rang for some time, then stopped.

They were silent for a while. He wondered what time it was, but didn't want to look at his watch. Then it occurred to him, suddenly, that he would ask her a few questions. But it was difficult for him to begin, to find the right words. He cleared his throat. "I noticed that your husband, I mean Mr. Loeper, had another novel published last year. . . ."

Marthe laughed. "That pathetic bastard," she said.

"I didn't read it myself," Alexander said. He spoke quickly, not wanting to let her sudden reckless, defiant mood pass, going on to tell her that his mother had bought the book, as far as he knew his mother had bought all of Loeper's books. . . .

"But you haven't read them yourself?" she asked.

"No. I never got around to it."

"That's just as well," Marthe said. Her face twisted into a look Alexander could not quite interpret—amusement, disgust, mockery. She was really a very pretty woman, in spite of her exaggerated makeup. "His books are all autobiographical and he hasn't exactly been merciful to anyone, including himself. But I don't intend to talk about him . . . I don't even know where he is. . . . Your mother, of course, would be interested in his books."

"Why?"

Marthe lifted the bottle of sherry and poured them each another drink, though Alexander indicated he didn't want any more. He felt light-headed and sickish . . . in a strange, impersonal, superficial way, as if it didn't matter. He heard himself asking again, "Why—?" and his voice rose shrilly.

Marthe frowned. "This girl of yours—the one you're traveling with—I suppose she's very independent?—I mean, very liberated?"

"I suppose so," Alexander said defensively.

Liberated!

"Things change so rapidly these days," Marthe said slowly. She sat back and crossed her legs; the stiff material of the dress rustled. Alexander could see that her shoe dangled from one foot, dangling there, swaying. . . . He blinked and concentrated his attention upon his aunt's face. She looked dreamy and yet formal, not quite meeting his gaze, as if she were saying words she had prepared ahead of time and didn't want him to get ahead of her. "Your mother and I . . . our generation . . . life was different then, it seemed to move very slowly. For long periods of time it would move slowly, like a glacier . . . then something would erupt, years would jump by, and then it would return to normal again. . . . Slow. Very slow. Over there, back home, it always seemed to me very slow. Of course things are different now."

"I suppose so," Alexander said.

They sat for a while, silent. Alexander tried to think of Marian, whom he had known now for nearly six months. When they argued she would not look at him, would stand turned from him, maddening him, her thin covert little face turned away. . . . Her short-cropped dark hair looked militant at times, like a cap. But his thoughts touched her and dissolved, fizzed away. He found himself smiling. Marthe asked him why he was smiling and he shook his head, he didn't know. She laughed. "Yes, life is very different now," she said. "What your mother and I had to discover, so painfully . . . well. . . . It's commonplace now. I suppose."

Alexander finished his glass of sherry. He felt suddenly hungry, shaky. He ate a few cashews and picked a grape out; fingering the overlarge grape nervously before he ate it, he had the strange idea it wasn't real, it must have been flown in from some tropical place, bulbous, exaggerated, swollen, a deep gleaming purple. . . . His aunt sighed and said something about getting dinner for them, she'd better, hadn't she? . . . or did he still feel the effects of his Soho lunch? At that Greek restaurant?

"Indian restaurant," Alexander said.

"You told me Greek!" she laughed.

"No, Indian. Indian. I told you Indian," Alexander said excitedly.

Then they fell silent again. Alexander didn't know why he had spoken like that, he felt his mouth twisted into a foolish smile, a grin. It was the truth, he hadn't lied. He and the girl had eaten at a cubbyhole of a restaurant, at a small table jammed in a corner, the entire lunch had cost only a pound and twenty pence . . . and afterward, when they'd walked away, he had felt his mouth and throat burn angrily from the curry.

"Well, I'd better feed you. It's very late. Come out to the kitchen with me and let's see. . . . Help me up, will you?" Marthe laughed. Alexander managed to push himself up from the squat sofa, swaying slightly. He pulled his aunt to her feet. Her hand was plump but rather cool, damp. He noticed that one of her rings was a carved figure, made out of what appeared to be ivory; it looked like a sphinx. "The refrigerator is crammed, I went on a shopping spree just for you," Marthe was saying cheerfully. "I hope you don't mind cold food . . . ? I went over to Harrods this afternoon, to the food hall where they have such nice things. I buy most of my food there, actually . . . I just get in a cab and go there, then get in another cab and come back. It's expensive but I can't help that. . . . You don't mind a cold dinner, do you?"

"No, not at all, no, no, I like cold food," Alexander said.

"But your mother—your mother is such a good cook! I should be ashamed of myself, offering a boy your age cold things—"

He tried to assure her it was fine, he wasn't even that hungry any more, but she kept apologizing. She led him down a corridor and into a kitchen with high, ugly cabinets and a single window overlooking some pavement; out there it was damp and dripping. The kitchen was so cold that Alexander shivered convulsively. It was like a cave in here. Marthe peered into the refrigerator, mumbling to herself: *Now let's see, let's see.* . . . Alexander shivered again. The other room had been so warm. His face was quite warm. There was a cold damp flow of air coming into the kitchen, the window didn't fit its frame properly. . . . Marthe was reading off the names of cheeses in a singsong, girlish voice: *Cheddar, Camembert, Port Salut, Stilton, Brie.* . . .

"All of them. Fine. Any of them," Alexander interrupted.

"Some of them are hard rocks," Marthe said. "Oh Christ. This Brie is withered, it's like a fossil. So expensive, now the damn stuff is withered like a fossil."

"I can eat it," Alexander said. "I can eat anything."

She laughed as if he had said something very clever. "All right, dear, we'll see. Can you reach that cheese board up there?—up on the shelf? It's too high for me to reach—"Alexander got it: a heavy, oblong cheese board, which felt weighted, it was so heavy, made of dark ebony wood. It was not very clean; tiny bits of cheese clung to it. Alexander blew them off.

Marthe loaded things onto the cheese board, quite gay now. "I feel so guilty about not preparing you a proper dinner!" she said. "And you'll be comparing me to your mother, you'll go home and tell her what a bad housekeeper I am—"

"I won't tell anyone anything," Alexander said.

"Oh but you will. You might."

"I don't communicate very freely with them. Either of them."

"Either of them?"

"Either of them."

Alexander carried the board aloft, like a waiter; in the other room his aunt dragged two chairs over to a drop-leaf table by the window. "Now we're all set. Now. Isn't this delightful? It's like a picnic. I hope you don't mind."

"Is this where you usually eat?"

"Sometimes. When I eat here at home. But sometimes I eat in the kitchen, and sometimes in the bedroom. . . . This flat is so awkwardly set up, the bedroom is as big as this room, but the bathroom is just a closet. . . . I suppose the place you're staying in, the room you're in, is all right for you?"

"It's all right," Alexander said, shrugging his shoulders. "It's cheap."

"Does your girl like it . . . ?"

"Watch out," Alexander said. A jar of something nearly fell off the table—he caught it, it was a small jar of Russian caviar. His aunt took it from him. Alexander looked at her, knowing she had asked him a question; but he could not remember it. He said, softly, "Aunt Marthe, you were telling me something about my mother. . . . About my mother. You were telling me something about her, weren't you?"

"You must be starved!" Marthe exclaimed. "Why, so much time has gone by . . . I lost track of time. . . . You're so tall, you're so thin, you must be starving. . . . It was the surprise of my life, to see you tonight, the size you are, when I remember you so differently . . . just a boy. . . . What was I saying? About your mother? . . . I thought we'd just have a drink or two, but so much time went by. I get a little light-headed from sherry."

Alexander shook his head, trying to make sense of this. "What about my mother . . . ?"

"You probably wish you'd stayed with your little girl and had dinner with her tonight!"

"She isn't little," Alexander said.

"Is she large?—heavy?"

"No."

"Is she as tall as you are?"

"I don't know, no, Christ no, she's just a short girl, she's shorter than you are," Alexander said. He had lost track of the conversation and was staring now at the food: a half loaf of Vienna bread, jars of olives and pickles and pimientos, a tall jar of cocktail shrimp, cheeses in different shapes, a heavy slab of what appeared to be turkey white meat, some processed ham, a long dark coil of salami. . . . He smiled at the food. His aunt was trying to slice off pieces of bread, but the loaf wobbled, so he steadied it for her. The bread was rather stale; crumbs flaked off, flew off, tiny bits of crust flew up into Alexander's face and made him laugh. "Did you buy all this today? You didn't buy all this today," he said.

Marthe put the bread knife down. "I knew I was forgetting something," she said. She went to a liquor cabinet nearby. When she bent over, Alexander stared at her—the material of her dress very tight at her hips, straining against her—and he still held onto the loaf of bread while she chattered about how disappointing the weather must seem to tourists, and how hard it was to get a cab out here, since everyone got cabs when they went by Sloane Square, and she knew he didn't really want to be here, she'd heard the dismay in his voice over the telephone—

"Hey, that isn't true," Alexander said.

—but did he want a martini?—or just some Scotch?

"I don't know. I don't drink, usually," Alexander said. "Anything is all right."

"Anything?"

"You want me to help you get that open?"

"No, it's open. It's already open."

She came back to the table. She poured them each a drink. She said, "Well, the strange thing is, I was always closer to your mother than I was to your father . . . I mean, after I met your mother . . . though I'm your father's sister, as you know, and should have been absolutely loyal to him. But your mother and I, we became quite fond of each other. In fact you owe your existence to me. You really do. You owe your very existence to *me*."

Alexander laughed. "How is that?"

"Well, she didn't want to marry him, she knew it would be disastrous. She wanted an abortion. But I talked her out of it . . . because I knew she would never survive, she'd never, never survive . . . she was far too gentle, she wasn't independent like me, she was terrified of life . . . and an abortion would have. . . ."

Alexander set down his glass. "A what? What? . . . What?"

"She confided in me," Marthe said. She looked over the things on the table, squinting. With one long, painted fingernail she poked at the gelatin that edged the ham. "I suppose I betrayed her . . . because perhaps I gave her the wrong advice. . . . I said, oh, he'll make a good husband, I'm sure he will, why don't you just grit your teeth and go through with it. . . . Because, because, things were quite different in those days. We were different."

"Who was different?" Alexander asked, confused.

"It always seemed strange to outsiders that I was closer to your mother than to your father, though I'm related to *him*," she said. "Is that paté? I like paté very much but I don't remember buying that. Do you want some?—it's liver—I think it's liver—let me

spread some on a piece of bread for you, dear. You must be fam-
ished."

"My mother wanted an abortion? When was this?"

Marthe sighed. "That's it: it was so long ago. Everyone is so
much older now."

"My mother never wanted an abortion," Alexander said evenly.

Marthe did not reply. She spread something on a piece of bread
for him, carefully. He took it from her but didn't eat it. He held
it for a while, then found a place to set it down, on the windowsill, out of the way. He stared at her. "What kind of a dress is
that? Is that a Chinese or a Japanese dress? I see lizards or dragons
in it."

Marthe laughed. She dropped the cover of the pickle jar and it
rolled across the table and onto the floor. "Oh this bracelet! These
things are so heavy, they just get in the way," she murmured. He
noticed a large, ornate bracelet, made of gold, hanging from her
wrist; it had slid down her forearm and hung heavily against her
wrist. He wondered if he should help her with the clasp, it worked
hard, but she didn't ask him. She managed to get it off herself.
Alexander, watching her, felt that he was close to shouting or
laughing. She continued her light, girlish chatter: ". . . well, no
one would know it from the external evidence, she's a sweet,
mousy-looking woman, like most of them. . . . But she's very
deep. Very. And tragic."

"Tragic? My mother?"

"Like most of them."

Alexander laughed coarsely. No, this was too much. He knew
now that his aunt was lying, she was lying, and wouldn't even look
at him now that he had challenged her. . . . "What do you
mean?" he asked.

Marthe was licking paté off her short, plump fingers. "She was a
beautiful girl for a while. You wouldn't know this, of course. My
brother wouldn't know it either. I was very, very close to her and
when *he* showed up, and threatened to have her committed. . . .
I nearly went mad, it was so horrible. You don't know what your
father is like."

"My father? What? When did this happen?"

"When she moved out."

Alexander shook his head. For a while he sat quietly, not eating, watching his aunt as she pretended not to notice him; pretended not to feel the agitation of the heartbeat in his body. Behind her the unfamiliar room seemed to waver. He had a confused impression of something mirrored—the ceiling reflected in the mirror above the mantel—and his aunt's head bobbing snakelike in his vision, the heavy stiff wings of hair, the part drawn carefully through the middle of her hair, her flushed luminous dramatic face, her exaggerated self. He knew she was lying. "She never—!" he shouted.

Marthe looked calmly at him. Calmly, fastidiously, she wiped her mouth with her fingertips; she had forgotten to give them napkins. On that hand she wore two rings. She smiled, in a pretense of sympathy. "The Polish lover in that novel, *À Trois*, Loeper's second-to-last novel—he's still in London, would you like to meet him? He lives in a pathetic little room in Chelsea, down at the far end near—"

"Who? What? I don't know what you're talking about," Alexander said. "Novel—! I didn't read any novel, I didn't read any of them—"

"—then you could write a postcard to your mother, and say you'd gone to visit 'P'—that your aunt Marthe had accompanied you—"

"I'm not going to visit anyone, I'm not going to write anyone," he said. "I can't even remember her. . . . No, I can't remember her. I saw her a week ago but now, now I can't remember her, her face is mixed up with . . . with someone else's face. . . . I don't know if I had a mother," he laughed. He felt his face, like Marthe's, glow dramatically. He wondered if his skin looked like hers, throbbing, shining with perspiration, the warm red-veined flesh beneath the skin swelling outward, pushing outward, so that the surface of his skin was flushed, ripe, golden.

Marthe poured an inch or two of liquor into his glass. He was holding onto that glass. He had been holding onto it, his forearm lying heavily on the edge of the cheese board. He watched her covertly, seeing how she frowned, pouring the Scotch, pretending to frown, seeming to frown, while all along she was lying . . . she paused, like an actress, not yet meeting his gaze. Then she met it. Sly, teasing. "You must know that your mother tried to escape? —that she came here one winter, oh maybe ten years ago—she came *here*—she came to me here, when I lived up in Hampstead, with a friend of mine—and with Loeper, too, of course, at that time—a dear friend of mine, Nicole Bergé—do you know who she is?—was? You must know these things."

Alexander could not speak.

"How old are you now?—twenty?"

"Twenty-four."

"Twenty-*four!*" Marthe laughed. She reached out to touch him, as if to apologize—as if spontaneously—and he drew his arm away, fearing her, but still she smiled, pretending not to notice this, saying, "But you look so much younger, like a boy!—But you must have been fourteen then. About that age. You must remember, you weren't a child. You must remember when she left you, you and him both, and came *here*. You do remember that."

"I don't remember. I don't remember anything," Alexander said. He wondered why he had jerked his arm away so quickly. He had almost upset something on the table. "I don't want to remember."

"Yes, well. Yes. Of course. You're like my brother, you're like him in many ways. I understand. And it certainly wasn't my intention . . . wasn't my intention," she said, with drunken caution, "to upset you."

He was poking with his thumbnail at a piece of cheese: hard as a rock it was, discolored in places, stale and cracked. After a while he said softly. "If she wanted an abortion, back then, it wasn't because of me . . . she didn't want to kill *me*. She didn't want . . . to do that to me."

"Of course not," Marthe said quickly. "Of course not."

"It wasn't me."

"That's true, very true. That's very true," Marthe said.

Alexander noticed bits of cheese under his fingernails. Suddenly the pressure of the crumbs disgusted him; he seized a fork and tried to pick them out. His aunt was speaking in a rapid, soothing, unconvincing voice, speaking of a Polish dancer with a troupe here in London, and an ex-ballerina named Nicole, and a big partly restored eighteenth-century mansion at the edge of Hampstead Heath—and somehow a woman found lying on the kitchen floor, on a rug she'd dragged in, lying there with the gas oven on, the oven door open, *too terrified of freedom because of the past.* . . . Alexander paid no attention. He ran the fork prongs beneath his nails, one by one. After a long, embarrassed pause, Marthe began speaking again: this time in a furry drunken murmur, as she patted his arm, petted it, as if to restore him. "But you don't have to believe all this, or even listen to it. It might never have happened, really," she whispered.

Alexander cleared his throat. He let the fork fall onto the table. "He says—he says you're the way you are, you live like this, like this—because you're sterile. You're sterile."

Marthe laughed delightedly. "The way I am—! But does he know how I am?"

"Unhappy—a failure—Because of the marriages," Alexander said. "Once in a while he gets onto the subject of you. He says you've always been like this—I've heard him talk about you lots of times, to my mother."

"I'm very happy," Marthe said belligerently. "I'm happy, very happy. But it is for the reason he gave—because I'm sterile. He's right about that, but he's got me wrong in every other way. . . . Because he has no imagination. Like most men. . . . Most of them are just animals, you know, they have no imagination, they're barely human. Without imagination you sink back into your physical body, you become bestial, stupid, fixed on one idea, like *him*. You degenerate. You really do, you sink back. You regress. The season for mating takes no imagination, it's all direct, physical, it's impersonal, but after that life is all imagination, and your father doesn't have that capacity. Most men don't. That's why they are impotent—most men."

Alexander looked up. His arm was oddly heavy. He saw that

her hand lay on it, absentmindedly, a plump beringed hand . . . abstractions like the glimmer of the room behind her and around her, all light, gradations of dim, dusky, tawdry-golden light, without strong outlines or divisions between things. "Are they?— most men?" he asked in a whisper.

"Yes. Of course—Didn't you know that?"

"I don't know," he said. "I don't know if I knew it. . . ."

"But you're so young yourself, you can't know much; you probably don't know anything. Why do you think your father wanted to marry that girl, what was her name, that girl who modeled at Saks—you must remember her, she's about your age—I even met her the last time I visited White Plains, out at your house at a big cocktail party—your mother didn't know about her yet, oh, her name was Stella, I think—and once in the city, in a midtown restaurant with your father—Why do you think he went crazy over her? He was forty-five years old then and—"

"What? Stella? *Stella?*"

"Yes, that thin girl, she was very pretty and very intelligent, and tried to back out of it gracefully, after she got enough out of him and saw how—well, how close to a nervous breakdown he was —it was her idea the three of us meet for lunch, almost at the first instant our eyes met I knew—I knew what the situation was, how desperately she needed help—Evidently you didn't know about this, Alexander? You didn't know the girl?"

"None of this is true," Alexander said.

"I don't know how we got onto the subject . . . it wasn't my intention. . . . Oh yes. Yes. I simply wanted you to consider why you thought your father was so devastated, why he was so sick during that period, sick with love for a girl twenty-five years younger than he was, a lovely girl if you like girls so vacuous and so skeletal, and he confessed to me himself he didn't even know her—but, well," she said, swerving back into her bright cheerful manner, "why do you think, Alexander? *Why?*"

"It isn't true. It really isn't," he said, smiling. The corners of his mouth lifted by themselves.

". . . because he was impotent everywhere in the universe

except with her, and she looked at me with her stricken eyes, just desperate to get out, to get out of that noisy, expensive, fake-French restaurant, just to get *out* and be free of him. I knew exactly what the situation was. The two of them didn't even talk to each other, he just stared at her, and she talked to me chattering away about college, she'd dropped out of college, about girl friends of hers at Bennington, and it was all to make him know how old he was, how free she wanted to be . . . she drank too much, she even squeezed my hand too often, her eyes were just terrified. . . ."

"That was in the summer, all that," Alexander said suddenly. ". . . I knew her. Stella. I knew her. Yes," he said, smiling, grinning, thinking of the dark-eyed soiled Stella, whom he had found kissing someone in a cloakroom at the country club once, Alexander a high-school boy then, blundering into a strange couple's embrace and gaping in surprise, and for years afterward—yes, now he remembered her—he had run and rerun that vision in his head, trying it on with other girls, feeling it float up, helplessly, into his brain. And his father also—! His father—!

"He lost so much weight. I felt sorry for him . . . in spite of everything, in spite of the past," Marthe said.

"Yes, he lost weight. I remember. . . . But I don't really believe any of this," Alexander laughed.

"You can believe it or not believe it," Marthe said happily.

"I know that. I know that."

"But they are all impotent, in their imaginations," Marthe said. "That's why women like your mother and myself and . . . well, other dear friends of mine, whom she came to know . . . before she got frightened by life, and let him take her back to White Plains . . . that's why we laugh at them so much, and never take them seriously. Yes," she said, still with that bright, happy voice, "they really are tragic, but they can't be taken seriously. If I took such things seriously I wouldn's be as happy as I am."

Alexander was thinking of Stella, Stella Reiner. His head was heavy and vaporous, with a perfumelike vapor; perhaps his aunt's perfume. Then he stopped thinking about Stella. His aunt squeezed his arm, sighing, "Yes, you're all tragic people," and it went through him like electricity, a pang of sexual desire. He felt faint.

"Tragic? Tragic?" he stammered.

He stopped thinking of Stella and thought of his mother, but her face, too, eluded him: plain, was she, or beautiful? He had never looked. He stared at his aunt's face. "Yes, tragic . . . tragic," she whispered. They looked at each other, Alexander breathing hoarsely through his mouth, faces rising and falling in his mind, a girl's face, Stella's or someone else's, a girl, a girl's face and body, no, his mother's face, his mother standing there in her expensive beige coat with the mink collar, hurt, trying to have a conversation with him and Marian while they waited for the plane to load, subtly snubbed by Marian, *who was Marian?*—and now their faces all blurred and glowed and his aunt was staring at him, smiling gently at him, that gentle throbbing smile.

"Why don't you finish your drink?" she said softly.

Alexander was breathing noisily. He could not believe this, but it was true: she was closing his fingers now, firmly, around his glass. She urged him to raise it to his lips. She helped him. She rose to her feet, she swayed over him. Radiant, damp, warm, very warm. . . . He wondered at her beauty, he wondered how he had got here to see it. She drew her hand up along his arm, up to his shoulder, to his neck. Every hair on his body stiffened. She said, smiling, "Are you tragic?—or? Maybe not, maybe you're different? Are you different? You, are you different? . . . you, Alexander, are you different . . . ?

He got to his feet. He felt the stammer rise in his throat, from his chest. *I think—I think—*She was so short! He glanced down and saw that she had slipped her shoes off, he could see that she was barefoot, he did not mean to take a step toward her but he swayed in that direction, helplessly. She was saying something out of a mouth that was curiously red, reddened, though the lipstick was smeared a little, she was saying, "Yes, I think you are different . . . yes, I think so. . . ."

No, Alexander thought. *Yes*.

"Come back here, back along here," she whispered. She led him out of the room, he followed, dazed, very tall, his shoulder brushed against the dangling leaves of a plant hung somewhere, shadowy spidery tendril-like leaves, and she was speaking rapidly, urgently, while he felt his body yearn to crouch over, the throbbing in him was so violent, so helpless. She hurried into a room and he came after her, his hands grasping one another, he was wringing his hands in that strange, drafty, cavelike room—her bedroom?—but it was so jumbled, so crowded with furniture, it smelled sour, it smelled of earth, somehow—he saw on the windowsill another of those plants, the cheap clay pot overturned and a small halo of dirt spilled out around it. His aunt turned away from him. Two big, ceiling-high windows seemed to move in upon him, out there *a street . . . a street upon which traffic moved. . . .* No, it was too confusing. He watched her, terrified. He wanted to stop her before it was too late. "Aunt Marthe? Aunt Marthe?" he whispered.

He stepped toward her, he bumped into something—one of the bed posts—she exclaimed as if she, and not he, had been hurt, but he interrupted her saying, sobbing, "No, no, no, I don't want to. . . . No, don't make me, don't make me do it. . . ."

He backed away. He ran out.

"Alexander!"

He looked wildly around—there she was behind him, standing there, calling his name—"Alexander, don't be afraid, don't be afraid like everyone else—Alexander—"

"No," he cried, "no," and ran out the door and down the steps to the foyer and out to the sidewalk, out into the fresh surprising air, panting *No no no no no,* and behind him she was still calling his name—He glanced over his shoulder in real terror and saw her, there, right in the doorway where anyone on the street might see her, calling out to him in that high musical shrill voice, "Alexander! Alexander!" She had snatched off the hair piece, she was shaking it at him, he heard a catch in her voice, a choked-off laugh —with her close-cropped gunmetal-gray hair she looked robust, delighted, crying out, "Oh Alexander, *you too*—"

He ran away, down the street, and halfway down the long windy

street he had to catch hold of something, an iron railing, to support himself. . . . His breath was tearing him in two. Out here
it was raining, out here cars and strange double-deck buses were
passing, in the rain. He stared, amazed. He was somewhere he
didn't recognize. It was strange to him, new to him, evidently
he was in a foreign city.

T*he Scream*

"Makes you wonder, don't it?"

Renée turned quickly to see a man standing close behind her. He was anxious about something and therefore grinning . . . his face creased, reddened. He must have been in his late fifties; he wore a herringbone-tweed overcoat which was unbuttoned and not very clean.

"I mean all these kinds of things, what they got hanging in the gallery these days," he said. "I mean . . . you don't know how to take them, eh? Makes you wonder, eh?"

Renée agreed, faintly. The man's smile broadened at once. His teeth were far too white to be plausible; they gleamed like porcelain and made the rest of his face turn sallow. He smelled of tobacco and dirty clothes.

They were alone together in one of the gallery's smaller rooms, on the second floor. Before them, taking up an entire wall, was an enormous canvas. Renée had been staring at it for several minutes, not seeing it—her mind was on other matters—and now the canvas seemed to materialize before her, powerfully, aggressively. *Lost Landscape III*. It was completely abstract: a swirl of colors, mainly browns, wet-looking, heavy, three-dimensional. Rather like sculpture, except it was on a flat canvas. The painter was quite young—in fact younger than Renée—born in 1952 in Regina, Saskatchewan. Very young. He had done something with his pigments to make them appear to be wet; they glistened, with an almost synthetic slickness. The canvas appeared to be not quite finished, as well. Renée felt a temptation to touch it, like a child. But no: mustn't touch, someone might be watching, someone might scold her. And it would not solve the mystery of the canvas anyway.

"Yes, it makes you wonder, don't it?" the man repeated.

Renée wanted to escape. But she lingered, to be polite; she read an explanation of *Lost Landscape III*, thoughtfully prepared by the museum's curator and Scotch taped to the wall: . . . *Strenuous but repressed emotion . . . "controlled chance" as in nature . . . the lyricism of the Canadian landscape as it passes beyond the dimension of the human. . . .*

She left the red-faced gentleman reading the explanation of the painting, walking from the room without appearing to hurry. She did not want to offend him, after all.

Renée was wandering through the Telford Art Gallery and Museum for the second time that week.

It was a Friday afternoon in April. A spring day. Sunshine, forsythia, a clamorous bunch of sparrows in a tree just outside an opened window . . . the world coming to life again, again. As always. It had been a drawn-out winter, bitterly cold in January and February. But now it was spring: people warned her against assuming that winter was really over, that there wouldn't be another freezing spell and maybe another blizzard, but she did not care. She stood by an opened window in a corridor, staring out, seeing nothing. Had someone been bothering her a few minutes

ago . . . ? A vaguely unpleasant, indefinable experience . . . ?
She had already forgotten.

A five-minute walk to her lover. He was waiting for her nearby.
Already it was one fifteen, already she was late. . . . He might be
looking at his wristwatch, noting the time. A twist of his mouth,
a bitter impatient smile. She stood at the window and could see,
not far away, that three-story mansion of dark granite at the corner
of Westbury and St. Regis. . . . Her lover was waiting for her a
few houses down; in the studio of a friend of his, the second
floor of a carriage house on one of the old estates. 788 St. Regis.
Friday at one. Renée? Will you? Can I trust you?

One minute before the hour she had telephoned him, from the
public phone downstairs; had told him she couldn't come that day,
she wasn't well, things were not right, she couldn't come to him
after all. . . . That had taken place on Tuesday. Three days ago.
She had driven past the carriage house and had been unable to go
to him; instead, she'd come to the art gallery and parked in their
lot and telephoned him. . . . Sorry. She was sorry. She detested
herself for her cowardice.

Mockingly gallant, he had asked if something had gone wrong at
home?—something with her husband?

No.

She just didn't want to see him that day, was that it?

No, no.

Renée and Karl had been lovers for two months now; but it
seemed a much briefer span of time, hardly more than a few
days. So quickly! . . . it had all happened so quickly, and without
any preparation . . . Renée had been unable to develop a sense
of irony, which might have helped her. A margin of irony had
always helped her in the past: not with love affairs, because she had
had none, before this, but with the perplexing disappointing snags
of ordinary life. She had always been a little older than her true
age, always the girl in charge of others, the child unconsciously
assigned responsibilities other children would have balked at;
Renée the honor student, Renée the young woman who, in a

crowded drugstore, would be the person to stoop and pick up a half dozen bars of soap some running boy had knocked to the floor . . . Renée the young woman whom old men or retarded boys approached, wanting to start a conversation. *Hello. Nice day isn't it. Hello, hello. What kind of a painting is this. Makes you wonder, eh?* Her husband might still love her; might not; only her intelligent, ironic, painfully acquired detachment helped her stay sane . . . in the postition of being loved, possibly, by two men . . . or by one man and not the other . . . or by no one at all, no one. She thought of her lover constantly, like a young girl. Fourteen years old, she knew herself to be, anxious, humiliated, uncertain. It did no good to imagine that her lover suffered, as she did; that made their predicament all the worse. She had hoped that falling in love would allow her to love herself, once again, or to halfway respect herself; but it had not worked out that way.

Will you come on Friday, then?—Friday at one?

Yes.

Now it was Friday; it was one twenty. The air was slightly tainted by an odor of malt from a brewery a few miles away, but Renée did not find that unpleasant. A bored worker in one of the gallery offices turned on a radio: shrill music, a Detroit station. Not really unpleasant. No. . . . Renée backed away from the window. A tall, hesitant young woman, who did not seem to know which way to turn: into the main exhibit room, or in the other direction, a corridor that led to smaller exhibit rooms. . . . Where was she? What place was this? The telephone was downstairs.

She followed a talkative middle-aged couple into the main exhibit room.

Striking English accents. Rather loud, for this place. Renée liked to hear such people talk, however, since they gave the impression—speaking so firmly, so archly—of knowing what they meant. Englishwomen, especially. Firm, confident, emphatic. By contrast her own voice was usually faint and unconvincing, as if she were telling lies.

Why are you so unhappy, so irritable?—her husband had asked.

I am not unhappy. I am not irritable.
Why are you so tired all the time? You look exhausted.
I do not look exhausted.
But then again he might ask, cunningly: *Why are you so happy?*
Always the same question, always the same answer.

She liked the art gallery, though everyone criticized it for being small and for being parochial. Why should it matter that it was rather small. . . ? The Canadians of her acquaintance were always mocking their own city, their own university, their own music and galleries . . . making sarcastic, defensive remarks about "their" own poets, like Karl, like his friends. Renée could not quite understand why. She wondered if they were deliberately testing her, and other Americans? . . . but no, they were sincere enough. If she pointed out something that was genuinely good, they resented her intrusion; if she said nothing they resented her silence. When they were most fiercely and unreasonably nationalistic—insisting that *their* work, *their* art should supplant Chekhov, and Picasso, and Yeats, and Faulkner, and Stravinsky, and even Shakespeare—she halfway suspected that they were grimly joking and that they wished to be saved, somehow, from the grimness of their joking; but she could say nothing. Their wild, hopeless wishes for insularity, for a kind of cultural protective tariff that would banish competition from the outside world (the "outside world" being, unfortunately, most of the world) was, in a way, deeply moving to her. But if she was sympathetic with them, they suddenly reversed their positions and said that the nationalistic movement was childish and grotesque and doomed, and they wanted no part of it, they had no intention of becoming involved with it: *their* art was international.

One of the worst blunders of Renée's life had taken place a few months after she and her husband had moved to Canada. She had discovered a painting in the local gallery that seemed to her marvelous—really beautiful—striking and original and moving. Of course she knew little about art; she had taken a few courses in art history, but that was all. She made no claim to know contemporary art. The painting she admired so much was *White Birches* by Tom

Thompson, whom she had never heard of. She had assumed, for some reason, that no one had heard of him . . . or that he was a local painter, a not-yet-discovered painter. . . . After mentioning his name to a group of people, she had learned, to her embarrassment, that he was famous; which accounted for the cold, amused looks, the patronizing remarks. . . .

Karl, too, disliked her. He claimed to love her, but he also disliked her; she could sense it. He resented something he could not have named. Though he knew very well how poor the Maynards were—how unhappy Renée's husband was with the work he did—he evidently believed, unconsciously, stubbornly, that since they were "Americans" they had money. It made no sense, of course. Yet it was there, an idea that could not be dislodged. And he believed, just as unconsciously, that they were naturally critical of Canada: that their presence here was a kind of adventure, an interim period in their lives, like camping out.

If she went to him now, they would make love on his friend's sofa bed. And she would be happy. And then unhappy. He would be glad to see her; and eventually resentful. Emotions rose and fell in them, ungovernable. Now happiness, now unhappiness. Now panic, at the thought of being discovered. And now guilt. And now jealousy. And then happiness again, a surge of spiteful, selfish joy. . . . Sometimes he was distracted. Sometimes she wept, which frightened him. Sometimes he spoke quite bitterly of "her" marriage: Renée did not dare speak of it, did not dare expose her feelings for her husband to her lover, and so he misinterpreted her silence . . . since Karl, himself, spoke at length about the problems he had, with his wife and with his children, with his friends, with everyone.

"This exhibit is quite an improvement, isn't it? It's real people, I mean, that you can make sense of. . . ."

The red-faced man again. Renée murmured agreement, forced herself to smile. What did he want, why was he following her? He was smiling so strangely. . . . Eager and anxious. Watery eyes, no color at all. She shied away from meeting his gaze but could not avoid speaking to him. The exhibit? The photographs? Yes, she liked it. Yes, she preferred it to the painting in the other room.

They were in the main room, looking at an exhibit of photographs. Quite a number of them, probably more than a hundred, and all so striking. . . . Renée wished she might be alone, so that she could really study them. But the red-faced man was beside her, pointing things out, chattering, praising one photograph and unaccountably damning another, and the English woman, nearby, was expressing her dislike of something: "Why, they shouldn't show things like this in public! Look at that woman—*look* at what she's doing, out in the street!" Some children trooped in. A boy of about ten giggled. Another boy said in a falsetto: "Somebody's going to get a bayonet through the guts!"

A number of the photographs had been taken in wartime. World War II. The Spanish Civil War. Other wars, near-forgotten wars, wars in Indochina and India and the South Seas. . . . An Oriental child of about four was crying, standing in a roadway, staring at the photographer; crying bitterly. The photograph was dated 1941. Was the child now an adult? . . . was he still living? . . . was he no longer living? Wounded soldiers. An emaciated Italian priest, tanks in the background, a dead chicken in the road. Faces blown up three times the size of normal faces, grainy black and white, staring in absentminded terror at Renée and the other visitors to the gallery. . . . The red-faced man pointed out something to Renée and she went reluctantly to look at it. A photograph of a German woman, plump, her hair fixed in ugly sausage curls, standing before the ruins of a church. Thick, flabby legs. Renée didn't know why the man had wanted her to see the picture. She noticed something odd about the woman's face . . . was she cross-eyed? A near-moronic expression. Yet sensual, cunning, knowing. The woman wore black stockings and high-heeled shoes and a kind of chemise or slip that was far too small for her, so that the tops of her stockings were visible. Posing for the photographer, hands thrust deep into the pockets of a man's baggy coat-sweater, she exposed her body, a vacuous half grin on her face, her eyes glazed. . . .

The man touched Renée's arm and began to say something

further, but Renée drew away. She was reminded, now, of an old man in a subway car, in New York City, showing Renée—then about twelve years old—an obscene advertisement in a pulp magazine. "No. Please," she said sharply. "Leave me alone."

"Was that man bothering you?"
"No. It's all right."
"I've see him in here before . . . he's a strange character."
"No, it's all right. I'm all right."

Once, Karl had said to her, fondly, accusingly: "You're too sensitive."
She had said immediately: "And you—aren't you sensitive too?"
"There's a difference between being sensitive and being thin-skinned," he said. "My wife knows me very well: she says that I call myself sensitive, when in fact I'm only sensitive of my own feelings. I'm thin-skinned, I suppose. An egotist."
He scratched idly at his bare chest. His manner was detached, subdued.
If he expected Renée to deny what he had said, he gave no indication of being annoyed at her silence.
They had become lovers because of his love for her, his pursuit of her. In the beginning everything had seemed simple. All romances are simple at the very beginning. Karl would ask, half seriously, whether she would marry him—if it were possible?— if his wife ever discovered them?—or her husband? They did not want to hurt people, of course; yet if the two of them were some-how discovered it would no longer be their fault. . . . Their relationship would have its own momentum, its own demands. He asked her such questions as if he meant them. Renée answered them timidly, fearfully, as if he meant them. *Would you? Would you leave him for me?* She told him that whatever happened would be a relief: she detested lying, the delirious state of in-decision, of not knowing, not daring to know. *Yes, but would you leave him for me . . . ?*
Yes.

*

She did not tell her lover how often she wanted to scream at her husband: Don't you know? Can't you guess? Why are you so indifferent?

Their hurried meals together, breakfast and dinner. He ate quickly, sometimes reading; he apologized but read just the same, journals in his field—biochemistry—or magazines like *Scientific American.* He was like a brother to Renée now, an older brother. Studious. Worried about the future, but worried in such a way as to exclude her; he did not care to expose his fears to her . . . that would be unmanly, perhaps. Unhusbandly. Before their marriage she had guessed at Evan's pride, but it had not occurred to her that his pride was really dangerous, that it would become a kind of sickness; it had seemed abstract, rather touching.

He had the idea, lately, that the work he was doing was funded, indirectly, by an American chemical corporation. He could not be certain; no one told the truth about such things. He suspected that everyone lied. For money, of course. For American money. He could not trust his supervisor, even.

But when Renée wanted to talk about his suspicions, he waved her away, laughed, dismissed it all.

Lying beside him as he slept, she thought of her lover. She would have liked to appeal to him, to argue with him. *Look at me, look how I suffer, how am I to blame for this? . . . how am I sinful, an adulterous woman scheming to take another woman's husband?* It was not possible. Not Renée Brompton. Not her. Her mother and her relatives and her friends, her girlhood friends, would not have been angry with her so much as astonished. *Renée . . . ? Must be some mistake.* Her lover was four or five years older than her husband. Both had dark hair, though her lover's hair was curly and thick; her husband's hair was straight. Her lover laughed often. Her husband laughed rarely. Her lover had not much money either—he worked for a down-river press and did free-lance writing, for the local newspaper, occasionally for the Toronto *Globe and Mail*—of course he earned nothing from his poetry, nothing at all. Her husband had hoped for an excellent job, and an excellent salary would have been incidental. But he had not the excellent job. He had emigrated to Canada; he had crossed the border and was now competing in an inflated job market, in a field that had become, in a single year, over-crowded. No one knew how it had happened. No one would admit knowing. Universities, governments claimed not to have foreseen such a shortage of jobs . . . yet new Ph.D.'s continued to appear each spring, hopeful, doomed. Her lover had not much status in the world yet seemed not to care; her husband cared very much. She loved one of them but did not quite trust him . . . the other she trusted implicitly, would have trusted with her very life. But she no longer loved him.

Renée? No. Must be a mistake.

One thirty-five and she had decided against him. She continued to study the photographs, as a kind of discipline. She would not give in to the despair she felt, would not begin to cry. . . . It was not difficult to become absorbed in the faces of black children in Harlem . . . elderly men and women in the American Midwest . . . immigrants in Quebec. Hundreds of people. Faces. Eyes. Pain-ful, it was painful to stare so closely into those eyes, into the souls of strangers. Many of them suffered, yes, but many of them were very happy. One face and then another and then another. . . . Renée might lose herself in them, in humanity. The German woman . . . children in a refugees' camp somewhere in Indo-china . . . an Indian woman holding a skeletal baby out to the photographer, her face contorted with rage or despair, her mouth opened in a wide, soundless shriek. . . . Renée shivered, looking at the woman. My God, it was too painful. It was far too painful. The woman's mouth was a gaping hole . . . her teeth hideous, stumps of blackened teeth . . . the eyes narrowed to slits that were not human. . . . The baby was a skeleton with a swollen belly. It was already dead, of course. Didn't the mother know? Yes, she must have known. She knew.

Renée stared until her vision seemed to glaze over. The woman's scream was everywhere around her: it forced the other sounds, the chattering of ordinary people, the sparrows' singing, into silence. How could it matter if . . . how could it matter. . . . Renée had to think, had to force herself to think. How could it matter if a young woman went to her lover . . . or if she denied herself to him. How could it matter. It could not. No. How could it. If she went to that place that stank of paint and turpentine, and wept in his arms, eager and shameless, loving him, as if he were life itself . . . so long draining from her, eluding her. It could not matter, could it? Could not matter.

She looked again at the photograph, as if hoping it might have altered. But no: exactly the same. A soundless scream. Immortal. Annihilating everything else.

Downstairs, by the front door, the old man was talking with another old man. Both wore overcoats in spite of the warm weather. Flush-faced, earnest, the man who had bothered Renée did not notice her at all, now. His friend was leaning toward him with interest and cupping one ear: ". . . one whole week I didn't get out, a bad cold in the chest, and coughing . . . you know where I moved to, after Lillian died . . . well, the IGA store is right at the corner but I couldn't get to it . . . didn't talk to nobody for a week, not a single soul, thought I would go crazy. People don't give a damn about you in that neighborhood. You could die in your bed and nobody would give a damn. A whole week can go by and you don't see a single soul, I mean to talk with. . . ."

Renée pushed the heavy oak door open, throwing her weight against it.

The carriage house of dark-red brick, with white trim: needed paint, but handsome. Forsythia had begun to bloom around it. Some of the bushes were gigantic, not like the feeble bushes around Renée's rented house. The last time she had been here, the forsythia had been no more than a cluster of stalks, not even green at their tips.

Was he watching for her, at the window? Or was he stretched out on the sofa bed, reading, not aware of the time? He read constantly, read anything. . . . Or had he gone home, had he gone down the stairs and slammed the door and left? *Damned bitch.*

Any of these. All of these. Or none.

T*he Liberation of Jake Hanley*

After seventeen years of marriage, the quarrels became so noisy, so ill orchestrated, and finally so tediously predictable—without even the advantage of stimulating Jake's imagination, and therefore his poetry—that he agreed to his wife's angry, unbalanced, and masochistic demands for a divorce. "If you want one, all right! Yes! I agree! I will cooperate!" he shouted. Raising his voice, Jake Hanley had been pleased to discover, disguised the tremulousness that had always shamed him in these encounters with Cynthia. Whereas she, when she surrendered to her emotion and began to shout at him, was revealed as shrewish and shrill, like an actress simulating female rage in a manner meant to provoke laughter rather than sympathy. "Yes, good!" he cried. "I do want my freedom, as a matter of fact—I want an end to this—to all of this—to *you.*"

Cynthia had already consulted a lawyer; she had evidently been planning this move for some time.

So Jake found himself signing papers, defiantly and carelessly; he agreed to begin with "separation," even to retaining a lawyer of his own, though he bitterly resented paying anyone fees of the exorbitant nature lawyers demanded; he agreed to the "removal of his person and his personal effects" from the house, agreed to visit that house only at times approved of by his wife and her lawyer, and not to make any attempts to "coerce or cajole the children" into any alliance in opposition to their mother. He agreed, he agreed, though he knew both he and Cynthia might regret all this later.

He packed suitcases, filled cardboard boxes from the supermarket with shoes, books, ash trays, a few pots and pans Cynthia did not want, and other of his "personal effects"—wondering whether to be relieved or bewildered that, after seventeen years of adulthood, he owned so little.

From one point of view, he was seizing an opportunity to be free once again—more or less free, within the restrictions set up by the attorneys; from another point of view, he was being kicked out of his own house by a white-faced, hysterical, self-pitying woman whose habit of clenching her fists so that her fingernails dug into her own flesh, and of bringing her fists down repeatedly on her own thighs, indicated the self-destructive nature of the entire process. *I want you gone!* she seemed to be screaming. *I want us both gone!* Yes, it was probable that friends and acquaintances, when they heard, would phrase the matter inelegantly. Jake was being kicked out.

A tiny kitchenette apartment in the University Arms would be his new place of residence. The University Arms was a stucco building, mustard-colored, which was convenient to the campus and the bus line; Jake was lucky to get a room, since it was October, and most inexpensive rooms in the area were rented back in September. He was lucky, also, to be near the bus stop, since the Hanleys' old Ford station wagon was, of course, in Cynthia's possession. She would need it to drive the children around and to buy groceries—Jake had not even contested the issue. Suddenly he had wanted to give it up, had been eager to give up those nuisance things—the washer and dryer, the television set, the phonograph as well—because they were always breaking down, it was always his responsibility to get them repaired, and now, though of course he would have to pay the bills, the responsibility for their maintenance would be Cynthia's. Yes, let her learn. Let her suffer a little, as *he* had suffered, being a husband for so long; being a *man*. It was peculiar, how easy and agreeable the process of divorce might actually turn out to be. . . . Once alone, a can of beer opened, his gaze fixed blankly on the slightly grimy pane of his window, he began to wonder if things might be too simple, after all. He was a poet: he possessed a romantic, passionate temperament, long repressed because of marital and academic demands. As a poet, he would not mind suffering a little. He spoke of the purgative, therapeutic benefits of suffering, in his classes, and often wrote of pain, despair, and sordid experiences in his poetry . . . though, in fact, personally, he had not suffered much, so far as he knew. He was a poet; he deserved more violent emotions.

More pain. More regret. He and Cynthia had loved each other at one time, after all. That love had been real, surely? It had not been an illusion? *I love you, Cynthia. I want to marry you. . . .* Yes, he could summon back a timid twenty-year-old, a mere boy, a nervous but stubborn incarnation of himself, daring to pronounce those sacred words to a girl named Cynthia whom he had met some months previously, at a party in Toronto. Then as now Cynthia had been an attractive person, with a manner that appeared to be sweet, even subdued and malleable . . . she had hidden the more wily, calculating aspects of her nature, even then, and had wept uncontrollably, in his arms. Nineteen years old. A nursing student with no family except a widowed mother, pretty enough, charming enough . . . and so . . . somehow . . . by some quirk of fate or circumstances or legitimate, commendable personal decision . . . so they had married. Sacred the moment of his declaration of love; sacred the moment of her surrender, as she wept in his thin but protective arms. And everything that followed was sacred, in a way, or must be considered so: the children, not well spaced but clumped together in a five-year period, all four of them; the thirty-year mortgage on the buff-colored brick house on Chandler Boulevard; the eighteen-hundred-dollar debt Jake had carried over from last year, a second mortgage his brother in Winnipeg had promised to help him with, before developing unfortunate financial problems of his own; a leaky roof, a garage whose walls were beginning to crumple, a front yard of crabgrass and a back yard of thistles, and a vicious, unforgiving woman, her face plain and militantly pale, more aged than she deserved. Hers was the dubious triumph of injured virtue; hers the pain of having been "betrayed." Her last words to Jake had been contemptuous ones—now the world would see him for what he was, *now* everyone would know how adolescent and egotistic and neurotic he had always been—hiding his true nature behind a weasely hearty good-natured façade—She had managed to laugh scornfully, without humor; her gaze held his, shiny-bright with tears of exhilaration, allowing him to know that she, alone of all the world, knew Jake for what he was.

"I've suffered too," Jake protested. "This hasn't been easy for me, I know what it is to suffer. . . ."

But perhaps it was not quite true. There had been dark moods, of course. And melancholy. He had muttered to himself, wiping at his nose with the back of his hand, opening cans of beer, drinking too much, not eating wisely. He had even managed to cry a few times. It seemed to him obvious, necessary—pain should have accompanied love, the loss of love. He would miss his children, of course. Of course. But he would be seeing them often: not much less frequently than he had seen them anyway, these past few years. And it was possible they would love him all the more, because he had been vanquished, exiled, a victim of their mother's insatiable lust for revenge. They would take his side, would come to hate their mother for the divorce, since it was she who had been responsible for it all. . . . Still, he would not have minded suffering, to some extent. Others seemed to suffer liberally, and to talk about it, to complain bitterly about it, like actors in a profound and tragic drama. But, for Jake, everything had seemed to take place in inappropriate or even ridiculous settings and to be heavily qualified by circumstances. The first time he had been with Ginny in her apartment, the first time they had been truly alone together, a fire had broken out in the building across the street and several fire engines had arrived, sirens blaring, red lights violating the cavelike sanctity of her little room. The girl had been terrified, Jake hardly less so. Many months later, drifting into the argument that was to be their farewell, not knowing why he felt so indifferent and sluggish, he had actually been on the verge of coming down with the flu . . . as always it attacked him in the stomach and bowels, and made romance, and even the memory of romance, grotesque. "You don't care! You don't love me! You don't *care!*" the girl had screamed.

Jake moved out of 779 Chandler on a Saturday morning; on Monday morning, as always, he unlocked the door to his office in the Humanities Building a little before nine. Shamefaced, guilty, his shy smile obviously the smile of a man whose wife has rejected him, he was surprised at the reaction of his colleagues—which was no reaction at all. Evidently they didn't yet know about him. His students were as friendly as ever; one of the departmental secretaries even complimented him on his necktie—an old blue knit thing he'd found in the back of a closet—and he was foolishly grateful that life should continue as always.

Perhaps nothing would really happen? Nothing would be changed?

Jake had the hallucinatory idea of being in costume; of playing a role, learned long ago and committed to memory. His colleagues said good morning, asked how he was, invited him to have coffee with them in the Common Room. The usual students gathered around him after classes, chattering about ideas he had touched upon in his deft, light, amusing way. He could see an image of himself in their eyes—Professor Hanley—that slightly overweight, creased, but handsome and lively teacher—not only a teacher but

a poet—one of the more popular members of the English Department. No one stared at him. No one plucked at his sleeve and
asked him if the rumor was true—after seventeen years of married
life! Monday passed without event. And Tuesday. And Wednes-
day. He had the idea, with the rational part of his mind, that
people now "knew" . . . or guessed . . . but, somehow, it made
little difference in their behavior toward him. They *liked* him.
They were not going to accuse him of the things both Cynthia and
Ginny had accused him of; they were not going to nag at him for
being selfish; they were not going to. . . . But, at the same time,
no one came around to ask him if he was lonely or suffering or
wounded.

One day there was a pink notice in his departmental mailbox
and his heart lurched—whether in excitement or dismay, he could
not judge; for such notices meant someone had telephoned in his
absence—but after he had snatched it up, and stood reading it, his
heartbeat slowed and his blood ran with a kind of neutral chill. A
message: Would he please telephone Cynthia? Absurdity of
absurdities, his own former telephone number was given.

Possibly she had changed her mind; had decided against continuing with the divorce proceedings.

Well, he would let her worry for a while. He had suffered this
week, in a manner of speaking, and so she could suffer a while
longer. *I hate you*, she had screamed. *I want you out of here, out
of this house.* He had said certain things too, which he had not
altogether meant—though in a way he did mean them, with a part
of his mind. But he had never screamed them so that the children
could hear.

He decided not to telephone, not to bother. Or at least not to
telephone for a few days. That way he would not appear anxious;
she would get the idea—a correct one—that his professional life at
the university, and his poetry, at the apartment, were absorbing
his energies, distracting him from grief or sorrow. He had been
rather heroic this past week: he had braved meeting people, had
taught his classes with nearly as much vigor as always, had gotten
drunk only twice. He had not shied away from friends and acquain-

tances, though a few of them had given him a certain inquisitive, pitying look.

No doubt it was up to Jake to tell people, to sigh and reveal the news, but he found it difficult to bring up in ordinary conversation. Even on Friday afternoon, when he joined a group of men from the university for drinks at the Ontario House, an occasion that lasted well into the evening, it was somehow easier to talk and joke about the usual things. Who wanted to be depressed by news of the Hanleys' probable divorce? Not Jake himself, certainly; life was too short.

There were only three taverns within reasonable walking distance of the Hillberry campus, and each was disappointing in its own way. The worst was a dim, noisy place frequented by young motorcyclists and workers from a nearby Chrysler trim plant. One evening Jake went in, against his better judgment, and in less than ten minutes someone was shoved into him—one leather-clad young man set upon by several others—and he fell heavily to the floor. Afterward, stumbling home, he had had to suffer the indignity of overhearing strangers discuss his condition as if he were deaf, or not quite human: *Do you see that man? Look how drunk he is! No shame! Isn't it awful!*

Occasionally Jake and a few friends went to the White Hawk, an English-style pub attached to a notorious hotel, but it was hardly a pleasant place—frequented mainly by the red-faced, bulbous-nosed, decrepit men of all ages who rented rooms by the week in the hotel. Its only advantage was a relative proximity to the English Department. Though the Ontario House was always filled with undergraduates, and Jake often discovered himself the oldest customer in the place, he preferred it to the others—at least there was a lively, cheerful atmosphere there. It was good to be among happy people. His first weeks away from home, Jake began to drop in at the Ontario House immediately after his two o'clock class; if things went well, and he didn't feel too uncomfortable, he stayed until six or even seven. After that, he didn't mind returning to the kitchenette apartment.

He was working on a poem. It was a long, complex poem, by far the most ambitious thing he had attempted in years. It might even be a series—a book-length experiment in the transmutation of private suffering into art: *Divorce and Other Diversions*. Or, possibly: *Elegy for Various Dying Gods*. But work went slowly, painfully. Sometimes he gave up, opened another can of beer, and turned on the tiny television set he had bought. Sometimes he thought of calling someone—his children—his family out in Winnipeg—even Cynthia. (But he dreaded speaking to his wife: he had not returned her call, and was waiting to hear about his misdeed through his lawyer.) It crossed his mind that he might even telephone Ginny. . . .

But no, better not.

She would have refused to speak to him anyway. And the cost of telephoning long-distance, to Vancouver, would be exorbitant. No sooner would she pick up the phone and discover who it was, than she would slam the receiver down. It wasn't worth it.

Sometimes the thought of Ginny inspired him, however, and he went back to his poem. A few lines, a few minutes of almost feverish creativity . . . then he found himself back again in the tiny apartment, alone. How unfair it was! During the months of his infatuation for Ginny, he had felt curiously alone, and lonely, as if his continual daydreaming about the girl set him apart from other human beings, irrevocably; even from Ginny herself, in a way. At home, he had made his wife suspicious by being so abstracted and melancholy. But he couldn't help summoning up, in his imagination, the girl's charmingly frizzy hair, her impudent brown eyes, her smooth, pale flesh. She was young, of course, and he knew that—yet it was a continual surprise to him that her skin, especially the flesh of her stomach and abdomen and thighs, was so unlined, so smooth and tight. And she was very pretty. Not particularly intelligent, he sometimes thought, the way she praised his teaching and the fragments of poems he dared show her—since he had a modest, realistic assessment of himself; but, on the other hand, Cynthia was hardly a brilliant woman, and it was at least five years

since she had even bothered to compliment him on anything. . . .
The problem was, the ludicrous problem was, that when he was
actually with Ginny in her two-room apartment he found himself
thinking about Cynthia. At home, he dreamed of the girl's apartment, and of the girl in it, opening her arms for an embrace; but
with her, he found himself thinking anxiously and guiltily of Cynthia. He feared her discovering them—had improbable, comic fantasies of her following him, pounding on the door and demanding
it be unlocked. Sometimes she was with a detective, sometimes she
had brought the children along, so that they could see what sort
of man their father was. *We know! We see!* The anxiety grew
worse instead of lessening, and Ginny came to hate him as much as
Cynthia did for his vague, distracted manner and his habit of insisting guiltily that he had been listening to what was being said.
She had held it against him, also, that he never took her out to
dinner—or to movies—or anywhere, in fact; she accused him of
being cowardly, of being terrified of his wife. She even accused him
of being stingy, though he had bought her several presents—a recording of *The Messiah*, a copy of one of his favorite novels, *Under
the Volcano*, and a lovely pale-green scarf from the Asian students'
bazaar. But it was Jake's preoccupation with his wife that really in-
furiated the girl and led to that final, near-catastrophic quarrel. . . .

Perhaps he should call her?

But no: better not.

As time passed Jake began to stay later at his office in the Humanities Building, since the weather had grown foul and it was an
unpleasant walk to the Ontario House, even to the White Hawk,
with the wind so strong from the river. And he had overheard a few
students' remarks, one night. Nothing too serious, he'd been lively
and good-natured and not really drunk, and the students liked him,
generally . . . but still, the next morning, he had made a vow to
avoid the Ontario House except on Friday afternoons. The tiny
apartment was depressing; other tenants in the building were noisy;
he had come to hate it, to prefer his office and the quiet of the late

afternoons. It seemed to him he could work better there than anywhere else. Even his long poem, which was still tricky and opaque, came more easily there.

He liked the Humanities Building itself, which had been built in the fifties, was "modern," and yet not so hideously modern as the high-rise Engineering and Sciences Building, all dark-tinted glass and precast concrete. He liked his office, comfortably cluttered as it was, bookshelves jammed with books and magazines, a cheerful though rather watery Impressionistic print on the wall behind his desk—a gift from Ginny—and a grimy, well-worn old braided rug on the floor, inherited from the previous occupant. Without having been conscious of it, he had grown attached over the years not only to this office but to the English Department itself. He liked the look of the corridor when no one was around; he was somehow comforted by the messy appearance of the large cork bulletin board by the chairman's office door, crowded with announcements and advertisements and notes. The common room was windowless and chilly, but he rather liked to wander in there and get coffee from the vending machine, and to sit for long blank stretches of time, leafing through aged copies of the *Times Literary Supplement,* or examining the work of rival poets in such small publications as *Skunk, And Elsewhere, Orc Review, Cabbage,* and *The Ant's Forefoot.* A few years ago Jake's poems had appeared in little magazines like these, but the pressures of hard work, a love affair, and family problems had crippled him temporarily. He believed it was only a matter of recovering his strength, his faith in himself. . . .

Ordinarily Jake stayed around the department no later than five or five thirty, but one evening, around six, he was sitting in the common room when another faculty member, Ron Blass, came in. They were startled to see one another at first. Then Ron pulled one of the lightweight plastic chairs over beside Jake and said: "I suppose you know . . . ? About Marcella and me . . . ?"

Jake stared at him. Ron was a short, stocky man in his forties, with a pleasant, bumpy face and a generally rumpled appearance.

He was the department's outstanding poet: he had written and published hundreds of poems, was the author of a book, and was invited nearly everywhere to read his poems—to New Caledonia College in the wilds of British Columbia, to Heart's Content, Newfoundland, to Sarnia, Ontario. From time to time Jake had been envious of Ron, even jealous, but Ron was so harmless and good-natured that it was impossible to dislike him. And it seemed to Jake that the department members who held Ron in contempt—nearly all the nonpoets, in fact—simply coveted Ron's success.

"I've tried to keep it quiet," Ron was saying sadly. "The way people spread rumors at this university . . . ! But Marcella is adamant and I guess I'll go along with her. It happened this way: she discovered some new poems of mine, some love poems, and . . . and, well, frankly the adjectives just don't apply to her, it was futile of me to argue that they did . . . futile and grotesque. She forced me to admit the truth. What a nightmarish scene it was, Jake, when I came home innocently from school one day and Marcella was all red-eyed, and ran at me with the new issue of *Mainline*, slapping me on the head and shoulders with it, crying like mad. . . . I was so astonished, I could hardly defend myself."

Jake was blinking. Then he began to smile faintly. "You mean . . . ? You and Marcella are breaking up . . . ? I'm really surprised to hear it, Ron, I've always thought . . . everyone has always thought. . . ."

"I drifted into it, actually," Ron said. His eyes glittered with tears. "I just noticed, gradually, that my poems were developing along certain lines . . . certain images kept recurring . . . and one day, actually it was one evening in my night class, I looked up and there the girl was. *The girl.* Turns out she'd been there all along, watching me. A very sweet honey-haired fourth-year student, very perceptive, superior to most of the other students in that class. Somehow it came out, I don't even remember how, we began to have coffee together . . . even went a few times to the Ontario House, but always with other people . . . it was like a miracle, a truly miraculous thing in my life, the way she seemed to step out of the poetry, to illuminate the images. It was as if I'd known her before, in another lifetime, or . . . or maybe . . . maybe the poetry gave me the idea. I don't know."

"Fourth-year student . . . ?" Jake asked.

Ron blushed. "Darlene McCarthy," he whispered.

"*Darlene McCarthy* . . . !" Jake repeated. Oddly, he felt tremendous relief—though of course the girl could not have been Ginny; that was impossible. But how strange, that a beautiful, intelligent girl like Darlene—who had been in Jake's contemporary-poetry course the year before—should be involved with Ron Blass, of all people. She was so pretty! She had always seemed, or so Jake had imagined, rather attracted to *him*. But he managed to say that Ron was certainly a lucky, lucky man.

"But do you think she might really marry me? *Me?*" Ron asked eagerly.

"Marry . . . ? Have you asked her to marry you?"

Ron began a long, complicated, excited story that Jake followed only in part. It was typical of the English faculty at Hilberry—and possibly elsewhere; Jake supposed so—that individuals spoke passionately and at considerable length of themselves, their academic or personal problems, even, at times, to the extent of brandishing mimeographed syllabi or students' term papers, failing to notice their listeners' glassy stares, and even more often failing to pause and to inquire whether their listeners had anything to say—any problems or remarks of their own? But Ron's story was more interesting than most. Evidently the girl claimed to be "hopelessly" in love with Ron, but she was also in love with someone else, a boy her own age. She was trying to "work through the relationship" with the boy and would need perhaps a year's time. . . . Unfair, Jake thought grimly. Ron was hardly an attractive man, how had he managed to delude so fine a girl as Darlene McCarthy? Of course Jake had no illusions about himself any longer; fifteen or twenty pounds overweight, or had been the last time he'd dared weigh himself—by an unspoken consent, he and Cynthia had pushed the bathroom scale farther and farther under the laundry hamper, an inch at a time, so that it was never used any longer, not even by the children in play. Jake had a drooping waistline, a pronounced stomach, his hair was graying in uneven patches . . . but he was still a handsome man, while Ron was merely an agreeably homely man, no more than five feet six.

"The hellish part of it is," Ron was whispering, "that Marcella kicked me out of the house. My own house! And Darlene is going through some kind of personality crisis just now; she's pretending to be angry with me. She's a very skittish girl, awfully proud and complex and moody for a girl that young, and surprisingly experienced. . . . At least I was surprised. She has roommates, too, who are suspicious of us, as it is. One of them is in my 10 A.M. creative-writing class and it's . . . well, it's hideously embarrassing for me. . . . So . . . you won't tell anyone, Jake? . . . I've been hanging around the department as long as possible, then going to spend the night at a cheap room I've rented at the White Hawk. A dump, I know, but at least it's . . . at least it's something."

For a while both men were silent. In the distance there were sounds—someone running on the stairs—voices—probably students arriving for night school. An office door was unlocked nearby. Jake was relieved that whoever it was, whichever of his colleagues it was, had not poked his head in the common room to see who was here so late.

"Better leave," Jake said with a sigh.

"Yes," Ron said, getting slowly to his feet.

They left the Humanities Building together, and walked down Telford Boulevard as far as the intersection with Mason. November now, drizzly and cold. Dusk seemed to begin as early as five in the afternoon; the sun disappeared behind a perpetual bank of clouds. Jake took the opportunity to mention his impending divorce—to speak of his emotional turmoil, concerning the children above all. Ron listened sympathetically but did not appear to be surprised. Evidently people knew all about the Hanleys . . . ? "I've visited with the children a few times now, on Saturdays and Sundays," Jake said, "and it's so . . . so heartbreaking . . . so difficult. I want to grab and kiss them and burst into tears, but of course I don't; at the same time, they seem to sense how close I am to doing it, to breaking down, so they keep their distance . . . even Bobbie, who's only six. I hear myself saying the most insignificant things, my voice sounds like a stranger's voice, I feel numb, not anyone at all . . . like an uncle no one has seen in years, who shows up one day, and everyone must be polite to him. I just can't get over. . . ." But his voice was distant now; he felt numb now, walking beside Ron Blass. It was comforting to talk at last. Ron was a friend, they had known each other for how many years now? —eight, ten?—and it was obvious that Ron was not judging him. Perhaps he was not even listening to every word—especially Jake's mild denunciations of his wife—but of course Jake had not listened to every word of Ron's. This was comforting in itself.

". . . if only Cynthia weren't so vindictive and bitter," Jake said. "Why, I told her I wouldn't have minded if she . . . if she had found someone else. . . . I wouldn't have minded in the slightest if she. . . . In fact, I hope that . . . well . . . someone might come along."

"I told Marcella the same thing," Ron said.

"Did you?"

"But no one is going to come along," Ron said flatly. "Not for Marcella or Cynthia. No one."

"No one . . . ?" Jake said.

They stared at each other, suddenly frightened.

Jake began to discover odd, intriguing things at the college. He was using the men's lavatory on his floor one night, having inadvertently stayed rather late—he and Ron and Frank Ambrose, another colleague, had been in the Common Room discussing various things, and hours had slipped past—and a member of the Philosophy Department, a man named Zinn whom Jake didn't know well, came in carrying a toothbrush, a tube of toothpaste, and a towel and washcloth—wearing bedroom slippers—though still dressed in his daytime clothes. Zinn was surprised to see Jake; he blushed angrily and muttered something about it being "rather late" for people to be hanging around, wasn't it? Jake stammered a reply and escaped.

Another evening, he strolled along the darkened corridor of the English Department and saw a light under the office door of one of the younger men, an instructor named Scoville whom he had once tried to befriend, without success. From inside the office came the sound of typing, a ceaseless clatter, and small murmurs or exclamations—Scoville was evidently talking to himself. Jake wanted to knock, just to say hello; he had been feeling a little lonely that evening. But Scoville might resent the intrusion. He was a fastidious, rather overdressed young man of thirty, a "born scholar," it was said; he alone, of the dozen or more members of the English Department who had applied, had been awarded a research grant from the university's Distinguished Scholars Program—he was working with the letters or private papers of an early twentieth-century English poet, Jake believed, though he didn't know the details. He was reluctant to disturb Scoville and crept quietly away.

On another occasion he ran into Zinn again—this time in the third-floor men's lavatory, where he had gone in the hopes of avoiding him. And that same evening he saw lights under the doors of two department members—one of them an unmarried woman, Wanda Barnett, whom he didn't know well; the other was Frank Ambrose, a friend. Jake knocked quietly on Frank's door and was surprised at the warmth with which Frank greeted him. "I hope I'm not disturbing your work," Jake whispered.

Frank was an attractive black man in his late thirties; during the day he was fashionably dressed, but this evening he was wearing an old pullover sweater with stains on the front and a hole in one elbow. And bedroom slippers. Jake was a little disturbed by Frank's chatter and hospitality—he was insisting Jake join him in a cup of hot chocolate. "It's cold out, starting to snow," Frank said. "You'd better have something warm before you leave." It was already nearing midnight, but Jake decided to stay a while and relax.

They talked of many things: at first Frank dwelt upon his scholarly work, which evidently took up most of his time these days. His project, begun in 1961, was a bibliography of works by and about the eighteenth-century satirist Lord Lewesbury. Frank was working hard, hoping to complete the project by the end of next year. "At first I disliked what I was doing," Frank said amiably, "I mean it was just . . . well, from a psychological point of view, according to my analyst, it was just some kind of 'house nigger' psychology, my trying to be a true white-man's scholar; you know, the way they trained me at Harvard. But as the years passed I got to actually like it: the research, the endless cross-references, the smell of the books, the tranquility of archives and special-collection rooms, that sort of thing. I even went to the Huntington Library once, in Southern California—have you heard of it? No? Well, it's of interest primarily to scholars in my field," he said with a smile. "Yes, I enjoy what I'm doing. I truly do. I've found my life's work, I think. . . . And of course I had to live down those terrible rumors that had been circulating about me . . . totally false, they were. But I had to create a new image fast; otherwise I might have been fired."

Discreetly, Jake pretended not to know what the rumors had been.

It was quite natural for them to move onto another topic now; and Frank was genuinely interested in hearing about the latest developments in Jake's marital problems. Not only was Cynthia harassing him through their attorneys, but she had taken to telephoning him in the early morning; and once, a few weeks ago, she had actually come to the University Arms to knock on his door. He had not wanted to let her in, fearing her tears and uncontrollable rage; after ten minutes of pleading and threatening—"I'll tell the children what you're really like! I'll tell the world, you selfish bastard!"—she had finally been driven away by the superintendent of the building. Jake had been humiliated and terribly depressed for hours afterward.

"Yeh, Eunice has that power too," Frank sighed. "She can break a man down . . . can change my temperament from euphoric to dismal in a matter of minutes. She never believed me about the girls. Never. I told her that the rumors were false—just scandalous lies made up by people who were jealous of me—of my advancement in the department, that sort of thing. And my scholarly publications. I was just breezing along too well; people started to get jealous. But no matter how I pleaded with Eunice, and even threatened her with walking out, she never believed me and of course she never forgave me. If I'd married a black woman—and I'm not saying I regret marrying Eunice—not at all, it's been quite an experience!—but if I'd married a black woman none of this would have happened; she would have wept and screamed and kicked and bit a little, but in the end she would have forgiven me. But, well," he sighed, "it didn't happen that way. . . . So you and Cynthia are definitely through?"

"The attorneys are working it out between them," Jake said vaguely. He dreaded knowing too much about the terms he was agreeing to; part of him wanted to examine everything suspiciously, another part of him wanted nothing to do with it. ". . . I suppose the process could be stopped at any time," he said helplessly, "but if Cynthia . . . if she really wants . . . and the children don't seem to miss me; Sandy has already taken over my corner in the basement, for a model-airplane workbench. I don't know. It just seems to be happening by itself. If Cynthia would come to her senses and apologize and ask me to come back . . . instead of always calling me names. . . . But. . . . It's as confusing as it was with Ginny. I've told you about her, haven't I? How irrational she was, the demands she made on me? It's just too much, Frank," he said with a sigh. "I can see why you've become so involved with scholarly work."

"I certainly am, it's no exaggeration," Frank said cheerfully. He went on to confide in Jake that he sometimes worked so late here in the office that he stayed overnight—"slept over" in his black-leather easy chair, which was much more comfortable than it looked; he simply stripped to his underwear and tucked himself in with a thermo-knit blanket he kept in his filing cabinet, and there wasn't the nuisance of driving home in the cold. Jake asked, surprised, if Eunice didn't mind? "Well, it was sort of her idea," Frank mumbled. "I mean in the beginning. She's touchy, you know, very proud and irrational . . . like most women . . . and the rumors really offended her. I think she was more insulted by them than by the fact that . . . the fact that her husband might have been, well, unfaithful to her; which wasn't the case anyway, but only a bunch of lies contrived by jealous people. So she sort of suggested it. At first. I was afraid of being discovered by the janitors or the night watchman . . . but nothing ever happened, no one ever caught me. After a year, I met old Stuart Findlay in the john, and it turns out that Stuart has been sleeping over for ages. . . . Of course, he's a bachelor and a little eccentric. Evidently he's been more or less living in his office all these years and does his cooking on a hot plate; gave me the idea for getting one of my own. They're very useful, Jake. You should get one for your own office."

"I don't think so, really," Jake said stiffly. He stood. It was time to leave: it was 1:30 A.M.

". . . poor Stuart, he published that study of Gower's metrics with Oxford University Press, years ago, and now his enrollment is down to practically nothing, he teaches only one course and it meets in his office . . . two or three students, that's all. Isn't it tragic? He's very proud, won't discuss such things, but Dr. Barth told me the administration has found some alternative work for Stuart, something to do with book orders, typing up lists, helping the secretaries. He's so morose these days, so sensitive . . . maybe you should stop in and see him, Jake, before leaving? . . . Of course it's convenient and cozy for him, having that class meet in his office. That way he can stay close to home. . . . Sure you don't want another cup of chocolate, Jake?"

Jake went back to his apartment that night; but a few nights later, working at his desk until midnight, he decided it was too much trouble to go home. The office was warm, he'd kicked his shoes off, he was sleepy and in no mood to trudge through the snow. Locked in his office, with only his desk lamp turned on, he did anything he liked: worked lazily on his poem, leafed through paperback novels, corrected a few student papers, reviewed his notes for the next day's classes. Jake had always enjoyed teaching and, as a consequence, tended to award his students mainly A's and B's. He liked being generous, he liked being *liked*; it was a pleasant sensation, and of course there were far fewer complaints about Professor Hanley than there were about the more severe, old-fashioned professors. Teaching was immensely rewarding as an end in itself: Jake felt no need to impose rigorous, unrealistic standards on his students. He was totally unable to comprehend either those professors who were difficult, or those who routinely cut classes on Fridays and Mondays and who occasionally disappeared from Hilberry for a week's impromptu vacation in the middle of the semester. He was very fond of the university atmosphere and was growing fonder all the time. The department, for instance, was absolutely quiet at night. If Frank was a few doors down in his office, if Vincent Scoville was typing industriously away in his, if Wanda Barnett or Stuart Findlay or Ron Blass or anyone else were in their offices, no one could have told; the English Department was wonderfully still.

A miracle, such quiet. Such peace.

Washing in the lavatory, Jake sighed with the luxury of it. He even enjoyed the special kind of exhaustion one feels from having read too long; it reminded him of his days as a graduate student, when he'd led an almost monastic existence in the library stacks, and his wife—even then—had seemed strangely unreal; both his wife and the baby had seemed unreal. It was unfortunate he had not planned on staying over, but perhaps he could borrow some toiletry items from Frank, in the morning. . . . He remembered the commotion and bustle of family life, remembered with displeasure those mornings at home: children bickering, Cynthia scolding, the bathroom a mess, the breakfast table too crowded. Unreal. All that unnecessary noise, confusion . . . why had he endured it for so long? He had allowed other people to sap his energies for most of his adult life.

And little Ginny: she had tried to trap him too. Kittenish, shrewd if not intelligent, twenty years old but in certain ways older than he. He eyed himself in the washroom mirror, wondering if that was the man Ginny had seen. Certainly she exaggerated, idealized, but there must have been some truth to it . . . she had claimed to love him "more than life itself" . . . and he had claimed to love her, had actually loved her very much, but could not handle the circumstances that developed. At first their love had been idyllic; they had been infatuated with each other. Then Ginny had become unreasonably jealous . . . had accused him of caring more for his wife than for her . . . of being more afraid of his wife, than he was of *her*. But why should Jake have been afraid of her? It made no sense. Her moods changed from day to day, from hour to hour. She slashed at him; she burrowed into his arms and begged to be forgiven; she turned coldly away; she stood on her tiptoes and kissed him. She did one thing, then she did another. And another. Her suicide attempt—or her pretense of a suicide attempt—had been simply one trick in a series of tricks, but at the time he hadn't quite caught on.

She had come out of her bathroom and announced, calmly, that she'd swallowed fifteen or twenty sleeping pills.

Jake had panicked at first—had believed her.

Then he realized it was only a trick—might only be a trick—she had been nagging him all evening—had been alternately pleading with him to marry her and denouncing him as a worthless person, not good enough for her to marry—and then she'd disappeared into the bathroom and locked the door and then reappeared—ghastly pale, triumphant, a vicious little bitch who really wanted him destroyed—reappeared and announced calmly that she'd swallowed all those pills.

"You're lying," Jake had said.

Alone in the lavatory he repeated those words: "You're lying."

And she had lied, it turned out. He hadn't the exact information—didn't know the details—had heard about her banging on someone else's door, after he had left, and insisting she had swallowed the pills—insisting even on why she had swallowed them. But evidently it had been a trick, a ruse. He didn't know. He had not wanted to find out, exactly, how much she had told people. . . . Fortunately nothing came of it; she had dropped out of school and was living now in Vancouver; and of his own free will, because he was miserable and drinking too heavily, Jake had confessed part of the story to his wife. . . . A mistake, maybe.

He should not have given that woman any information that could be used against him.

Jake had been staring at himself in the mirror. What was surprising was that look of subdued pleasure: he hadn't seen it in himself for months. Unshaven, bleary-eyed, and *yet.* . . .

For a moment he could not remember where he was, that he should feel so free at last.

*A*n Incident in the Park

A man staggering-drunk, babbling-drunk. Several days' beard, filthy trousers, a raw amazed accusing voice. . . . Not Evan, not Evan Maynard. It wasn't Evan, it was a stranger, much older than Evan. It wasn't anyone Evan knew. Eleven thirty in the morning and the man was drunk already. Evan was not drunk. People were beginning to notice the drunken man—a young mother, pushing her baby in a stroller, was staring foolishly at him—several boys were giggling at him—but no one was looking at Evan Maynard, who was unobtrusive as always. His clothes were not filthy, he had shaved only a few hours ago; he shaved every day. Of course. The drunken man was muttering to himself but Evan never talked to himself—not out loud—and he would never have said such things in a public park, at midday. *Who the hell you think you are . . . What . . . ? What the hell you pulling . . . ? I told you once'nf'rall . . . son of a bitch. . . . What the. . .*

The man was alone. Of course. Evan was alone also, but his presence was unobtrusive, as always, and no one would dare to point at him, giggle at him, not as they did with the drunken man. Drunks like that one, barely able to make his way along the path, are always alone, always solitary . . . no one will approach them, except the police. Evan was alone also, but he was not drunk. He had had a few beers. But he wasn't drunk, he never got drunk, couldn't even remember the last time he'd been light-headed from drinking . . . no, couldn't remember. His wife Renée never got drunk either. They were a well-suited couple, intelligent and fairly attractive and very nice, very well mannered, from good families, both Americans. . . . Evan had a wife, he was married, had been married for quite a while now, so close to his wife he could almost forget her; he had always loved her, of course, hadn't meant to forget her, hadn't meant to. . . . But he lost his line of argument. The drunken man was approaching a park bench, still mumbling to himself. Evan watched: he wanted to see if the man made it safely.

He did. He sat. He raised his face, blinking in the sunshine. A bumpy, sickly complexion, eyes nearly hidden beneath his thick eyebrows, blinking, blinking, a character in a cartoon. Yes. Evan was nothing like that and *never would be.*

"What's so funny?" Evan asked two teen-aged girls. They were probably no more than thirteen, but their movements, their shrill giggles and the way they lifted their shoulders, were eerily adult. Halter tops, tying around the neck; very short shorts. Red polka dots. Mustard yellow. They stared at Evan, they hadn't even noticed him, their long straight curtains of hair swung with the surprise of his irritated voice. "He isn't going to hurt you, leave him alone. You think he's funny? It isn't funny. There isn't anything—"

But they had hurried away, giggling.

A weekday in Phillips Park. Few men Evan's age, of course. They would all be working. The drunken man had no job—had probably been unemployed for a long time—he looked caved-in, horrible, his eyes lost, nearly erased. A mouth that kept moving, mov-

ing. . . . *Thought I told you once'nf'rall . . . goddamn bastard
. . . trying to cheat me. Paid up for the week, I told you. . . .*
Evan wondered who the man was, how old he was, where he lived.
One of the cheap downtown hotels, probably. *Transients. Weekly
Rates.* Evan was a child of the middle class, had never even stayed
in a cheap hotel, had never had a few drinks before noon in his
life, so it was all a puzzle to him—not exactly attached to him.
Was he groggy? It might have been the sun, and the long walk
from the Institute; he wasn't accustomed to walking any longer;
had gotten into the habit of driving everywhere. . . . No, he
wasn't groggy. But it bothered him, that the man on the park
bench should continue to mutter. *Who'n hell you sonsabitches
think y're talking to. . . .* Evan didn't want people to think the
man was addressing him.

Might be a good idea to walk away. Stroll along the gravel paths,
like the tourists. Admiring the roses. Beds and beds of roses,
arranged in an immense circle, half the size of a city block.
Tourists from the United States taking snapshots. Red roses,
yellow roses, pink, white, peach-colored, pink edged with yellow.
Pale roses, blood-red roses, dark blood-red roses. At the center of
the rose garden was an airplane, on a pedestal. Hard to believe.
Yes, but there it was, Evan had seen it once before, he and Renée
had stared at it one Sunday a few months ago, had made a few
jokes. Relic from World War II. A bomber with four propellers,
"historic," painted with dim blue-green spots meant to be cam-
ouflage. A brass plaque explained it. *Liberator.* Evan and Renée
were too young to have known about World War II, couldn't
be anything personal, anything emotional, but must make the
effort—try to get into the consciousness of the past—people
terrified that Canada and the United States would be invaded,
Germanic hordes, Teutonic beasts, that sort of thing: movies,
late-night reruns. A few months ago there had been beds of tulips,
not roses, and children had run happily up and down the gravel
paths and on the grassy borders and around the airplane, giggling,
happy, oblivious to the bomber but perhaps absorbing its bulky
shadow. A political lesson here. Moral lesson. Aesthetics sub-

ordinated to politics, and don't you forget it, the flowers pay homage to the bomber and you'd better pay homage to it as well. Even shaded his eyes and gazed at the plane. Why, it was sad. Touching. Without his wife beside him, without the conversation and the little jokes, the touching of hands, brushing of arms . . . why, the scene was vulgar and depressing and not funny, not funny at all. He was an American citizen in a foreign country and the bomber was an American bomber, a liberator, and don't you forget it, its shadow fell across the tulips and the roses and the children. . . . But he was exaggerating, dramatizing. It was just a bomber on a pedestal. Phillips Park was just a park. None of this mattered.

Tourists glancing at him—old man in the company of a younger couple, small children tramping along—someone glanced at Evan —why was he talking to himself? No, just grinning. The incongruity of the airplane, the roses, a kind of ironic grin. Intelligent grin. He was nothing like the drunken man, sprawled on the park bench a hundred feet away. Why glance at Evan? Neatly groomed, tieless but not staggering, not a drunk. A solitary man is incongruous in such a setting: so many families, young mothers and children, no place for single adult men. If Renée were with him it would be different. . . . *Did you lie? Are you lying? Are you in love with someone?* But he was not arguing with Renée, not in this public place. He wasn't moving his lips, even. The most he had done was grin and maybe laugh out loud, because of the airplane and the idiotic tourists from across the border, snapping pictures of such things, of ordinary sights, anxious to experience a "foreign country." The young couple towing the old man along, must be a widower, exasperated young man glancing at Evan— about Evan's age—but no sympathy with him, no recognition, the bastard didn't comprehend the irony of the airplane but why bother—most people were stupid anyway.

Evan yawned.

He wondered where the men's room was. Probably back in that direction; but he wanted to avoid the drunken man. Sprawled on the bench now . . . might be asleep. Right in the sun. Evan yawned, rubbed his eyes, wondered what to do. As a student he had never had any time—always harassed, anxious—now he was an adult, nearly thirty, and things were different. There was no connection between this Evan and the other. The other had been a boy, called a "genius" (what right had they to predict so much for him? the bastards!), supremely ignorant. Gone now. Rest in peace.

Not even noon yet, unless his watch had stopped. The day was going to be a long one. It had begun many hours ago, showed no signs of accelerating, night would be a long way off. He couldn't go home for hours. Couldn't go home for hours. He wanted to find a men's room and after that maybe a quiet place to sit, relax, doze. Was that against the law? Might it be considered vagrancy? . . . Of course not, nobody gave a damn.

If a policeman questioned him Evan had any number of answers. He had an identification card; he had his draft card. Anyway he wasn't drunk and nobody was going to question him. The thing was not to wander in one direction and then turn in the other, as if he were lost. He wasn't lost. Phillips Park was bordered by Pelee Boulevard and Elmhurst, and he knew his way around the city well enough, he knew how to get home when it was time to leave for home, it was impossible to get lost in so small a city. The grogginess from the beer was wearing off. He'd never drunk beer before noon, never in the past, was beginning to feel sick about it: sickness in the stomach, in the chest, rising up into the throat so that he gagged.

Perhaps Renée and her lover would be in the park. Ah, yes. Strolling hand in hand. The graveled walks, the lush green grassy banks, the roses. They would see him. *She* would see him. A cartoon scene: his wife staring, her hand raised to her lips, shock horror shame. She would have no time for guilt, seeing Evan like this. Why wasn't he at the Institute? What had happened? Had he been fired?—asked to leave without notice? *Was he drunk?* Couples strolled and admired the tulips, no, the roses, it was summer now and the tulips were gone, roses now, and lovely they were—absolutely gorgeous—deserving of all the snapshots, people squinting, crouching, adjusting their cameras. A number of couples, but Evan didn't see Renée. Might not have recognized her, in this setting. Anyway it was all imagination, wasn't it, Renée and a lover, Renée and adultery, his intelligent young wife caught up in the mindless vulgarity of the times, the cover stories, statistics, interviews. . . . Really, he didn't suspect her of adultery; he suspected her of not loving him. The bitch! He would go home immediately and—

"Could you tell me the time please sir?"

A girl in tight-fitting jeans and a halter-top blouse, coming up behind him. For a moment he was confused—thought he knew her—no, the other girls were younger, had been wearing shorts. No. He stretched out his arm gallantly, so she could see the watch face herself. Twenty-five to twelve.

"Hey, is that all? . . . No, hell. It's a lot later than that, your watch must have stopped."

"Stopped?"

"It's past noon," the girl said.

Evan shook his wrist. He wound the watch. His face was burning, the girl watched him so closely, studying him, smiling slyly, maybe could smell his breath. . . . No, when he looked up she was drifting away. Barefoot, about seventeen years old, odd vacuous look about the eyes: probably on drugs. He was relieved she'd walked away. Disappointed. But he wanted nothing to do with her. He was nearly thirty years old, an adult, a husband. . . . One of the research assistants who worked with him, young man in his early twenties and only married two years, bragging about . . . giggling, hinting . . . It struck Evan as horrible, the shallowness of such behavior; he wanted no part of it. No part of anything.

He had left the Institute saying he didn't feel well—asthma, headache—but he couldn't go home, what if she wasn't home, he had telephoned several times after their argument that morning— no answer—but of course she could have walked over to the branch library a few blocks away, could be working out in the yard, and if he went home he would know—might discover—so he couldn't

go home. The argument had been shapeless, dreamlike. A mystery.
Somehow they were in it, plunged in it, and he was accusing her of
always finding fault with him, of being ashamed of him, of the
job he had—though of course she never expressed these feelings,
not overtly—and she had screamed at him, a desperation he had
never heard in her voice before, had screamed for him to let her
alone, to stop staring at her, listening for innuendos where there
were none, and he had denied it all—for it wasn't true, it wasn't
true that he was suspicious of her—She needed more friends, he
said, they both needed friends, it was too lonely here, and she
screamed at him that he never cared for people she tried to befriend—he was suspicious, ironic—he wanted to destroy her, he
couldn't see how she was being destroyed—

The budget at the Institute was going to be cut. He might be
asked to leave: he was an American citizen, after all. Not a
Canadian. Didn't she give a damn about that, didn't she know
what he was going through? He seized her by the shoulders and
shook her. Shook her hard. Never had he touched her before like
that; it woke her up, it made her look into his face for the first
time in weeks. *Do you love someone else?* he shouted. *Who is it?
How are you being destroyed?—who is destroying you?*

She was not his wife. He did not recognize her. Bitch! Deceitful
bitch! He shook her, sobbing, he wanted to do more, wanted to
knock her against the wall . . . until she confessed her adultery,
until she begged him to let her go, to forgive her.

Instead she had cried: *I hate you! Don't you know how I hate
you. . . .*

She had not meant it, of course.

Could not have meant it.

But he fled: was fleeing still.

Nobody hated him, he told himself. That he was an American—
that he was morose, hard-working, rather absurd in his carefully
pressed trousers and always-clean shirt, when even the director wore
sports clothes—that he'd had such promise, had earned advanced
degrees and worked with famous men—"famous" men—Nobel
Prize-winning men—humiliating to recount, and humbling, those

marvelous letters of recommendation that meant so little now, like
Confederate money—that he was merely himself, Evan Maynard,
and no one else: nobody hated him for these facts. They just didn't
care. What value has talent without a context to nourish it? In the
States his talent had been hired to manufacture death, the Great
Defense: the "frontier" he and his team-mates had cultivated was
a tiny scaled-down universe of pathogenic creatures, allies of democ-
racy, "biological cloud agents" that, released in enemy territory,
would do a great deal for the survival of the free enterprise system.
Disease, a war waged by invisible soldiers, panic, madness, chaos. . . .
In the States his talent had been valued highly but he had left the
States, he had not even told his wife exactly why he must leave, and
here, now, in Phillips Park on an ordinary weekday, he was an
anonymous man, a citizen of no country, really, his "new life"
nobody's concern but his own. He had given up a great deal, he
supposed; he had certainly given up a handsome salary. But nobody
cared and, indeed, why should they care? Why should these strangers care for Evan's quixotic gesture? Whatever identity Evan had
possessed had been abandoned on the other side of the border . . .
and he had never guessed, had never dared imagine, that the value
of a human being might be irrevocably bound up with an entire
culture. . . .

Do you love someone else, he had asked her. Not shouting now,
but frightened; frightened that he would kill her. *Is it someone
here . . . someone you've just met. . . . Who is it?*

But she had turned away. Turned away from him and refused to
answer.

Yes, she loved someone else. It was obvious.

No.

No: impossible.

Impossible, Evan told himself.

There was a commotion by the fountain. What was happening?
Startled, Evan got to his feet. He was very nervous; his pulse
jumped. Was it—? Yes, the drunken man. He was doing something
over there, calling attention to himself again. Evan didn't want to
see but he couldn't stay away, couldn't resist. A small crowd was

gathering. Evan drifted near, not wanting to see but staring, fascinated. *What* the hell . . .? The man was wading in the pond. Shouting. Flinging his head from side to side, waving his arms. Was it possible that he wasn't drunk—that he was insane? Evan had not thought of that before.

"Don't let him hurt himself!" Evan cried.

He made his way through the crowd. Suddenly he was important—he seemed important. People stepped aside to let him pass.

"What's wrong? What's wrong?" Evan asked the man.

He was staggering. His eyes, fixed upon a spot just to the left of Evan's face, were darker than they had seemed before; a shiny plum black. His mouth worked soundlessly.

That man is crazy, someone whispered behind Evan.

Evan tried to take the man's arm; the man jerked away. Bold, desperate, pressed with an urgency he did not understand, Evan began to ask the man questions. What was wrong? Why was he so upset? Had something happened to him? Had someone hurt him? Where did he live—what was his address? Was there anyone Evan could contact? The man was not very old, probably no more than fifty. He didn't seem drunk now. He stared at Evan, his mouth still working. Evan had begun to tremble, he couldn't slow down though he knew his questions were only confusing the man: Was he ill? Did he need help? Did he need help getting home? Why was he crying? Why was he so unhappy? If he didn't calm down something terrible would happen—the police would come —he would be hospitalized—sedated—Didn't he know how dangerous it was, to behave like this in a public park?—dangerous and futile?

The man made a swipe at Evan, but missed.

". . . dirty sonsabitches. . . ."

"But—I only want to help—"

"Killya sonsabitches. . . ."

Someone was speaking sternly to Evan. He turned. He turned blindly, saw a young patrolman. He began to explain: "I only want to—"

The patrolman told him to step aside. He would take care of the situation.

"But—"

"Step aside, please."

Evan stepped aside.

He watched the scene from a distance, a safe distance. The young, competent policeman in his trim uniform; the staggering, broken man. About them, a ring of spectators, silent out of respect for madness. A day in the park, a day like any other. One of many. One of thousands. Evan's eyes burned with resentment. *I only wanted to help.* He turned away, still excited. He had been treated unfairly, had been brushed aside . . . so well-meaning, so generous, and yet he'd been brushed aside. What did it mean? He couldn't comprehend. He couldn't remember. . . . Why had he come to the park, why today? For what purpose? . . . He knew there had been a purpose, but at the moment he couldn't remember.

*F*alling in Love in Ashton, British Columbia

She was twenty years younger than he. No more than eighteen or nineteen. Her shoulders wide and boyish, out of proportion to the rest of her body; her skin fine, high-colored, lovely; and her hair—! Incredible. He was falling in love with a girl who wore her hair as no other girl wore it, as his wife had never worn it, nor the now-legendary high-school beauties of his youth . . . her pale-blond hair braided and wound in two separate coils around the sides of her head, exactly like earphones.

Amazing, that she should exist. That he should feel himself falling in love with her, the symptoms rising one by one. . . . Where was he? Where . . . ? Ah yes. A town called Ashton. In British Columbia. In Canada. Amazing, that he should discover himself, one summer day, falling in love in Ashton, British Columbia, with a girl who wore her hair in braids and whose name card, protected by a neat plastic device, announced her as simply *Anna*.

She was coming in his direction. He sat with both elbows on the table, staring at her, helpless and saddened to see her head on like this, a big-bosomed girl, with wide, generous thighs and legs that were certainly muscular, a peasant beauty, no doubt a farmer's daughter, coming innocently to him. *Anything else, sir? More coffee, sir?* Yes. Yes, thanks. *Is that air-conditioning thing too cold?—it's right overhead.* What? No. Oh no. He stared at the girl and hardly heard her words, so intent was he upon . . . upon her being, her soul. What was that accent? Must be Slavic. Possibly Russian. Polish? . . . He wanted to think of her as Russian, a Russian peasant's daughter, an immigrant to western Canada whose daughter was so beautiful, it made that terrible crossing worthwhile. It made Leslie Knox's transcontinental journey, terrible as any oceanic voyage, worthwhile.

She went to the next table, generous with coffee, brushing past Leslie as if it did not matter in the slightest that she should pass so near him . . . that he should be staring at her, bemused and melancholy. Yes, certainly: her accent was Russian or Polish. But her words were perfectly contemporary, her appreciative laughter at some remark another customer made was just right, just what was needed. Her body, her facial structure, the wide flat strong cheekbones and the slightly slanted eyes . . . her braided hair more than anything else . . . and that confident, rather heavy tread of hers, as if she walked quite frankly on her heels: old-world, otherworldly, a young woman out of a history book or a mural. A peasants' procession, maybe. Carrying the cross and the Virgin Mary through snow and blood, maybe, hordes of people with her looks, her amiable expression . . . which could, of course, turn in a few seconds into bovine rage.

Leslie finished his coffee, his third cup. He could see a distorted, comic image of his face in the paper-napkin dispenser: but no, he didn't take that seriously, of course he didn't really look that degenerate. The girl had smiled at him, had blinked at him. Did she know? Could she guess? Probably not: she struck him as rather slow-witted. Her eyelashes thick, childish, innocent. The eyelids naturally shaded, it seemed to him. Eyebrows sturdy, like a man's.

She was strong-bodied, already a mature woman, while the girls he knew—daughters of his friends, daughters of his neighbors back in Long Beach—were flat-bodied and narrow-hipped, mere children by comparison. For all he knew Anna might be married. He had not thought to check her ring finger: the sort of reflex his wife Sylvia would make automatically.

So he was falling in love, sadly, wearily, perhaps automatically, since it had happened so often. In the last decade it had happened so often. . . . No matter that she was twenty years younger, no matter that she was a waitress at a restaurant called, improbably, wonderfully, La Geisha, in a near-featureless town called Ashton, in a part of the world he knew nothing about and had no interest in, other than to survive his stay here. No, it didn't matter. For now the tone of his interior monologue seemed to change, the fiber of the voice thicken, and he realized he must be justifying himself to his wife: running through all the logical statements, the qualifications, the ironic contingencies. . . . No matter that the girl was truly beautiful, her eyes strikingly beautiful, no matter that he felt slightly ill, incapable of competing with the younger men who sat at the counter . . . truck drivers, were they? . . . or local boys? He was lonely, anxious, tired of his own interior monologue, his ceaseless witty voice, he was tired of justifying himself to Sylvia, who did not love him, and the bulging book of traveler's checks he carried in his coat pocket did not console him in the slightest. What did it matter that he was a fairly famous man in another country?—or that his income-tax returns were audited now each year, cruelly and minutely, by Internal Revenue agents who were outwitted—but only by inches!—by his Park Avenue tax lawyers? It made no difference to Anna, who was laughing now at someone else's jokes. The man wore bib overalls; bearded, dark-faced, he might have been a logger or a seaman for all Leslie knew.

La Geisha was at the corner of Ashton Avenue, the town's main street, and a hilly, narrow street called Wellingtonia. Not that he needed to memorize the street names; he could have found his way back to the restaurant in the dark, by touch. Blessed with a marvelous memory for directions, details, names and faces . . . or cursed, was he, since it was getting more and more difficult for him to forget; more maddeningly difficult for him to experience anything for the first time. And he was only forty, after all. Which was not old. He felt old, certainly; but in fact he wasn't old. . . . Twenty, thirty, possibly even forty years yet to go. He and Sylvia had been married for fifteen years, an anniversary coming up on October first, but it seemed they had always been married, be-trothed as children and thrown together in a rude, endless cere-mony. Sylvia had repeatedly said she loved him, far more than he loved her—for was he capable of loving anyone? she would ask reasonably—but she said only what women always said. His mother, his aunts. Complaining of their husbands. His friends' wives, complaining of his friends; and of him. Leslie wanted only to worship them but they kept talking to him, nagging him, mak-ing comparisons, stating terms, restating promises he could never remember making—promises he knew very well he had not made in some instances, though possibly another man had. He wanted only to enslave himself to his wife's elusive, capricious essence, but she kept getting in the way with her chatter, her repetitive jeal-ousies—*Do you think I don't know you, from the inside? Do you think I can't guess where you've been this afternoon? And who she is?*

It was a ten-minute walk from the restaurant to the Five-Star Motor Hotel, out Ashton Avenue; Leslie felt his soul darken, as he drew back into the sphere of his wife's consciousness.

But she was sleeping when he returned to the room.

Sleeping? Still sleeping?

. . . Saturday evening, Leslie and Sylvia had decided to stop for the night in Ashton; they had planned on driving farther that day, at least to the outskirts of one of the glacier parks, but Sylvia had begun to feel sick. Vancouver had upset her: they stayed there a few days, at one of the big hotels, and though Leslie himself had been vaguely disappointed, he was always vaguely disappointed with most things, so it didn't matter. Had they driven thousands of miles, their first vacation together in six or seven years, only to arrive in a big American city? Alas. The quarreling between them had begun to ebb, somewhere in the Badlands, perhaps because they were both chagrined at the desolate land, godless spaces that knew them not, and cared not at all for Sylvia's disgust with Leslie's infidelity, and her growing, rather alarming emancipation from him. . . . So the quarreling died down; Leslie began to be hopeful; if he could not talk her out of divorcing him, and causing a "scandal" (her term: Leslie very much doubted whether scandals were possible any longer in their part of the world), he had only to keep his mouth shut and the continent itself would humble her. But Vancouver was too much like New York City in certain respects . . . the thunderous hooves of secretaries and shop girls, in the season's fashionable three- or four-inch stacked heels, hurrying from work in high-rise office buildings whose chic tinted plate glass savagely reflected the light of the sun and made Leslie think, for a terrible sickening moment, that he was back on Lexington Avenue and had never left . . . the girls, the men in stylish sideburns and suits and bat-wing-framed sunglasses, the unmistakable pollution of the air, the traffic, the spotless expensive high-rise hotel in whose carpeted corridor Sylvia herself suffered an alarming moment of disorientation: it was just like the dreadful hotel in Chicago, wasn't it? . . . Their long, hopeful walks in the park did some good, but not enough. Sylvia began to pick at him again. He dreaded her light, acrid comments, the way she might suddenly slip her arm through his and lean against him, like a bride, and ask him who it was, that girl he had been seen with in a midtown restaurant, an enormous mane of ash-blond hair, she'd been told, and a bare midriff, and a rather shrill voice . . . ? Leslie could not remember this girl; he doubted her existence. He could not imagine who had told his wife about her. But it had all taken place two years ago, now, an incident or a nonincident reported to his wife by evil, jealous people, and he had so often denied it, so often scratched in comic, exasperated despair at his head. . . . Hopeless.

She insisted they leave Vancouver, though they had planned on spending more time there. They must leave, must escape. She wanted to head home. The trip had been a mistake, she should not have listened to him—Leslie Knox, trying to imitate the actions of real people, driving out to the West Coast!—Leslie Knox, who cared for his writing and for his fame, which he called his "reputation"!—she should not have listened to his absurd boyish idea, that they would isolate themselves from the pressure of their world, and from the past itself, in order to discuss the future of their marriage. It had no future, Sylvia said viciously. It was finished.

Sylvia did most of the driving, heading east on Highway 3. Leslie sat slumped beside her, hesitant even to call her attention to the scenery: when she was unhappy she did not care to be cajoled out of her unhappiness. He had the idea that she was waiting for him to say something friendly, so that she could scream at him. The mountains, the pines, the sky. . . . No, she did not care for them; she was passionately unhappy.

Should he ask her forgiveness once again? Again? Should he insist he loved her? It was true; yet somehow not convincing. He wanted to tell her quietly that he loved her very much but that she—a graduate of Radcliffe, after all, and for years a highly paid translator in Washington—was simply too intelligent to consent to love on human, instinctive terms. Leslie wanted only to worship her and to enslave himself to her, in theory; but she was too skeptical to accept a relationship like that. No, she wanted ordinary equality. She wanted citizenship in his world, she wanted him to conform to contractual clauses that bored him . . . amused and antagonized him. But he did love her. She could not deny that love. He insisted, he insisted. . . .

She told him suddenly that she felt ill. Suddenly she felt ill.

. . . She brought the car to a stop, quickly. Leslie drove and she half lay beside him. What was wrong? She didn't know; dizziness, nausea, confusion. . . . It was frightening. Leslie drove and kept glancing at her, stroking her arm, squeezing her hand. Honey? Are you all right? . . . He thought sadly that her life, his life, their married life, were really not in their control at all.

He was now driving their car, but had no idea where they were headed.

So they stopped in Ashton. The Five-Star Motor Hotel: the only reasonable, decent place in town. Sylvia recovered slightly . . . and they went out to a restaurant in the Ashton Hotel, which advertised authentic Russian dishes; but the place was dim and smelled of insect spray, and there were only a few other customers. They left without ordering. A block away was Hodge's Restaurant, glass-brick façade and dingy neon and no indication of a liquor license. . . . They walked on, too tired to quarrel. Sylvia was a few paces ahead of Leslie, as if she were trying to escape him: an attractive dark-haired woman in her late thirties, in a green cotton shift wrinkled from travel, and probably not warm enough now that the sun had set—it was quite windy, here in Ashton— a woman Leslie might have guessed, had he seen her from the street, to be drunk or drugged or a little crazy.

La Geisha: a revolving neon sign. What good fortune. . . . Nothing else was open, only a few dismal taverns and a coffee shop.

During dinner Sylvia was quieter than usual, but did not seem upset. Leslie tried to be cheerful; he kept whispering, *This place isn't too bad, it is?—honey?* He squeezed her cold, passive hand. He smiled a great deal. La Geisha was an interesting surprise, in the middle of the wilderness: the menu boasted authentic Chinese dishes as well as several Russian dishes, and even "Canadian" dishes. And drinks. . . . Leslie saw that his wife was not eating the Russian dish she had ordered. A kind of fatty stew in a very small dish, with a side order of doughy bread. Leslie himself had ordered a Chinese dish, which turned out to be a kind of stew also, into which tiny tasteless overcooked shrimp had been stirred. But he did not mind; he was trying to be cheerful. When the waitress strode over to them to ask if everything was all right, he was delighted with her: an eager, effortless smile, a strong, striking face, a look of robust health. . . .

"The check. Bring the check, please," Sylvia said dully.

"Sylvia—?"

"I can't stand this place. I want to leave."

The waitress continued to smile at them, though less forcefully.

That was Saturday evening; it was now Monday. Sylvia lay in bed most of the time while Leslie wandered about town, had meals sent in, sat for long uncharted periods of time drinking coffee and wondering what would happen, whether it was true, as Sylvia had said, that the future was not available to them . . . and at the same time falling in love with Anna.

"I'm not sick," Sylvia said. "I'm just tired of traveling. In that car. With you, in that car, in such close quarters."

"I understand," Leslie said.

"You don't understand, how could you? . . . I'll be well in another day, I'm sure I'll be well. But now I want to sleep."

"Sylvia, you've been sleeping all day."

"What time is it?"

"It's five-thirty."

". . . I haven't been sleeping, I've been lying here and thinking. As soon as you left I started to analyze the situation and . . . and I'm just temporarily exhausted. . . . My freshman year at college, I got very tired for some reason, demoralized and homesick and exhausted, and . . . and I recovered. Why are you staring at me like that? There's nothing wrong with me."

"It's Monday."

"Monday?"

"It's Monday, and this will be our third night at the motel. You know where we are, don't you?"

"British Columbia."

"You don't want me to get a doctor, really?"

"I told you that I'm not sick; I'm just tired," Sylvia cried.

Haggard, yellowish-skinned. His wife of fifteen years? His lovely wife? . . . Smoking his cigarettes, crudely, as if imitating him; her idea of how a man might smoke. She kept flexing the fingers of both hands. Her mother's hands were crippled by arthritis; it was Sylvia's fear that she was doomed to arthritis as well. But she never spoke of it. She saw him watching her and said, irritably: "Why don't you go out to dinner? Why don't you go out alone? I can't stand you analyzing me all the time. Judging me. Comparing me to other women. . . . You and your moral fables, your precious cameo pieces . . . your fame. . . . I can't stand you always *there*."

"I thought you wanted me to be faithful," Leslie said. He was more hurt than annoyed. His voice sounded like a boy's.

"I don't want to think about you at all," Sylvia said.

Her blue rayon bathrobe was wrapped around her but not tied. Her hair was a mess. Eyes blurry, lazy, as if it were too much effort for her to get anything into focus. Of course she was taking those sleeping pills her doctor back in Long Beach prescribed for her: but Leslie did not dare accuse her.

"What good does my fame do me here in Ashton? . . . here in the Five-Star Motor Hotel? . . . What good does it do either of us, this far from home?" he said. As always, he tried to cajole her out of hating him; he had a charming, hopeful, rather intellectual manner she sometimes found appealing. The ugly implications of her last remark had not escaped him, but he thought it wiser to ignore them. Forty years old, yet good-looking in the style of the fifties—clean-jawed, practical, a husband and a citizen, with handsome gray eyes often described as "penetrating" and "filled with a premature wisdom." He was a best-selling novelist whose first book had been published only a year after he had graduated from Princeton—a critical success and, surprisingly, a popular success as well, since his editor, a woman, had been a very close friend of the president of the publishing house and had arranged for an enormous sum of money to be allotted to his book for advertising purposes. What good fortune. . . . Yes, good fortune. He was, in many ways, a child of good fortune; and so he felt at all times a half-serious sense of guilt, a sense that some terrible mistake had been made, decades ago, and that he had been given the worldly success really meant for another man. He would have to pay it all back, of course. With interest. . . . Yet his novels were published to critical acclaim and popular success every four or five years, time after time, and still disaster had not struck. He had married an exceptionally beautiful woman whom he'd loved very much. He had a number of friends, a number of affectionate acquaintances and memorable ex-friends, whom he thought of, from time to time, with genuine pleasure . . . sometimes with remorse, chagrin, jealousy . . . but always with pleasure. An enthusiastic reviewer had said once of Leslie Knox: *He seeks the eternal in the temporal, the joyfully essential in what is passing.*

A bit exaggerated, perhaps. Still, it had been cruel of Sylvia to snort with derision, reading it aloud to him. She had flexed the fingers of her right hand, like a fighter, and told him that the reviewer was quite correct: Leslie Knox sought the eternal and the joyfully essential, wherever he could find it. It was real life he could not take seriously; real people, human people, whom he exploited.

"Yeh, well. I guess. I guess so."

The girl giggled. Awkward, fleshy. Unaccustomed to such urgency, perhaps. She shied away from Leslie's anguish as if she could smell it.

". . . well, like I said, *sure.* I like it here a lot. First we were in Montreal, where we landed. But there wasn't any work there. . . . There's seven of us, I mean the kids. Seven counting me. Now my father has a farm up that way," she said, pointing over Leslie's shoulder, "but he works whenever he can at the sawmill. You must of seen the sawmill coming in, if you were on three . . . ? No? Anyway he works there and also my brother, the oldest one. And . . . uh. . . . There's nothing else to tell you," she giggled.

"You're from Poland, originally?"

She lowered her gaze; made an attempt to appear solemn. It might have been the sobering effect of that word *originally.* It sounded like an important word. "Yes. Warszawa," she said softly.

"Warszawa," Leslie repeated.

He wanted to take the girl's hands in his. He was quite moved, enchanted. But she might have misunderstood . . . might even have shoved him away. Anna was not so light-boned and fashionably docile as the women he knew back home.

"And so you like Canada very much," he repeated.

"Yeh, sure. Like I said, sure."

She sipped her beer. After a moment she sighed, shrugged her shoulders, and said in an undertone: "Well, it's okay. I mean some of the people are okay and some of them . . . well, you know. People are people anywhere." She glanced around; the tavern was nearly empty. They were sitting at a table in the rear of The Roadway Inn, a sad-looking place just outside Ashton. "What happened was, when we got to Canada there wasn't, you know, the right kind of understanding. See, my father came over here first. He was here for a few years. In Toronto. Then he came back to get us and it took a while, on account of some family problems . . . my grandmother was dying and, you know, we couldn't leave her . . . and . . . and when we got to Canada, I mean to Montreal, it was different because of, uh, something about the economy. Now, you know," she said, so sorrowfully that Leslie leaned forward, "my father could start his citizenship papers ahead of us. So he got to be a citizen before us. Then the rest of the family, even the little kids. . . . But when we got here I was twelve years old. I couldn't speak English, you know? Couldn't speak English. . . . At home they spoke Polish; they wouldn't speak English, even my father. So what happened was . . . I had to go to grade school with the little kids, I had to start first grade. First grade. I was twelve years old and had to sit at the back of the room with the little kids . . . and everybody hated me and laughed at me because I was so big . . . and. . . . So I hated them back," she whispered. "Sometimes I still do. I still hate them. Now it's supposed to be different, I read that somewhere, that people in Canada, I mean the regular people, don't laugh at foreigners like they used to, but anyway they did when I was a young girl and it got to the point that I wouldn't go to school but just stayed home with my mother and the little kids and wouldn't go out and . . . and I just hated them all."

"But you speak English perfectly now," Leslie said.

"Well, thanks. . . . I don't know," she said, shaking her head, "it just didn't seem right to me, to sit in first grade with the little kids. You know, the nuns didn't like me either and never were nice to me, until I got a little older and could speak English better . . . that was the whole thing," she said bitterly, "if you could speak English or not. My younger brother and my younger sisters, I got two younger sisters, they caught on faster than I did . . . and my brother Stefan, who's older than I am, he's twenty-three now, he was the worst of all, he dropped out of school when he was sixteen and was always cutting school before that, because kids laughed at him and the nuns were so damn nasty to him. It just didn't seem right to me, either, that the school put my brothers ahead of me, started them in third grade, and put me in first grade, just because they were boys. *It wasn't right.* They couldn't speak English any better than I could. But the school put them ahead because they were boys. It wasn't right—"

She was speaking rather passionately. Leslie tapped her arm, to get her off that unfortunate subject; he asked her if she wanted another beer. She stared at him, blankly. Another beer? Yes? Good.

". . . then we moved out to B.C. where we are now," the girl said slowly. "I don't know if I like it or not. I guess so. People come through, driving on trips, vacations, with them trailers . . . travel vans . . . whatever they are, must cost ten thousand dollars, some of that equipment; lots of Americans come through, back and forth, going camping at the glacier park, fishing, that kind of stuff. On account of the mountains, huh? It's pretty out here." She spoke mechanically, almost glibly, as if she had heard someone say that British Columbia was pretty; she had not discovered this fact for herself but certainly would not contest it. *Pretty.* "The farm isn't any good, just between you and me. I guess I'll go to Vancouver, maybe next year. I was sort of going to get married . . . but the plans were changed . . . anyway I got a close girl friend, her and I are planning to go to Vancouver, you know, get jobs there. . . . Not a job like the one I got now, either, but something better. The problem is, at the place where I work, there's so many local people coming in and the tourists don't even see the place or maybe don't want to stop in Ashton because the next town is bigger and more interesting . . . Cross Falls, that's a *lot* more interesting . . . so the people that live around here come in and don't leave tips, sometimes, or leave a dime or fifteen cents, they're so damn stingy. You wouldn't believe it. . . . People traveling from the east, like from far away like Ontario, now, they will tip better; but Americans are best of all." She looked at Leslie and smiled, embarrassed. "Like, mister, right now at the restaurant there's some certain people mad at me . . . you know why? Because every time you come in you're *my* customer. You come right over to *my* station. The first night when you and your wife came in, you know, the girls were all wondering . . . on account of your accent . . . and Beverly, that seated you, said for sure you were from New York City; so they all wanted to know how much you left me," she said, blushing. "I couldn't help but tell them. . . . I was kind of pleased, you know. It was a nice thought on your part. And like I said . . . well . . . the people around here don't leave much for us, sometimes they don't leave anything at all . . . like they're pretending, you know, they forgot about it. Cheap bastards. . . . So I couldn't help but tell them and they were real surprised, but nobody thought you would show up again the next day. And the day after. . . . Well, Christ. I mean, that just doesn't happen around here. So . . . so . . . anyway they're kind of mad at me, jealous, you know. But they'll get over it."

Leslie tried to smile. He felt obscurely deflated, insulted.

"There was an American driving through here all by himself, a few years ago," Anna said slowly, "before I went to work there, but they still talk about him . . . somebody thought he was Howard Hughes, you know, that millionaire? . . . that has something to do with Las Vegas, and some airlines? . . . well, this man was just driving through all alone, which is unusual, and it was August and lots of tourists on the road . . . and they seated him just anywhere, you know, because he was by himself, and sort of soft-spoken, that kind of man. And according to what they said afterward he left his waitress a twenty-dollar tip. A *twenty-dollar tip*."

Anna shook her head. Leslie could not think of any adequate response, so he fumbled in his pockets for a cigarette. Imagine, a twenty-dollar tip! . . . But, as if fearful of having offended him, the girl went on to say that probably such money didn't mean as much to a millionaire as it would to other people . . . probably not. . . . Leslie agreed. He mumbled something that sounded agreeable. Anna spoke dreamily of Vancouver, of the sister of a friend who was working there in a bank . . . of all the well-to-do people . . . Leslie thought it ironic that the girl should speak of millionaires and the "well-to-do" as if they were a species distinct from her own, and from his: Leslie Knox had earned well over a million dollars by his writing, though of course he hadn't much of it left after taxes. The amazing thing was that a million dollars could come rather quickly . . . once you began to soar beyond a certain point, say two hundred thousand dollars, the rest was not difficult, but seemed to happen by itself, according to inexplicable laws. . . . Leslie did not pretend to understand finances, of course. He had no interest in money. His income-tax returns and his accounts and investments and tax-loss projects were handled by tax lawyers whom he rarely saw, whose names he did not even know; these men were hired by his attorney, an excellent man employed by a number of American writers to deal with their snarled, heartbreaking financial problems. These writers—including Leslie—were as helpless and desperately credulous as children when it came to financial matters. Their I.Q.'s dropped to about sixty; they had to resist the urge to bow down before their attorneys, seizing their ankles, kissing their polished Italian shoes. . . .

No, no. He did not want to think about such things. No. He had offered to drive Anna home, had offered to buy Anna a drink . . . weeks ago, he had begged his wife to take this trip, a kind of "second honeymoon" (shameless, that Leslie Knox should resort to sentimental language!), in order to forget such things. Money, fame, love affairs. Fame, love affairs, money. Love affairs, loveless affairs. Money. Money: taxes. The more you earned the more you paid. The more you paid the more often you were audited. As for fame, what good did it do him tonight? . . in The Roadway Inn? Anna was patting her beautifully braided hair, sighing, dreaming wistfully of millionaires; Leslie was no more than a wraith, a kind anonymous "American" who had tipped her well and who had even bought her a few beers. Introducing himself to her, he had not even bothered to give a false name—Larry Fox was the absurd name he sometimes used—since he knew Anna would never have heard of him. His six novels, four of them best sellers and one of them an exceptional best seller—totally unknown, out here. Totally unknown to Anna. For some reason this endeared her to him; she struck him as precious. He did not want to think about the bland mess of his life. No, not at all. No. He did not want to think about Leslie Knox. . . . Was Sylvia still sleeping her drugged sleep back at the motel? Were his tax lawyers telephoning his attorney with "unforseen" news? Was another ex-beloved threatening to sue him, claiming that a certain character in his most recent novel was based upon her? No, he did not want to think about such things.

Anna smiled at him. He forgot whatever he had been thinking about.

She lived in a single room above *Heinmann Bros. Hunting & Fishing Equipment:* a meager little store with a dusty window, behind which a life-size dummy, a male, stood with a fishing rod in one hand and a net in the other. He wore thigh-high rubber boots and what looked like a white cap. . . . Leslie made a joke of some kind. Driving back through the darkened, empty streets of downtown Ashton, he had made several humorous comments . . . at least he had meant them to be humorous . . . imagining the girl to be uncomfortable. But what could one say about Ashton that did not turn out to be ironic rather than amusing? A school that looked like a small prison. A post office. A single movie house where *The Aristocats*—a Disney movie of many years back—was playing, evidently on weekends only, since the theater was darkened. The radio-TV appliance store. The pharmacy, with an enormous red leaf embossed on its sign—must be a maple leaf? —symbol of Canada? "A nice, quiet town," Leslie murmured.

The girl made a noise that might have been a snicker, or an assent.

Her room: the first thing he noticed was her mirror, above a chest of drawers. Snapshots stuck into its frame, quite a number of them. Some in color, some black and white. Some evidently quite old—yellowed and curling. But he drew back from the mirror, not wanting to catch sight of himself. Jesus, if he looked as degenerate and unraveled as he felt. . . . Unfortunate, that overhead light. But there was a bedside light; he turned that on. Orange-pink lampshade, with gold tassels. Dust on the lampshade. He muttered something about bright lights hurting his eyes. . . . Anna switched off the overhead light.

She turned on the radio.

"Do you want that on?" Leslie asked, shocked.

She stared at him. "I always turn this on. . . . What's wrong? It's nice to have it on, kind of low. Like this. I come back here and make some hot chocolate and go to bed and have the radio on, you know, like company. It's a Vancouver station; they play some good records."

"All right," Leslie said.

He had begun to get a little angry; which was good, good. Otherwise he might have yawned and walked away. The secret disaster that might overtake him someday was simple apathy— but it would not get him tonight, not tonight. He was irritated with the girl, his voice had sounded almost coarse, grudging. That was good, wasn't it. . . . Must be. Any feeling at all must be good. . . . She was chattering away, making coffee at a tiny two-burner gas stove, telling him about a girl friend . . . about an older brother who worked in the Arctic . . . about her ex-fiancé." You've had a hard life," Leslie said sympathetically. She shrugged her shoulders and turned to look at him. A grimace. In that position, her chin bunched against her shoulder, she did not appear to be beautiful, or even very young. A peasant girl. A cleaning woman.

But she smiled at him as if grateful for his remark. "Well, yeh. It was my boy friend—what happened with him—last year— It was that part of it that was bad, you know; I was going to have a baby and we were going to get married and then something happened, I had a miscarriage or maybe it was a mistake and I was never pregnant . . . I don't know and I'm so sick of arguing about it . . . and it turned out his mother was the one pushing him into it, because she was so ashamed, and . . . and he didn't want to get married . . . but he said he loved me . . . and, and well . . . well, it was a bad time for me; but I'll get over it. That's what everybody says."

Leslie went to her. He touched her arm, then gripped her shoulders with both hands. She was nearly as tall as he: must be five feet eight or nine. She stepped backward, clumsy. Surprised.

"Don't you like me?" Leslie heard himself saying.

A voice that was a whine, pleading. *Don't you like me?* My God. Would hear that voice the rest of his life, jeering at him.

Anna was too surprised to protest. He saw her expression alter, crudely. She felt sorry for him; she was embarrassed; she would now try to be polite. Should he kiss her? . . . She blushed, tried to smile. Her teeth were strong-looking, even, white. Ah, that was good. Such a fine healthy sane girl: full-bodied, long thick blond hair that would probably fall below her waist, beautiful eyes, mouth. He did kiss her. She stood there obediently; then, as if an instinct overtook her, she lurched out of his embrace and brought her arm up, against his face. . . . What! The surprise of it, the stinging pain! Leslie was astonished. For a moment he couldn't see. He touched his nose, wiped it; his fingers were dripping bright-red blood.

"Oh my God, I'm sorry," the girl cried. "Oh my God. Oh Jesus. I didn't mean it . . . what happened? . . . oh my God, oh dear, oh. . . . Is it broken? Is your nose broken? Oh Mr. Knox, oh please forgive me . . . oh, oh this is awful . . . I don't know what happens to me . . . I just go sort of wild and . . . and hit guys like that . . . guys I even *like*. . . . Oh Mr. Knox, it isn't broken, is it? What will your wife say? . . . There's some Kleenex over there, and maybe if you run cold water . . . oh, thank God it isn't broken . . . oh I'm so sorry, so *sorry*. . . .

She was half sobbing. Really frightened: maybe she believed he might have her arrested. A warm, big-boned, marvelous girl. . . . He allowed her to dab at his nose with Kleenex: allowed her to fuss over him, to comfort him. How kindly she was, and how ignoble he was! But he loved her. He was weak with love for her. The nosebleed was nothing. The pain was gone, now a sensation of numbness, a vague tickle. . . . He would survive. Blood had splattered on his shirt front, his hands were sticky with blood, but he would survive. Something like this had happened many years ago, in fact. Leslie Knox as a boy of eighteen: gawky, acne-skinned, underweight. A nosebleed at someone's house, a party, high-school graduation party, people giggling at him, a girl giggling and rolling her eyes. *Leslie, you're so clumsy.* Well, other girls had paid for that remark: had paid dearly. Had paid many times over, with interest. Eventually he would have negated all the women in the world, simply by conquering them: and then he would be free. But not tonight.

Seven o'clock. A cold morning. Leslie parked a few doors down from their motel room, in order not to wake Sylvia. The motel hadn't done much business last night—only a few cars. He tried to open the door as quietly as possible, but Sylvia was awake. "Oh hello," she said. She was awake; just returning from the bathroom, where she had evidently showered. Her hair in a big white towel. Face shiny, eyes big, shrewd. . . . Awake, his wife: and staring at him, at his unshaven ghastly face and his blood-speckled shirt. She bent forward suddenly and he thought—my God!—she was going to faint. But no. No, she was merely toweling her hair, drying it. She said nothing at all.

"I'm glad . . . glad . . . glad to see you're better now," Leslie whispered.

"Of course I'm better," she said. "Didn't I tell you?"

She straightened. Drew the towel away, shook her hair out. It looked surprisingly thin. Short, dark hair. And her face was so shiny, as if she'd scrubbed it. . . . She went to Leslie and kissed him dryly. He could not judge the meaning of the kiss: forgiveness? affection? indifference?

They checked out of the Five-Star Motor Hotel; did not linger in Ashton, not even for breakfast. Leslie was driving, anxious to escape. It was a clear, chilly day: the sky postcard blue, the mountains superb. Sylvia was humming to herself. She had not questioned him at all. Had not even alluded to what he had done, in her usual deft, ironic voice. . . . Beautiful scenery, wasn't it? The trip had almost been worth it. Beautiful day for driving. Fortunate for them, wasn't it, that the border was so near, less than an hour's drive? They were both curiously eager to get back. "I'm glad we didn't bother to drive any farther north," Sylvia said. "I've seen all of Canada I care to see."

Leslie was trying to remember what he had promised the girl. Surely not marriage? No. He hadn't been that deranged. Not marriage—not even money, for that would have insulted her, hurt her feelings—but hadn't he promised her something? Maybe to see her again that evening. He could not exactly remember though he supposed he would remember eventually . . . might even work her into a story or a novel somehow, someday. But at the moment he could not remember what he had said. It was all falling away, fading away behind him.

The customs official at Gold Creek, Idaho, was a portly old gentleman who only glanced into the back seat of their car at the luggage and loose clothing. He did not even ask Leslie to unlock the trunk. Nice man. A few perfunctory questions. No trouble, no rudeness.

"Anything to declare?"

No, nothing.

"Any goods acquired, any merchandise . . . gifts. . . ."

No. Nothing.

*T*he Tempter

Last Tuesday he made his first appearance in seventeen years; there he was, waiting for me by the MacArthur Street bridge, just standing there waiting. Staring and smiling. The bridge there is only a wooden footbridge that runs along the railroad, and if a train goes by while you're on the footbridge it's very noisy and everything shakes. Used to frighten me, but no more. I just laugh. When you get a certain age the old things don't frighten you any longer, you just laugh at them, try to remember whatever frightened you about them—what power they had over you—but you can't even remember, it's lost. So there he was, trying to smile at me.

It wasn't me, but him. Made the first gesture. Made it with one hand, a feeble, embarrassed swing of the hand. Hello! . . . Was wearing gloves, shiny brown leather or maybe it was imitation leather, but why would anyone wear gloves in April? It wasn't cold that day. Could see him lick his lips before he started talking. Sickly-white. Scarecrow. Wasn't fooling me, with his expensive-looking clothes—a black-and-white checked jacket with narrow lapels, a white shirt that looked fresh, small black bow tie like nobody wears except some of the salesmen downtown or the bank clerks. And black trousers with a sharp crease that fell almost straight down, not wrinkled. His knees must have been no more than knobs, you see. Skinny. He didn't fool me for a minute, Had wire-rimmed glasses and the lenses were tinted blue. Lots of wrinkles spreading out from those lenses, X's that crossed and crisscrossed, and his neck was flabby, too, with many lines cut into the flesh, and that Adam's apple of his—hardly changed at all. The sight of him was like somebody shoving you in a crowd, jamming his elbow into your back, but if you're strong you don't show what you feel, only glance around, calm. Anyway, he didn't fool me for a minute.

He walked alongside me, across the footbridge. Talking. Trying to talk. Asking a few questions about the family like he wasn't afraid to ask them or afraid of the answers. I was hoping a train would come by—he hated this route—never went downtown by this route—frightened of the way you can see the river through the boards you're walking on, hundreds of feet below, and frightened of the possibility of a train, though of course would never admit it. He didn't lie, you couldn't call him a liar. Not a liar. There is no word for him: somebody who doesn't tell the truth but doesn't lie either. Just manages not to say anything you can hang onto and use against him. . . . Gulls flying around us. Herring gulls with white heads and silvery backs. Must be a hundred of them, a real mob. But they're not noisy and don't skim against your face like pigeons. They dive down into the water to get garbage or dead fish or whatever is down there, lapping up against the sides of the canal. It smells bad in certain places.

He said: . . . what's that smell along here? . . . something dead in the water?

I didn't bother answering.

He walked with me to the hardware store. Had to get some light bulbs, sixty-five-watt and a hundred-watt. It was Miller's Hardware, but with the new shiny-white façade I don't think he recognized it. Just stood there trying to keep his poise, his eyes hidden behind those stupid blue glasses, while I made my purchases, waited on by a young man who seemed in a hurry and had a cigarette in his mouth all the while. Hardly bothered to look at me or at him. What good does the fancy outfit do, or the skinny shoulders held so straight?—lots of people don't bother to look at you anyway. Then to the Chippewa for meat and groceries. Meat-market wasn't crowded today, I didn't have to take one of those plastic numbers. He was asking me did I live alone or was my sister with me now or was Jamie there . . . but I just shrugged my shoulders. Bought two pounds of ground round steak, very expensive for what it is. Just hamburger. Bought some chicken gizzards and necks for the cats. Was going to buy some liver, but it was too expensive—was afraid he could read my mind, would offer to pay for it—but he must have seen how closed-up my face was, my lips pressed hard together. He didn't dare speak. The butcher just glanced at him or maybe didn't even glance at him, must have known we were together because he didn't say *Are you next?* Just ignored him.

Got some bread. And a quart container of skim milk. And wanted some lettuce but the heads were so small, the outer leaves already brown, and so expensive—forty-nine cents—for hardly more than something the size of your fist! He followed me along. Offered to carry the things or maybe push a cart, but I told him I only needed a few things, never mind about the cart, I went shopping every day to get fresh things. Bought three little pies, a quarter each, one cherry and one apple and one pineapple. He said something about a picnic at Waterberry Park, did I remember, something about Uncle Clement eating a pie all by himself, did I remember him being sick leaning over the drop-off to the river, but I shrugged my shoulders. Said I didn't remember.

Lots of Easter candy by the cashier. Marked down. Big chocolate eggs with pink-and-white frosting on them, looked like toothpaste. Bunnies big as my arm, that waxy cheap chocolate, a rabbit that had been two ninety-eight marked down to ninety-nine cents, inside an Easter basket with green cellophane grass and lots of little eggs like plastic balls. I had to laugh. It was just a few weeks ago in my mind that the Christmas junk was marked down and a few weeks before that the Hallowe'en junk. I wasn't having any. He tried to make a joke, asking me did I want that big bunny?— but I pretended not to hear.

Outside it was sunny for a change. Only eleven-thirty, but the junior high was recessed already; three or four girls ran past us, in their short skirts, giggling, showing off for anybody who cared to watch. But he didn't even glance at them. Didn't notice them. . . . Forgive me? . . . he was whispering.

I kept on walking. Headed uptown now, up that hill from the Chippewa to Main Street. I knew it was something he would be wanting, money or a place to stay or goddamn tears like all of them, they always wanted something. A coincidence that he should mention Uncle Clement, who was the worst of all if you looked at it from a certain angle.

He said he knew he didn't deserve to be forgiven. But. . . .

I was heading home the long way around, to the Harrow Street bridge. Always took this route. Made a kind of stretched-out circle. Especially when it was sunny I enjoyed this walk; my legs are stronger than they look. And I am stronger too. Three operations in four years and I do my own shopping and housework and there's no problem except sometimes shortness of breath, the doctor said it was high blood pressure but what does he know?—his own father dropped dead one day at the hospital, supposed to be the leading doctor in the city and look what happened to him. Dropped dead. It was in the newspaper, "exact cause of death unknown." I had to laugh even though I liked the old man. Because the exact cause of death is always unknown. They just make up something to fill in the blank on the death certificate. _____ is there and they fill in the blank. Anybody could do it.

He said I was looking good. Was my health good, he asked. I said my health was my own business.

We were passing the Metropolitan Five & Dime but I didn't want to go in. Sometimes I browse around, for something to do. Maybe buy something—a spool of thread or some thumbtacks. But I didn't want to go in because he'd follow me and people would see us together; there's Mrs. Chesney who lives a few houses from me, works at the candy counter and would notice who was with me and would ask all kinds of questions, a nosy woman, so I walked by the Five & Dime and didn't even pause by the big show-windows of Marcus Department Store that I like to look into most days. And he followed me. Kept alongside me. Asking more questions, but in a frail voice now, like he's caught on; knows there won't be any answers.

How is Dan? . . . Jimmy Glover? . . . Bessie?

I walked at my usual pace. Did not quicken my step, did not slow down. Might have been my imagination but I thought I could see how his left foot dragged. . . . We passed the King Wah Chinese Restaurant, which I have never stepped inside and never will. Restaurant food is just garbage. You can't trust any of them. Passed Velko's Barber Shop, where Jamie had his hair cut when in town. And the Lacey Sisters Dress Shop, never opened for business after Agnes Lacey had a stroke. And a florist's squeezed in between Kresge's and a Revco drugstore where Easter lilies and mums and tulips were for sale, marked down. Big shiny satin bows around the pots. . . . He asked me did I want some flowers or a corsage, maybe, and I made a noise like laughing and said no. No thanks. . . . Did anybody think I was going to start crying? . . . and the two of us would start crying right on Main Street? Like hell.

There were big wreaths and things called "grave blankets" for sale, too, in the window. I almost said to him, why not buy a wreath for my mother's grave, but kept my mouth shut. . . . We passed the Embassy Hotel where the reception had been held, also Janice's and Rosemary's receptions, a long time ago and things tend to get mixed up, like things in a junk drawer. There's no harm in things getting mixed up. Life is easier that way. Why should he come back to Rockland, why should he be waving his gloved hands around so nervous and pitiful . . . so that my skin was starting to prickle. Especially on the back of my neck. Like when there is a noise in the house at night and I just lie there, so helpless; and half blind too, without my glasses.

The Canal Street Bar & Grill: twin plants in the window, same as always, with leaves like spears. Very dusty. He asked me did I want a drink, just one drink. I looked at him: was surprised to see how runny-eyed he was, you could see through the blue lenses if you stood close to him. And that dead-white skin. Looked fifteen years older than he should have looked. I could smell something strange about him—mint?—mouthwash?—something metallic yet like ashes. Should have told him no thanks again. But we ended up in the tavern, at the bar. A beer for me, an ale for him. Bob Swanson's boy was tending bar but didn't recognize us. Fat-bellied, going bald, though he wasn't much more than forty. Had Bob Swanson's face but not his friendly manner. The television set was on fairly loud. A daytime show, people giggling and applauding. . . . He was leaning against the bar, maybe tired, telling me about how he lived in Des Moines then Seattle then Vancouver then took a chance, went to Nome, Alaska . . . signed on for trucking . . . then there was a union dispute, some tires shot out, maybe I had read about it? . . . years ago. I shook my head. No, couldn't remember, couldn't remember. What the hell did I care. There was news coming on the television right now, the noon round-up it was called, and what the hell did I care or anybody in the bar care; Bob Swanson's boy switched the channel from some man saying "Holiday Traffic Deaths All-Time High" to the electric bingo show. . . . Well, he said, he had gotten mixed up in it and somebody turned state's evidence and a few men were sent to prison; it was just bad luck.

Now do you think this surprised me? It did not.

. . . Is Bessie alive? He asked that suddenly, as if trying to surprise me. Or maybe he had not known he would ask it.

I told him no, what the hell did he think? . . . people lived forever? Aunt Bessie was sixty-two when he left, he knew that. What did he expect? He leaned toward me and cupped his hand

to his ear. Must be going deaf. Maybe senile. His jowls wobbled
as if shivering. *What the hell do you expect, people live forever
waiting for you?* . . . There was a table of young men, probably
workers from Ford's, laid off. They were having a good time, laughing, ordering more beer. One of them was pretty drunk, though
it was only noon. He had dark curly hair like Jamie and I was
uneasy for a moment, thinking it could almost be him, and there'd
be a fight. But of course it couldn't be him. That was not possible.
. . . Anyway, Jamie was older than that man.

Now he was whispering to me. Would I forgive him? He was
sorry. He had been sorry for years. In prison, so much time to
think. In the prison hospital. There were lots of men his age
there, all of them far from home, and sorry. Jesus, were they
sorry. They wanted to get out and go back home and. . . . But
I didn't say anything. I sipped at the beer. He wasn't drinking
his ale, but was leaning toward me and whispering. I wanted to
push him away because of the smell; the smell was his breath.
But I could not touch him. I thought: if he touched me I would
start to scream. I would scream and scream. But he knew better,
he just hovered by me and kept adjusting his glasses and trying
to smile, showing his ceramic teeth, so perfect you would want
to laugh at them. I was afraid I might laugh. I might laugh or
scream or start slapping him. I didn't know what would happen,
especially with the bingo program and that funny spiraling music
they have, like a siren; it makes you think you're going crazy.

He said that some men got religious again. Cried and moaned
for Jesus. Really. You could never tell who it might hit—Sundays
and Wednesdays—prayer meetings. But he hadn't succumbed. It
hadn't happened to him, just hadn't happened. He didn't know
whether to believe the other men or not—maybe they were lying.
. . . Would I forgive him? he whispered again.

I had nowhere to look but the television screen. My skin was
all jagged. It was like goose-pimples frozen in place. I thought that
if he touched me I would start to scream. Forgive? Forgive him?
. . . He went on, embarrassed, something about a lump under
his arm . . . eighteen months ago . . . and he went to be ex-

amined and the doctor said . . . and the doctor arranged . . . and there was a preliminary operation or whatever they called it . . . and. . . . And he was dying, that was the news. Dying. At first he had not believed it because he just didn't believe doctors, he knew of too many times they were wrong, but after a while he knew it was true because he could feel himself dying. Said he could feel himself dying.

What does it have to do with me? I put the glass down, couldn't finish it. What does any of it have to do with me? But I was beginning to tremble, could feel the trembling begin inside me. O Lord. Jesus. Wanted to yell at him, what does it have to do with me?—why are you here?—why didn't you die out West or up in Alaska or wherever you escaped to? Instead I heard my voice talking to him. It was going fast. The words came along without pause, flat and quick as if I knew ahead of time what I was going to say, but I didn't know. . . . Jamie living with some woman down by Crescent Beach. Two small kids, she had. Husband gone. Lived in a big expensive trailer up on blocks, a trailer court. They got along okay. A little drinking but not too bad. Jamie not working right now. . . . Suellen went to Cleveland, years ago. Probably married. Never saw the grandchildren, no. What the hell. It was a long time ago. Clement and Royal and Adelaide fought over the will—he knew about that, didn't he?—yes. They all got lawyers. One of the lawyers was from out of town, said to be very good, expensive; but he didn't seem too especially bright. Real nasty things said. Case dragged on for three years. Royal claimed he had done repair work and carpentering for the old lady for twenty-five years, unpaid services. What a liar! . . . They all lied. Or maybe they told the truth as they saw it, getting so angry they invented things and then believed them. You know how Uncle Clement always was. Anyway, the lawyers got one-third of it all. . . . Then Clement came over one Christmas Eve with his daughter that had the leg-brace, and he was drunk and crying and Adelaide wouldn't come out of the kitchen for a while, then she came out, then they made up and telephoned Royal and he came over so by midnight they were made up again and there was old Aunt Adie, two-hundred-fifty pounds, her face wet with tears and blushes in spots, like measles. Then we all played gin rummy until two in the morning . . . finished up the leftovers from dinner . . . they were all giggling and crying from time to time, like children. They played gin rummy their own special way, according to their own rules, as they had when they were children together at the old place, the farm. . . . He was listening hard to this, his breath sucked in. I was afraid he would grab hold of my arm and bury his face in my neck . . . I was afraid he would start to cry and I might not be able to stand back from him, I might give in. . . . Clement? Royal? Aelaide? Bessie? Jamie? . . . Were they still . . . ? Could he . . . ? It wasn't too late, was it, for him to see them . . . ? It wasn't too late . . . ?

Things worked out in the end, he said. He knew it now. He had faith in it now. When he was young, he hadn't known— hadn't known anything. But now he knew. Things worked out and came to a happy ending, all the arguments faded away, it was meant to happen before people died . . . somebody at the prison had told him that, a very religious man, eighty years old. A lifer. Judge sentenced him for three hundred years plus life forty years ago and there he was, still in jail and didn't even care for parole, wouldn't apply for it, said he had made his peace and was just waiting to die and anyway his loved ones were all scattered and dead so there was no point in living beyond them. . . . Things worked out in the end. It did not matter how.

I felt lightheaded. The shakiness was inside me, in my stomach and lower chest. I got away from him . . . went back to the ladies' room . . . the same deep-pink walls I remembered from a long time ago, except now they're quite dirty, lipstick scrawls, eyebrow-pencil scrawls . . . drawings of nasty things. I had to get away from him. He was so powerful, leaning against me. And his voice. And even his breath. It was like something hypnotic. . . . I ran a little water, but it came out tepid. The sink was filthy. Hairs in it, crumpled-up tissues. It never used to be so dirty here, I would swear; never used to smell so bad. . . . Sickening. If I gave a damn, which I did not, I'd tell Bob Swanson's boy about the conditions back here. But why waste my breath, what did I care? Not my business. I'd never come back, neither of us would come back to the tavern. It was too late. In the mirror I noticed my own face but wasn't much concerned about it. Too late?—too old? You get to the point where you don't give a damn, not because you're angry or even tired, but because you're free of all the crap around you and free of the people around you, whether they show up streaming tears or begging you for favors or dying on their feet, their breaths stinking poison. . . . The shakiness was going away. I was going to be all right. I soaked some paper napkins and dabbed them against my face, careful to lean far over the sink so I didn't get the front of my coat spotted. Face was burning. Cheeks red-hot. High blood pressure, he said, warning me. My grandmother used to say *Six of one and half-a-dozen of another.* If you don't die of one thing, you die of something else.

It stank so much in there, I hurried out. Went back to where he was leaning against the bar. Touched his arm, just touched it lightly. Good-bye. I was over the dizziness and all right again, just needed some fresh air; I told him good-bye. Started out of the tavern. He caught up with me. Mumbled something more about dying . . . didn't I know he was dying . . . didn't I understand what he had been saying. . . . He was dying and he wanted me to forgive him. He had come nine hundred miles. He wanted . . . wanted his wife to forgive him. . . . Now I was getting tired of this. My face was so hot, maybe I had been angry all along without knowing it. Should I forget seventeen years of my life, should I lie to myself about how I hated him and how sick I was with hatred for him, should I erase it all, should I give in just because of some bastard telling me lies . . . breathing poison into my face . . . telling me stories about a stranger who took a Greyhound out West and ended up in Alaska and then in prison and was now dying on his feet, a scarecrow swaying beside me, as if everybody didn't die, tempting me to go back on my own self?

But I walked out of the tavern without another word. Left him there. It was sunny outside, which confused me a little, because I remembered the weather being dark and chilly . . . hadn't it been raining? . . . but it was spring out now, you could smell it in the air. Spring. Warm weather. You could smell it even downtown, with all the exhaust from the cars and buses. Somehow I remembered it being cold, like winter, but I must have been mixed up. Obviously it was spring.

I went back home across the Canal Street bridge. Felt good. The fresh air was good. Old men were feeding pigeons on the bridge, on the wide walk. The pigeons scattered when I went by but flew only a few yards, then landed again. Nothing scared them. I said hello to the old men, same as always, though I didn't exactly recognize them. Some were my age and some were very old. A few were the age my father would be if he was living. . . . They had names and we all knew one another all right if we stopped to puzzle it out. But why fuss? After I walked by, the pigeons filled in again and pecked at the bread crumbs; nothing scared them for long.

R*iver Rising*

Dear Karl:
   I think that the decision we reached together is a wise one.
As you can imagine, I have been hearing again and again certain
conversations of ours . . . certain parts of conversations . . . and
I do agree that, though we love each other very much, it is a
good idea for. . . . I seem to feel the necessity for us not even
to continue to see each other as friends, occasionally, because
of. . . . The basic decision is a wise one. . . . Your children and
of course your. . . . I did not mean to give you the impression
that there was anything seriously wrong in my marriage, but
as I suppose you can imagine there is tension between . . . there
are occasional arguments, outbursts . . . misunderstandings.
Complicating the relationship is. . . . I think that the decision
we reached together last Friday is very wise and sane and certainly
for the best, considering our commitments to other people, and
as long as you have the opportunity to take advantage of a move
to the West Coast I think that. . . . I try to imagine myself with
you but have difficulty, I have difficulty seeing us as a couple, in

the street, in daylight in the street . . . having difficulty somehow
hearing us speak to other people, as a couple, as couples do.
Married couples. . . . The decision was far more sane than. . . .
The possibility that. . . . A few times Evan and I have come close
to. . . . Once things are said of course they cannot be unsaid.
You know that of course . . . you have been married much
longer . . . you know from experience . . . sharing, bitterness,
anger, broken dishes, a chair fallen over backwards from the table
and your wife threatening you with harm to one of the . . .
which I fully believe her capable of, in spite of . . . of appearances
to the contrary. . . . Yes, I think that the decision we reached
was the inevitable one, and looking back I. . . . The future is
not so complicated as the past, and once things are straightened
out here. . . . We did not know each other well: perhaps we
could write, after a while, after you are settled out there, and
come to see how what happened was inevitable. . . . Your claim
that I seemed to you unmoved is based on misunderstanding . . .
I have never been one to . . . even as a child I made every effort
to . . . now I am usually in control of . . . though there are
occasional breakdowns, temporary of course, hidden and shameful
because I lack that spontaneity that. . . . Our meeting by accident yesterday made me realize that more must be said, our
conversations must continue, even if the subject is no more
than an intellectual grasp of what. . . . I sensed that you . . .
that I . . . that we. . . . I did not mean to give the impression
that. . . . I think the decision is so sane, so wise, and certainly
did not mean to give the impression that. . . . I . . . I . . .
I. . . .

Then the words ballooned suddenly into patches, star bursts, and
a face bobbed weightless in one corner of her eye, while another,
that of a plump, pale stranger, sailed in out of the darkness; behind them an immense greenish wave; and through the giddy
silence an impression of furious waves of music, beating and throbbing and plunging in layers . . . layers upon layers upon. . . .

"What is it? What is that?"

She was awake now.

Her voice woke Evan, who sat up at once. They said nothing,
listening to the wind, to the lapping of waves. Then both spoke
at once. Renée said, "The river—" and Evan said, "But I thought
it—"

The crashing of waves, usually distant, rather melancholy and romantic, was very loud. And it was still raining, even more heavily than it had been around midnight; and they could feel the wind, driving itself out of the northeast, across the lake and the river, against their house.

"My God," Renée whispered. But she was not frightened: her voice was not frightened at all.

"Don't be silly," Evan said.

November. The first storm of the year.

Rain had begun just after eight, pelting against the windows at the rear of the house. At first it had sounded like hail. The sky darkened, there were flashes of lightning in the distance, across the river; but the thunderclaps were remote. Renée recalled storms from her childhood, storms during the summer in Maine, offshore squalls, bursts of lightning, beauty and terror and. . . . Small craft driven to shore, occasionally swamped. Occasionally there were serious accidents. Near-drownings. Drownings. Deaths.

But it had seemed to be dying down, after ten. They listened to the local radio station, they comforted each other with repeating the announcer's prediction that the worst of the storm was over, that sleet mixed with rain and winds "of hurricane force" were now moving up into the Georgian Bay area. . . . Renée had even felt a little ashamed, to be grateful for this news; the odd, ungovernable sensation of relief, of actual optimism, she felt when hearing of a plane crash shortly before she or someone she knew was about to fly somewhere—disaster had already happened, it could not happen again so soon. But her shame, her gratitude, had both been premature.

Now it was 2:30 A.M. They could see waves in the back yard, they could see waves at least three or four feet high, and whitecaps, they could see water from where they stood, close together, like children, in the kitchen of their little house. Water? The river? Visible from here, at night? It did not seem possible. Yet they could see it . . . could see actual waves, lapping in the back yard, the familiar terrain of the back yard suddenly changed, a new landscape, remorselessly alive. "I thought that—At midnight it—" Evan said. His voice showed surprise, dismay, reproach. They had been alarmed for a while, and then they had been comforted; they had gone to bed, had fallen asleep hearing the rain, hearing the wind in the poplars, in the partly dismantled dead elm, hearing it seem to withdraw, to dissipate itself. Then they had been awakened by the wind again. A moaning, whining, throbbing, beating, pounding impossible noise. Earlier, the storm had sometimes looked beautiful: flashes of silent lightning, miles away, across the border and in another country. Beauty to it, the beauty of distance. Now everything was up close. The churning waves, the noise, the lapping, the beating . . . no longer rhythmic, no longer pulsed, contained. "Do you think—Is it really going to—Evan, is it really going to—"

He turned on the radio. At once they were in the middle of a conversation, two men earnestly speaking, vying with each other to both convey and suppress excited alarm. "—and for the residents of the area bounded by the river on the north and, what was it —Caledonia on the—" "Caledonia on the east, yes, and Pelee Boulevard on the—" "—on the west—" "—as far down as—" "—that would be, uh, on this map it would be—" "—emergency crews are now helping to evacuate home owners on the lake— residents in the area of St. Anne's parish—the district bordered by Matthew Brady Elementary School on the—" "Excuse me, Bill, there's a special announcement from the—" "The Royal Mounted Police have issued requests that—a request specifically for people to remain in their homes unless—Can you get that telephone, please? The telephones are ringing like mad here tonight—" "Folks at home, the Mounties are advising to *stay put* unless your home is in danger of flooding—the latest bulletin—flooding along Pelee Boulevard with the possibility of—There are several cars stalled— What is this word? Manx? Marx? Mahr?"—"the Genesee Overpass—" "Emergency volunteer workers at St. Anne's parish hall are requested to confine their rescue operations to the area bounded by Caledonia on the east and Pelee on the—" "It's of utmost importance, it can't be stressed too much, folks, the Mounties and the city police are adamant about this, to stay put at home and off the streets many of which are blocked because of stalled traffic—here is Dan Baker of the Ontario Provincial Police with a—"

Evan turned the dial, but got only static, then dim, querulous voices, like birds' cries; then rock music and more static. He was strangely calm, standing there in the kitchen, his lips pursed, his pale narrow feet close together on the linoleum floor. "Why did you—You'd better turn it—" Renée said. He turned the dial back, and now another voice, a man's voice was speaking quite sternly. *A need not to panic. To stay put. In cases where there is basement flooding . . . in cases where there is the probability of being washed out . . . along the lake, north of the general area of Lineham. . . .*

"That's miles north of here," Evan said.

"Where? Lineham . . . Are you sure? Do you know Where. . . .?"

"Lineham is north of here, three or four miles. . . ."

"Should I telephone? Who should I telephone?"

He did not hear her question. He stood in his pajamas, bent over the radio, his head inclined slightly to one side. Renée found herself walking into the bedroom. She was saying aloud: "Now where is. . . . Where did I. . . . If we could. . . ." Her hand switched on the overhead light, and the room was revealed rather harshly. Eggshell walls, scuffed behind the bed; a ceiling of queer striped wallpaper, off-white and silver. The carpeting, of course, was filthy. It was not their fault, they hoped to find another place, they had fully intended to be living elsewhere by now, but the rentals were so scarce and so expensive and. . . . She was taking one of their suitcases down from the closet shelf. A summer nightgown of hers was tangled with it and fell about her feet. She said aloud: "No, I don't need that. I have one on. This one . . . flannel . . . this is warm, warmer, and in case of. . . . Evan? Evan? What do you want me to pack of yours?"

He shouted something inaudible.

She lay the suitcase atop the rumpled bed. She opened the top drawer of the bureau and began to transfer Evan's socks to the suitcase . . . at first in their neat, bunched pairs, then in handfuls. Evan was saying something, from the kitchen. "I can't hear you, the wind is too loud. I can't hear you," she cried. The drawer was empty. She opened the next drawer, filled with her underwear. She stopped to think, tried to remember. "The telephone," she whispered. She had been going to use the telephone. She let her things fall back into the drawer and hurried, still barefoot, out into the tiny foyer where the telephone stand was; but it was dark, she bumped into a chair. Evan was asking her something. She squatted, got the telephone book out of the place where it was kept, turned on the light with her elbow, felt a surprising shock there, hadn't known she was so sensitive. Evan was behind her now. "Should I call the police?" she said. "Who should I call?"

"Better let me call," he said.

"No, it's all right. What did they say on the radio?"

"Dial the operator."

"I've started to pack—"

"Here, let me—"

He reached to take the telephone book from her, but it slid away, fell onto her bare toes. She cried aloud. "Jesus, I'm sorry," Evan muttered. He was leafing through the book hurriedly; Renée knew that the information he wanted was at the front, on the inside cover, but something in his manner intimidated her. He seemed very angry. He was murmuring to himself: "What the hell. . . . Now where is. . . ." Finally he gave it back to her. He grinned, ran a hand through his disheveled hair. "I'll check the radio," he said.

She dialed the emergency number for the police, but the line was busy.

She dialed the emergency number for fire, but the line was busy.

From the other room Evan called to her. She let the book fall and ran into the kitchen. "Oh my God," she whispered.

An enormous log had been wedged in one of the forsythia bushes out back—propelled by the water, now jammed in place. How far away was it? Renée could not judge. Ten feet? Twenty?

The waves were higher than before. It was possible to see how the wind from the northeast was fanning them higher, even higher. "I think we should leave," Renée said. "I think . . . before the driveway is flooded. . . . What if the driveway is flooded, Evan, and the car won't start?"

"The size of that log! Jesus! What if it had been. . . . Do you see that, Renée? It's part of a wharf. Someone's wharf from up river. Or maybe it's part of a boat . . . what is it? Over by the hedge there. . . ."

"What if the Volkswagen won't start? The engine—the motor—what if it gets wet, a car motor won't start, will it?—if it gets wet?"

"I don't think we're in any danger."

"What did the radio say?"

"I really don't think. . . . Look, that's part of a boat, isn't it? You can see the hull. . . . It must be terrible for people who live on the lake; my God, their houses will be flooded, they might be in danger of. . . . There was an announcement about evacuees being welcome at one of the firehouse stations. And they need volunteers, they need blankets and coffee, that sort of thing. . . . I think we'll be all right. I don't think the water will get any higher."

"Did the radio say. . . ."

"Look, the log is moving . . . no, it's stuck. What an enormous thing. . . ."

Renée listened: someone was announcing the time, the weather conditions, the situation on the lake and the river ("water rising in some areas as quickly as a foot an hour"). Then there was music. Incredible. Music.

"Evan, it said the river was rising. I think we should prepare to evacuate."

"Honey, don't be so nervous. Don't talk so fast."

"I wasn't talking fast, I. . . . Did you hear what that announcer said? I was doing something in the other room, I'd better get back to it, maybe you should . . . maybe you should check the car, see if the car is working. Maybe we should change our clothes."

"It isn't that serious. The flooding is north of here, miles north of here."

"If we don't leave in time the roads will be flooded. It said something about stalled traffic, and. . . ."

"Those people dramatize everything," Evan said vaguely. He was standing on his toes, staring out at the water. His expression was both alert and abstract, as if he were looking a considerable distance. ". . . that radio station is notorious . . . false alarms, catastrophes, bad news every hour. . . ."

Renée backed away. She meant to do something urgent. Was it the telephone, or something in the bedroom? The overhead light was on in the bedroom; she detested that light. She went into the bathroom, instead. She licked her pale, dry lips, her gaze sought her reflection's gaze in the mirror, hoping for encouragement. How the wind blew! The little house was shuddering. But there were no windows in this bathroom so perhaps it was safe. . . . Renée staring at Renée, hoping for a smile, a nod of encouragement. *You will be safe. Nothing will happen.* As a child she had often found herself in the bathroom somewhere, locked in, safe against intruders, staring hungrily at herself. *Will it be . . . ? Will I survive . . . ? What will happen . . . ?* Her ankle-length flannel nightgown looked unusually pretty: many-petalled pink and red flowers on a pale-green background. Her eyes picked up that green, drew upon it, seemed to glow with light; but it was the light of terror. She was going to scream. She was going mad. Her skin was bleached-out, bloodless. She was going to. . . . Ah, she remembered her lover, her ex-lover. Ah yes. Then it was good, this punishment was good, it made sense that she be in here, cringing, her hair wild about her face. The door was locked, no one could discover her. Karl could not get in—could not embrace her. Her husband might shout for her, but who could hear?—the wind made so much noise.

She had been in love with a man, had been loved in return. Yet they did not know each other. They had been together less than ten times . . . that is, they had lain together less than ten times;

but over and over in her imagination, over and over, feverishly, in her memory, they grasped at each other, kissed and embraced, grappled together as if drowning. . . . They called each other's name, across the rain-swept miles of the city. She had fallen asleep, composing a letter to him. Letters. A constant, continual, ceaseless letter to him, and only to him. *Karl? Should we . . .? Or is it better to . . .?* He and his family lived far from the river, would be in no danger tonight, would perhaps be sleeping. Safe. Indifferent. Untouched. He loved her, so he claimed; perhaps it was true. She loved him. But already she was testing her love for him, already she was composing a letter that began: *Dear Karl, I think you deceived me, I think you deceived your wife and me both, I think you are a hypocrite, I never loved you.* . . . But no: erase that. Begin again. *Dear Karl, I think the decision we came to the other day was the wisest one, considering your family and my.* . . . They had wept in each other's arms. Even Karl had wept. His breath heated, urgent. His arms tight around her, his mouth pressed against her throat, her shoulder. . . . No, he had not deceived her. It might have been something else, but not deception. He kept repeating: *In the beginning you were so happy, like a young girl. Now you're miserable, always . . . now I've hurt you . . . everything has gone sour.*

Yes, he had wept. Had wept in her arms.

A few days later Renée had been driving along Telford Avenue, heading downtown, when it began to rain suddenly. She noticed a hitchhiker on the curb, not a boy but a man. For some reason she slowed the car . . . for some reason she stared at the hitch-hiker, recognizing him at once, and yet peculiarly detached from him, unmoved, as if they were strangers. There he was in the rain like a fool, hitchhiking—very well, then, let him get wet! He had a car of his own, didn't he? Did his wife insist upon taking it? Very well, then, he deserves to be stranded in the rain, how can he stand there in public begging for a ride? Why should anyone stop for him?

Yet she stopped.

He stared at her, astonished. "Christ, what a coincidence. . . ."

She felt, still, that curious, pleasurable independence. She had not had to stop for him; he might not have noticed her drive by; she had stopped out of her own free will, not coerced, not even especially moved by the sight of him. He was speaking irritably of the repairs that had to be done on his car . . . the brakes needed overhauling and it would be expensive . . . and the car had just been serviced a few months ago. Renée was quiet. He changed the subject and told her some good news: a small press in Vancouver was going to publish a volume of his poems, *The Sirens*. He was very, very pleased. Very pleased. Excited. . . . Then he shifted to his wife, not mentioning her name but alluding to her simply as *her*. She hadn't had much faith in him, evidently, in his ability as a poet; now she would be forced to reconsider him, now she would be surprised. . . . Renée listened in silence, disturbed at how bitter and boyish he sounded. She wondered if her lover knew what he was saying. *Now she would be surprised! Now . . . !* It alarmed her, that her lover's wife should seem so dominant, suddenly, so much stronger than he. Karl was like a boy, a gleeful boy. A number of people in this town would be surprised, he said. But of course people were always jealous. . . .

"Congratulations," Renée said faintly.

"Thanks! . . . You're sweet, you were always so sweet," he sighed. "And what a coincidence, you driving along like this . . . rescuing me. . . ."

"Just a coincidence," she said.

She managed to get her call through to one of the firehouses.

"Hello? Hello? Can you help me, please? My husband and I . . . we don't know what to do, we're afraid of the flood and . . . and . . . and we're. . . ."

"How high is it in your basement?"

"We don't have a basement—"

"Where do you live?"

"Telford. In the 1200 block."

"Well, is it flooding?—How old are you?"

"What, how old? I'm—I'm twenty-six."

"You sound like a child. Do you people need help, are you stranded?"

"No—"

"Just a minute, please—"

There was noise in the background.

Evan squatted beside her. "Look, Renée, I think it's going to be all right. Who are you talking to?"

She turned away from him, shutting her eyes. She sat with the earphone pressed against her ear.

"The police? Who is it? What do they say? Is there any danger?"

The line went dead.

Renée got to her feet. "I think . . . I think we should leave."

"Honey, I'm sure things will be all right."

They wandered back into the kitchen. Renée saw with a shock that the waves were closer to the house—washing within a few yards of the house. Evan had been watching all along and had not noticed. He spoke in a mild, hollow voice. "It probably won't get any higher tonight. It's quite high, isn't it? . . . but it can't get much higher."

"What's wrong with you?" Renée cried.

"What? What do you mean?"

"Why are you acting so strangely?"

"What do you mean? I've been out here listening to the radio —I'm a little tired—You're acting strangely, you're the one who's hysterical."

She had begun to tremble now. She pushed him away.

"I'm sure the house is safe," he said stubbornly.

"The driveway might be flooded already. If it's flooded we won't be able to leave."

"Where do you want to go? Why are you so anxious to go some-where?"

"Why are you standing here like this? Evan, you look—you look hypnotized—"

"I'm a little tired, that's all. Stop staring at me like that!"

He had put on his bathrobe over his pajamas, but he was still barefoot.

It was three o'clock.

"You don't care what happens to us," Renée whispered.

"I don't think the situation warrants—"

"The house is going to be flooded! It's going to come in here—look at those waves, for God's sake!"

"We won't drown—how can we drown—It's a little high but it can't get much higher—"

She stared at him: this usually intelligent man, now drawn, haggard, lines of sheer stubborn spite on both sides of his mouth. In that instant she did not know him at all, did not know if she loved him or hated him or feared him. She did not know if what he said was correct, or whether he was slightly out of his mind. She was trembling, shivering, but he seemed quite calm.

She ran into the bedroom. What to do—what to do—This was the first time that—There was danger, yet she did not know what to do. Their neighbors? Had their neighbors evacuated their homes? Renée considered telephoning them. *Can you help us? We don't know what to do, we're having a little disagreement—who is sane and who is mad*—But their neighbors on the left had built a seawall that summer, and their house was on higher ground; they were probably not in danger. They were probably enjoying the storm. And their neighbors on the right . . . a large family in a ramshackle house like a barn . . . seven or eight children . . . would probably not know what to do either. And Renée intensely disliked those people. Or perhaps she disapproved of them, morally: the mother did nothing to prevent the older boys from teasing or even hurting the younger children, and occasionally the father came home drunk and yelled at them all. *I'm going to kill one of you!* Incredible, incredible. . . . So she must not call upon them for help. Was this panic, that she should stand paralyzed, unable to move? She would do something. She would take off her nightgown. Must change her clothes, put on something warmer. But the suitcase caught her eye. Filled with

Evan's socks, it was. Why? Why would he need so many socks?
She took most of them out. She turned, twisted awkwardly at the
waist, looking around the room for help. It was an utterly
familiar room, yet it was subtly altered. What to do, what to do—
She took some of her underwear out of the bureau drawer, and a
sweater, and some of Evan's things, and put them in the suitcase—and then it struck her that they had nowhere to go. A
motel? One of the downtown hotels? But they would be filled to
capacity. . . . One of the church halls? One of the firehouses?
Her mind reeled. Blankets, hot coffee, people weeping, huddled
together. She had seen photographs of a small town in Alberta
that had been devastated by floods that spring. People on stretch-
ers. Survivors. Victims of. Raging uncontrollable floods. Damage
estimated in the millions: human life, livestock, property.

. . . She decided to keep her nightgown on. She put a heavy
sweater over it. And a tweed skirt, an old comfortable shapeless
thing that dated back to her undergraduate days. Ah, this was
better. This made sense. She could slip her bare feet into boots.
Her coat was in the front closet. She would be safe, would be
safe, would not drown. She would be safe.

When she returned to the kitchen, she saw that Evan had
turned off the light so that he could watch the storm better. He
glanced at her, surprised. "You're dressed," he said, hurt. "Where
are you going? Where do you think you're going?"

"How is it?"

"See for yourself—we're in no danger."

The waves were now within a few feet of the house.

"Evan, aren't you being . . . aren't you being unreasonable,"
she said. But her voice was curiously flat. He could not even hear
her, over the wind. "I think that . . . I think. . . . I think we
should. . . . I. . . ."

She came to stand beside him. She pressed her forehead against
the windowpane. It was fascinating, the storm. The waves, the
chunks of debris, the churning lapping noises on all sides. . . .
They had taken the river for granted. At times, they had forgotten
it. Now it was here, two or three feet from the house itself.

Hypnotic, in spite of the noise. And there was a rhythm to it, beneath the cacophony of air and water.

Renée stared. There was someone she wanted to think of . . . but the storm drew her attention . . . it was fascinating, brutal. Ah, her lover. She had no lover, now; but she wanted to think of him. Was he thinking of her, worrying about her? Listening to the emergency broadcasts? No, probably not. She would have liked to think so. But no. He was probably asleep. And he could not have helped her anyway, with her life. She could not have helped him with his. *I've hurt you . . . everything has gone wrong. . . . My wife will be surprised. . . . I love you, I don't want to hurt you. . . . My wife never had any faith in me, in my talent . . . she's really an ignorant, complacent, unimaginative woman, but our relationship is, our marriage is . . . all marriages are . . . workable in ways that can't be described. And she'll be surprised. She will be surprised.*

It was after four when they went back to bed.

"I told you there was no danger," Evan said.

Renée was laughing, in relief. The wind had died down; the waves had retreated a foot or so. The storm was spent. She was laughing, laughing. Evan laughed. He set the suitcases on the floor. "Didn't I tell you? I told you! And you were ready to abandon the house—ready to run."

"People have died tonight, in this storm," Renée said numbly. "On the radio they just said—"

"That was north of here. Miles away."

"—heart attacks, a drowning—"

"Miles away."

"Only a short distance away!"

They went to bed. Renée was shivering and Evan's teeth were chattering.

". . . you wanted to evacuate, wanted to abandon everything," Evan whispered.

"We were in danger. It was real. People died tonight."

"Aren't you glad we didn't leave?"

". . . the storm was so real, so terrible . . . the river was so real. . . ."

The wind was still loud. They huddled together, shivering.

"So real, so very real," Renée whispered in awe. She was tired, exhausted. She was too tired to be frightened now. Her terror had faded to an odd blank relief, and had changed then to disappointment . . . for what, she did not know. Disappointment? She was not going to be punished after all.

"You wanted to abandon our house," Evan murmured. "Our marriage . . ."

But he too was exhausted. His voice fell into a rhythm, a singsong, a lullaby. "No danger . . . never was any . . . I told you, didn't I? . . . should have had faith in me. Now it's safe, we're safe. You see? Never was any danger."

Renée laughed, pressing her face against his neck. She groped for his fingers—they were cold. She meant to massage them but she was too tired suddenly. She could not remember why she was disappointed or why she was relieved or what the danger had been.

". . . safe, in our own bed," Evan said sleepily. "You see . . . ?"

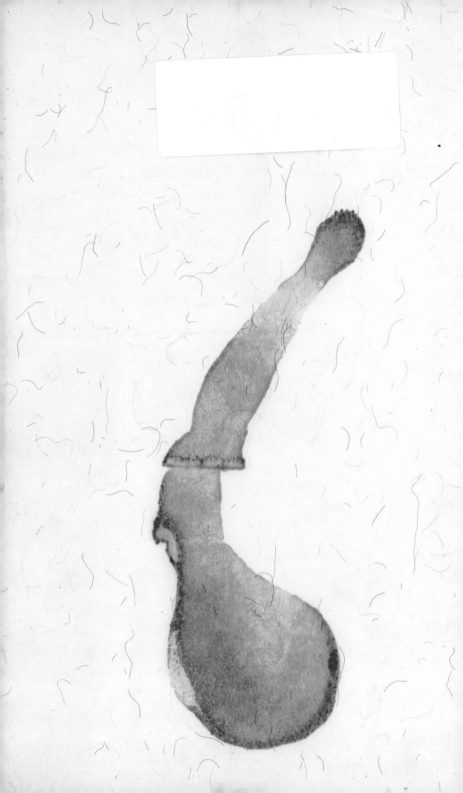